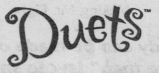

**Two brand-new stories in every volume...
twice a month!**

Duets Vol. #43

"If you seek escapist fare, sensuality,
romance and a good story, look no further..."
than talented Temptation author Jamie Denton, says
Under the Covers. Joining her this month is new
writer Holly Jacobs with the delightfully funny
I Waxed My Legs For This? Enjoy!

Duets Vol. #44

Popular Jacqueline Diamond returns to Duets
this month. *Romantic Times* notes she always
"delivers a wonderful romance...and combines
it with a quirky cast of characters." Paired with
Jacqui is Isabel Sharpe, "a name to watch in the
romance genre for her excellent characterizations
and smooth plotting," says *Affaire de Coeur.*

Be sure to pick up both Duets volumes today!

"Anybody can be made over... just like that." Jaycee snapped her fingers.

"Reginald Dwight was once a quiet, unassuming lad with a remarkable talent for the piano," she continued.

Simon shrugged. "Who's Reginald Dwight?"

Jaycee held up an outrageous picture of Elton John in his role as the Pinball Wizard from the old rock opera *Tommy*.

Simon frowned. "You want me to wear diamond-studded glasses, platform shoes and green coveralls?"

"This is a really old picture. I'm thinking of something a little more conservative for you." She pulled out the cover of a *GQ* magazine that sported a lean, sexy hunk who had Simon's body structure—when he stood straight.

"So what do you think?" she asked, excitement in her voice.

Simon took the magazine for a closer look. "You think you can make me look like *this?*" he asked incredulously. "Ms. Richmond, I don't think anyone has *that* much money!"

For more, turn to page 9

I Waxed My Legs for *This?*

"Carrie! Where are you?"

"Right here," Carrie shouted to Jack as she jumped out at him from behind, knocking him into the water.

"You scared about ten years off my life." He now had her around the waist and dunked her. She came up sputtering and he continued. "Repeat after me, I will not scare Jack ever again."

"Never," she yelled just before she was dunked for a second time.

"Say it."

"No! You deserved it for throwing me in." And in she went again. "Jack," she screamed as she coughed and laughed. "I'm sorry I scared you."

"You don't look very sorry," he grumbled.

He seemed to be considering her apology, and Carrie moved in for the kill. She scooped her right leg behind his left knee, pushing him under the water. "Threaten me, will you?" she asked as he came up for air.

"You're walking a fine line here, lady."

"Nope, I'm running," she yelped, moving as fast as the warm ocean water would allow, with Jack right on her tail.

For more, turn to page 197

HARLEQUIN DUETS

ISBN 0-373-44109-6

MAKING MR. RIGHT
Copyright © 2001 by Jamie Ann Denton

I WAXED MY LEGS FOR *THIS?*
Copyright © 2001 by Holly Fuhrmann

This edition published by arrangement with Harlequin Books S.A.

® and TM are trademarks of the publisher. Trademarks indicated with
® are registered in the United States Patent and Trademark Office, the
Canadian Trade Marks Office and in other countries.

Visit us at www.eHarlequin.com

Printed in U.S.A.

Making Mr. Right

JAMIE DENTON

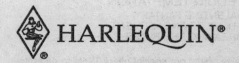

HARLEQUIN®

TORONTO • NEW YORK • LONDON
AMSTERDAM • PARIS • SYDNEY • HAMBURG
STOCKHOLM • ATHENS • TOKYO • MILAN • MADRID
PRAGUE • WARSAW • BUDAPEST • AUCKLAND

Dear Reader,

My love of the movies was a gift from my mother, especially the romantic comedies of the '40s and '50s. Mom was, and still is, a huge movie fan. Forget teen idols like David Cassidy and Donny Osmond. My heroes were the leading men of the silver screen: Cary Grant, Spencer Tracy and Clark Gable.

When Harlequin asked if I wanted to write *Making Mr. Right* for Duets, I was thrilled. What could be more perfect for a gal who was weaned on romantic comedy? Although *Making Mr. Right* doesn't contain half the zany antics of Cary Grant in *Arsenic and Old Lace* or Claudette Colbert in *It Happened One Night*, sexy Simon Hawthorne is the perfect Clark Gable*esque* straight man for Jaycee Richmond, a heroine with enough spunk and determination to have made any of the screen legend comediennes eager to play the role.

I really enjoy writing for Harlequin Temptation and Duets. I'd love to hear what you think of my first attempt at the lighter side of romance. Write to me at P.O. Box 224, Mohall, North Dakota 58761 or send an e-mail to Jamie@jamiedenton.net.

Happy reading!

Jamie Denton

Books by Jamie Denton

HARLEQUIN TEMPTATION

For Bobby
1955–1988

1

JAYCEE RICHMOND crumpled the fortune from the cookie she'd had at lunch. She crammed it into the oversize black bag slung over her shoulder and stepped off the elevator. How many others had received the exact same words of wisdom from Chan's Chinese Kitchen? Or worse, she thought, heading down the corridor to the door marked Private, how many would actually fall victim to such silliness?

She didn't believe in bad karma, good fortune or Confucius's mass-produced fortune-cookie wisdom for a buck ninety-nine a dozen. Fate had little to do with success or failure, and silly daydreams were fine so long as they didn't shadow the present. She did believe hard work was rewarded, and while her employer brothers shared her philosophy, they didn't apply it to her. She'd spent eleven loyal years working in one capacity or another at the image consulting firm they'd taken over when their father, John Richmond, retired four years ago, but had little to show for it.

Fortune-tellers, psychics and horoscopes fell in the same category as snake-oil salesmen, and the last thing Jaycee Richmond would ever waste her time believing in would be a little piece of paper tucked inside a fortune cookie stating, ''Mr. Right will walk into your life today.''

At two minutes before one o'clock, Jaycee pushed through the private entrance into the corridor of the offices of Better Images. She'd been playing the good girl for the past six months in hopes of furthering her cause toward the promotion she so desperately wanted. Better Images was a family business. And she was family, too, even if she was a woman.

She walked into her office. The once very roomy broom closet had been a reward from her brothers when she'd graduated from college with a degree in business administration. She been thrilled with the private, albeit tiny, office. Until she'd figured out geography was the only change in her job. She was still a secretary, but at least she no longer doubled as a receptionist.

Her education hadn't stopped with her bachelor's degree, and for the past three years she'd spent her nights enrolled in the master's program at the University of Washington. Six months ago she'd achieved her goal and had been positive she'd be made an equal partner in the family business.

She couldn't have been more wrong.

Instead of the promotion to account manager with a partnership buy-in option, her brothers had surprised her with a two-year membership at a local health spa...for singles.

The Richmond philosophy stated that if a "girl" wanted to work, then she belonged in a more traditional job like secretary, bookkeeper or nurse.

"Traditional? Subservient is more like it," she grumbled, and cast a glare at the small stack of files piled on her chair.

Common phrases like *equality* and *women's rights* were nearly foreign to the Richmond men, but unlike Rick, at least Dane didn't mind making fresh coffee or getting his own copies. The fault lay with her parents, or even her grandparents, she thought, scooping the files off the chair and slapping them on the top of the filing cabinet. Richmond women didn't work. They went from their fathers' homes to their husbands'. The fact that Jaycee worked for a living, was educated and determined to have a career, not to mention was living away from home and still painfully single at the ripe old age of twenty-seven, was a source of embarrassment to her traditional family.

Maybe she was adopted.

She slid her purse into the top drawer of the lateral filing cabinet that pulled double duty as a credenza. She had to find a way to prove to Rick and Dane she was capable of doing what they saw as a man's job. And she couldn't very well do that locked away, day after boring day, in a broom closet with a computer, having nothing more intellectually stimulating to do than type up proposals and business plans all day.

"Are you Ms. Richmond?"

Startled to hear a strange man's voice in her office, she pushed the drawer closed and winced when the metal pinched the tips of her fingers. Her usual welcoming, professional smile slid into more of a grimace as she struggled to ignore the stinging pain in her fingertips.

"I'm Jaycee. And you were supposed to be here yesterday," she said a little more sharply than usual. She rounded the desk and brushed past the repairman. "The copier is this way."

"I'm not here to fix your copy machine," he said, his rich, smooth voice a sharp contrast to the tall, gangly frame of the guy wearing black-rimmed glasses and a plain white short-sleeve shirt. He slouched forward slightly as he stuffed his hands inside the pockets of a pair of navy polyester-blend slacks. More polyester than blend, too, she noticed.

He frowned. "I want to *hire* you."

She took a deep breath and counted quickly to ten. Just because she was irritated with her current employment situation didn't mean she had the right to take her frustrations out on a total stranger, especially a stranger with eyes the prettiest shade of green she'd ever seen, even though they were practically hidden behind thick, black-framed glasses. "You want to hire *me?*"

He let out a rough breath after a sharp nod of his head, then his slumped shoulders relaxed even more. "They said I needed a life."

They? Who was they? Esteemed members of the medical profession? Or perhaps law-enforcement officials? He didn't look crazy, but then again, Jeffrey Dahmer had been a nice, quiet boy, too.

She inched toward the door. "Excuse me?" Fiona, her best friend and the firm's bookkeeper, was undoubtedly still at her usual extended lunch hour. Other than Juliana, their new receptionist, she was alone...alone with a guy claiming he needed a life.

His glasses slid down the sharp slope of his nose. "A life," he said, scrunching up his nose to position the thick glasses in place.

Look, Ma, no hands.

"You know. With people."

Jaycee stepped into the hallway, hoping to lead

him to the lobby and closer to the exit. "I think you're in the wrong place."

He shook his head. "You don't understand."

And Ted Bundy was just a misunderstood law student.

"You're an image maker, right?" There was a note of desperation in his voice that had Jaycee trying to recall the necessary self-defense moves that would slow down, if not altogether stop, an attacker. "Well, yes, but..."

Was that right elbow to the solar plexus and left foot to the instep? Or left elbow and right foot?

"Better Images," he said, following so close behind her she was certain she wasn't imagining the warm whisper of his breath on the back of her neck.

He stopped and pointed to a framed picture on the wall, the one with her father and brothers standing in front of the Better Images logo in the lobby the day of her father's retirement. It was no coincidence she and her mother weren't in the picture.

"*I* need a better image," he explained, leaning over to tap his fingers on the wall beside the dark wood frame.

Jaycee let out the pent-up breath she'd been holding, the one that would have had the entire fifth floor up in arms when she let it out into a bloodcurdling scream. "So you're not a...I mean, what kind of business do you have, Mr...." She really needed to stop watching the True Stories cable channel so late at night.

"Hawthorne," he said. "Simon Hawthorne. I'm an accountant."

"An accounting firm," she said quietly, and bit her lip, an idea forming. No one was in the office today. Just "the girls," as her chauvinistic brothers referred to their support staff. There had been occasions in the past where she'd had to do the initial client intake, but Rick or Dane always took over the actual handling of the client. If she kept Simon Hawthorne and his accounting firm temporarily off the books, then there'd be no account for them to take away from her.

The idea, regardless of how it stretched the ethical boundaries of the profession, held a whole lot of merit. She wasn't thrilled about the deceitful angle, but how else could she prove she was more than capable of managing her own accounts if they never gave her the chance? Of course it would've been nice if she'd had something a little more exciting than an accounting firm to prove her value, but lying cheats couldn't be choosy. Besides, she mused, an account was an account, and more importantly, a client with a potential for public relations.

And her future within the family business.

She flashed Mr. Simon Hawthorne her most brilliant professional smile. "Right this way, Mr. Hawthorne," she said, leading him down the hallway toward Rick's office. Rick, as the eldest, had claimed her father's old office, the one with the best view of Puget Sound in the afternoon and away from the heat of the sun glinting off the Pacific Ocean.

She indicated a wing chair and took the buttery soft leather executive chair behind the massive mahogany desk for herself. She looked over the desk at her possible promotion and smiled. "Why don't you start by telling me what kind of image you're envisioning?"

Simon drummed his fingers on the wood below the padded arm of the chair. "The term my secretary used was 'more user-friendly.'"

She caught a hint of embarrassment in his voice. "That's nothing to be ashamed of, Mr. Hawthorne," she offered sympathetically.

Tap. Tap. Tap.

"Accounting firms are well-known for, and take great pride in, their stoicism," she continued.

The tapping grew more determined and rhythmic. It was also distractingly familiar.

"I personally would feel more at ease knowing my company's finances are in the hands of professionals in a professional atmosphere rather than an excuse for an office with a frat-house mentality.''

Tap-tap-tap...tap-tap.

"Excuse me, but is that 'Jingle Bells'?"

"'Mary Had A Little Lamb'." The look he gave her was sheepish and apologetic. "Nervous habit."

"As I was saying," she continued, "there's a level of comfort knowing your account—"

Simon cleared his throat. "Ms. Richmond?"

"Yes?"

"It's me."

Jaycee blinked, confused.

He shifted in the chair, propping his foot over his knee. His nod was slow, and he slid his former nursery-rhyme-tapping fingers carefully around his blue argyle-covered ankle, the movement conscious and practiced.

"*I* need the image, Ms. Richmond," he said in that rich, smooth voice that reminded her suddenly of...

Phone sex!

That's the kind of voice he had, like a starving college student earning extra money by being on the giving end of one of those 976-HUNK lines. If she closed her eyes, she could hear the smoky undertones and practically feel the warm richness cascading over her. Decadent and...

"Me, not my firm," he said, pulling her reluctantly out of her temporary fantasy.

She opened her eyes and forced her attention on Simon Hawthorne and not the silly things his rich, deep voice made her feel.

"Well, it's not my firm," he explained. "I'm just an employee, but they said I'm not user-friendly enough. At least not for the clients."

"*You* want a new image," she clarified. "Not your accounting firm."

He smiled, and she couldn't help notice that he had a very nice smile. And a sexy mouth, too. At least from what she could determine, Simon Hawthorne wasn't quite the geek he believed everyone thought him. He really was kinda cute, in a pocket-protector sort of way.

"At Eaton and Simms, if you're not promotion material, you're unemployable."

The firm wasn't even his! So much for her chance to prove herself. With nothing left for her to do but show Simon Hawthorne the door, she stood. She tried not to feel too discouraged. Her chance would come along. It just wasn't going to happen today.

"I'd like to help, but Better Images is an image consulting firm for corporations." She circled the desk and extended her hand, signaling an end to their meeting. "Please don't take offense, but perhaps a self-help group would be of more assistance."

He stood, and she had to tip her head back. She wondered what he'd look like without those thick glasses, or maybe wearing a pair of wireless frames.

A flash of irritation flared in his eyes. "There isn't enough time," he said abruptly.

"There's always time for self-improvement," she murmured, skimming her gaze over his tall body. Like maybe a shopping trip for a new look. She frowned. And a stop at the hairdresser for a more updated style, something different than the wet, combed-back look that did nothing to soften the sharp, angled features of his face.

"I only have a few days, Ms. Richmond."

That hint of desperation was back in his voice. "For what?" she asked.

He slouched forward again and stuffed his hands into the pockets of his trousers. "Until the partners at Eaton and Simms make their decision. I've been passed over twice already for a promotion. The annual partnership weekend is coming up, and if I'm passed over again... The third time's the charm, Ms. Richmond. I miss out this time around and I'm history."

"Are you sure it's only your image?" she asked, even though there was nothing *she* could do to help him. Accountants were typically stuffy sorts. If Simon Hawthorne was more comfortable with his columns of numbers than interacting with the rest of the world, wouldn't that make him the ideal accountant?

A hardness crept into his gaze. "I'm good at what I do," he said in a voice that matched the look in his eyes. "If you must know, my secretary overheard the partners. They said I'm a... She said they called me a nerd."

Jaycee winced. Somehow she didn't think this was the first time Simon had been branded with that less-than-glowing term. "I wish I could help you, but Better Images doesn't—"

"I need a better image if I'm going to have personal contact with our existing client base," he interrupted her, reciting the latter as if by rote, "or I look elsewhere for a job. I'm sorry I wasted your time."

He turned to leave, and Jaycee felt her first stab of regret. Hadn't she had enough personal experience to know exactly what Simon Hawthorne was going through? She knew all about the need to be appreciated for your abilities, not the exterior packaging. For years she'd been held back by the prejudices of others. Like her father, her brothers maintained an antiquated bias that was keeping her from what she really wanted, not just a promotion, but to become a legitimate partner in the family business.

He slipped through the door and quietly closed it behind him. For reasons she didn't understand, she felt as if her chance was slipping through that same door. A ridiculous notion. What Simon was looking for just didn't exist at Better Images.

Or could it?

With a shake of her head, she left Rick's office. A guy like Simon probably faced his own prejudices all his life. No matter how unfair, he faced the myth of the perfect male perpetuated by the images found in magazines and television commercials. Those guys could afford personal trainers and probably had enough steroids pumping through their systems to list their reproductive organs on the endangered species list. Not every guy had the perfect body of a sports hero or the spit-and-polish perfection of an airbrushed male model. Some guys were just like Simon. Plain, simple and hardworking.

She stopped at the door to her tiny office. Maybe she hadn't lost her chance to finally prove herself, after all. Maybe it was still within her grasp, just waiting for her to take it.

Better Images might be a consulting firm for corporations trying to put on a new face for the public, but for the life of her, Jaycee couldn't think of a single reason those same principles couldn't be put into practice to create a new public image for an individual. The challenge may be slightly different, but the result would be the same, a new and improved client with a renewed public image.

All she had to do was keep her work with Simon away from the office. And catch Simon before he got away.

So why was she hesitating? If she didn't hurry, her chance would be gone. With Rick and Dane out for the day schmoozing a client on the golf course, she'd never have a better opportunity.

She bolted down the hallway, past a startled Fiona, and into the lobby. Empty.

"I'll be right back," she called to Juliana, then yanked open the double doors and flew down the corridor toward the bank of elevators.

The ding of the bell sounded as she rounded the corner. Simon stepped into the car. Jaycee dashed in after him seconds before the metal doors slid closed.

She leaned forward, bracing her hands on her

nylon-covered knees, pulling air deep into her lungs. "*I'll* help you." She raised her index finger to signal she had more to say once she caught her breath. "We can…help…each other."

He pushed the red button, and the elevator slid to a halt. "You can help me?" he asked carefully. "Not Better Images?"

She nodded and managed a weak grin before pulling in another deep breath. "Better Images doesn't handle individual clients. Our business primarily consists of improving corporate public relations. This would have to be between us."

She would have held her breath if she'd had any left in her lungs to hold. He stared at her, his eyes filling with skepticism. Considering she'd charged after him like a lunatic, she couldn't really blame him for exercising a little caution.

And she'd thought *he* was the lunatic.

"How can we help each other?" he finally asked.

Jaycee straightened and with her hands behind her back used the brass rail for support. "Let's just say we share a common goal, Mr. Hawthorne. What do you have to lose?"

"A lot," he said, and pushed the red button again. The elevator continued its descent.

She shoved off the rail and pushed the button, stopping the car again. "So do I."

He reached around her and pushed the button. "Such as?"

She pushed it again, then stepped in front of the control panel. "Everything that's important to me," she said, determined that he at least listen to her. She planted her hands on her hips. "Look, you came to me for help, and I know I just said I couldn't, but I really think I can. Let's meet for a drink at the Harbor Inn around six. If I haven't come up with a viable plan for you by then, we go our separate ways. Okay?"

He might be looking at her as if *she* was the crazy one, but lunatic or not, she was all he had, and they both knew it. "What have you got to lose?" she pressed.

He let out a rush of breath. "All right," he finally agreed.

With a grin, she pushed the button to send the elevator to the bottom floor and moved away from the control panel.

The doors slid open, and Jaycee preceded Simon out of the elevator car. "You won't be disappointed," she said, extending her hand.

The warmth of his hand slipped over hers. "Thank you," he said, then let go and gave her one last look before turning and heading out the double glass doors of the building.

Curious, Jaycee watched him cross the busy downtown street, wondering why the simple touch of his hand caused her heart to beat just a little too fast.

Exertion, she told herself.

Too bad her breathing was no longer labored, or she just might have believed it.

2

THE DAY was never going to end.

Simon's frown deepened. The world *would* come to an end before he got to see her again, he thought, then checked his watch for the third time in as many minutes. The need to see Jaycee was far more personal than the professional relationship she'd proposed, an indicator of just how pathetic he was starting to feel.

He leaned back in his chair and closed his eyes. Pathetic or not, he imagined walking into the Harbor Inn at precisely six o'clock, suave and debonair, oozing Pierce Brosnan confidence. He'd melt her with a Mel Gibson smile and hide a knowing grin when her eyes skimmed over his iron-hard Schwarzenegger pecs hidden beneath the latest in Armani. With the polished charm of James Bond, he'd stroll casually through the trendy, upscale pub. Women would openly admire him. They'd attempt to gain his attention, but his sole focus would be on the search for one woman.

The woman with a lightning-bright smile and sleek, chin-length chestnut hair brushing against skin as smooth as porcelain. The woman with the longest, sexiest pair of legs he'd ever had the pleasure of watching dive into an elevator after him.

A light rap at the door to his office brought him hurtling to reality. He looked over the rim of his glasses to find Stella, his secretary, shaking her head. "Care to tell me when Uncle Harley's Hog Parts added cashmere scarves to their inventory list?"

"Excuse me?"

Stella's hot-pink painted lips curled into a grimace Simon suspected was supposed to be a grin. "I know the coffee's strong, but I doubt Carlene's Coffee and Creme started giving away free oil changes."

With a quirk of his nose, Simon shifted his glasses in place. "I don't have time for guessing games. What are you talking about?"

His painfully thin secretary slapped three thick files on the center of his desk. "These quarterly reports, Simon," she said, snapping her gum and drawing a long, hot-pink fingernail over the file labels. "I don't know what you did, but they're a mess. You've got the coffee shop's cost of goods recorded in the Calming Waters Boutique ledgers, the motorcycle shop's receipts for services rendered mixed up with Carlene's Coffee and Creme, and both Carlene's and Calming Waters's year-end inventory reports are mixed up with the motorcycle shop. Boss, this just ain't like you.''

Simon let out a sigh. Stella was right. It wasn't like him, but he'd been distracted since he'd returned from Better Images. Concentration at a minimum. Erotic fantasies starring Jaycee Richmond at an all-time high.

''Just leave them,'' he said. ''I'll take care of it.''

Stella popped her gum again then curled her lips into another one of those grimacelike grins. ''They're due tomorrow, boss,'' she reminded him, then turned on her spindly legs and left his office.

Great. He was supposed to meet Jaycee at six. There was no way he could repair the damage done to the quarterly reports in less than two hours. Maybe it was for the best. He didn't feel comfortable meeting her in a crowded pub anyway, not to mention that he wasn't exactly thrilled about discussing in a public place the type of business they planned to conduct.

Despite his preoccupation, he was under no false illusions. After thirty-two years of conditioning, he didn't need a reminder that women like Jaycee Richmond, sexy, alluring and extroverted, never really noticed guys like him. He tapped the files

Stella left on his desk. Apparently the delectable diversion of the memory of Jaycee's long, lovely limbs created too much of a distraction.

He slid the business card for Better Images he'd snagged from the receptionist's desk from his wallet and dialed Jaycee's office number. There'd be no weaving his way through the thick crowd while scanning the bar for Jaycee, he thought. He'd never liked crowds much, anyway. He'd be more comfortable asking a total stranger to perform a miracle in private. And beyond all that was the little voice in his head telling him he was who he was, and nothing could change that fact. He was Simon Hawthorne, CPA, and as Stella had overheard the partners comment, he was dull, boring and no longer the kind of accountant they envisioned representing the new hip, trendy image of Seattle's oldest accounting firm.

He admitted to being shocked by the news. As Jaycee had pointed out, stoicism and accounting firms were practically synonymous. But even Stella had finally admitted the truth, that the other secretaries and bookkeepers considered him the least user-friendly of the accountants in the firm's employ. He was a nice guy. He just kept to himself. Socializing was never a priority for him. Now it looked as if he needed a crash course on the subject despite his instinct to shrug his shoulders and turn his attention to the same accounts and ledgers that had been filling his days for fourteen years. Why should anyone care so long as the client was satisfied with his work?

The problem was, the client cared, according to Stella. In today's world of automation, Eaton and Simms's new image was one that would pride itself on providing personal service to their clientele. People preferred speaking to a warm body rather than an impersonal computerized voice. Personally, Simon preferred the computer.

"Jaycee Richmond," he said when the receptionist answered, then waited for her to put his call through.

"This is Jaycee."

Regardless of the varying degrees of sensual delight swimming through his oversexed mind all afternoon, a wave of longing ripped through him at the sound of her voice, stunning him into silence.

"Hello?"

He cleared his throat.

"Can I help you?"

He tried to speak, but his vocal cords were tied in knots, matching the tangled mess in his gut.

"Who is this?" A slight trace of irritation canted the husky nuances of her voice.

He cleared his throat again. Then coughed.

"Simon." He managed to speak around the dryness.

Silence. She'd forgotten him already.

"Simon Hawthorne," he prompted, wincing at the hopeful note in his voice.

"You can't call me here," she said, dropping her voice to a strangled whisper.

They were lovers, clandestine lovers caught in a forbidden liaison. "Come to my place instead," he said, enjoying the temporary fantasy.

Silence again.

So much for forbidden liaisons. She was supposed to ask when, or maybe even say something like, "Of course I'll meet you."

"Ms. Richmond?"

"I'm here." Her reply was another hesitant whisper.

"Considering the nature of our business," he said, dragging himself reluctantly out of the fantasy, "wouldn't it be better if we met in private?"

"Well…yes, I suppose."

"Would you feel more comfortable if I came to your place instead?"

"No!" she shouted into the receiver.

Simon shoved the phone away as he heard clattering noises. "Sorry," he heard her say after a moment. "Phone slipped. Uh, go ahead and give me the address."

Not only did he provide her with his home address, but also his phone numbers for work, home and pager. "Would you mind changing our meeting from six to eight? I had something come up at the office."

"Maybe tomorrow would be more—"

"That's okay," he cut her off. Not only did he need her help, but he wanted to see her again. Lustful musings aside, time was at a premium. "What I mean is...I'd rather discuss your plan tonight."

"All right," she agreed, albeit reluctantly. "I'll see you at eight then."

Simon hung up the phone and tried to remember the last time he'd actually invited a beautiful woman to his apartment.

An hour later, he was still contemplating the answer.

JAYCEE HUNG UP the phone and turned to face her computer monitor, pretending her best friend Fiona hadn't been blatantly eavesdropping on her stilted conversation with Simon. Ever since they were kids, the rule had been if you wanted someone to know something, simply tell Fiona. Unfortunately, the aging process had done absolutely nothing to still her friend's wagging tongue.

Fiona took the three steps from the door to the front of the desk, making her officially inside Jaycee's office. "You might as well tell me who he is now, Jay, and save us both a lot of whining and arguing."

Jaycee continued typing. "I don't whine."

Fiona dropped into the hard white plastic chair to the side of the desk. "Okay," she said with a laugh. "*I'll* do the whining, but I want details. And *you* can argue and tell me to mind my own business."

Jaycee let out a melodramatic sigh that did nothing to dampen her friend's curiosity, then spun in the chair until she faced her longtime pal. "Do you ever think that's because I might actually consider that my private life should be, well, gee, I dunno…*private?*"

Fiona Goldwyn often referred to herself as a bowl of mixed nuts, or on bad hair days, a mutt. The truth was, the half Irish, one quarter Jewish, one quarter Chinese woman was nothing short of an exotic beauty. Her thick, shiny black hair hung straight down her back, the blunt-cut ends brushing her backside. Almond-shaped eyes a stunning shade of aqua were filled with laughter and a sassy, determined glint, while her perfectly shaped lips slid into a wide grin. "You haven't been able to keep a secret from me since the ninth grade. What makes you think you can start now?"

"And you haven't *kept* a secret since then, either."

Fiona examined her perfectly manicured nails. "I'm turning over a new leaf."

"And I'm running for Congress," Jaycee returned dryly. Snagging a stack of files from the edge of her desk, she turned her back on Fiona and opened the filing cabinet.

"Oh, give it up, Jay. Who was the hunk on the phone?"

Jaycee's fingers momentarily stilled. "He's not a hunk," she said quietly, then slipped the files inside the appropriate hanging folders. Simon Hawthorne was...nothing. At least nothing more than a means to an end. Whether or not he was the next poster boy for Calvin Klein or Accountants Anonymous made little difference to her. He was a client—even if he wasn't technically on the Better Images roster, he was still a client, just one who belonged exclusively to Jaycee Richmond, Image Consultant.

"He's a man, isn't he?" Fiona countered.

She couldn't argue with that logic. But the fact that he was a man meant nothing to her. To Jaycee he was a client...period. So what if he had eyes that reminded her of a forest glade in summer? Big deal if her breath stilled and tingles raced up her arm and shot down her spine when he shook her hand. She'd been running and had been out of breath. And Fiona Goldwyn, her lovable big-mouthed friend, was the last person she wanted to share in the knowledge of her latest professional liaison.

That thought firmly entrenched in her mind, she said, "You don't know him."

Fiona leaned back and kicked her feet up on the edge of the desk. "Then you simply *must* tell me all about him," she said, folding her arms and set-tling in for what she thought was going to be a juicy bit of gossip.

"I hate to disappoint you, but there's nothing to tell." At least nothing that included her and what Fiona probably thought was a much-needed man in Jaycee's life. "Don't you have work to do?" she asked helplessly.

Fiona's grin deepened. "No cat on the premises. Time for these mice to play."

Jaycee spun in her chair and contrived a look of concern. "I promised Rick I'd have the Henderson Corporation proposals on his desk before the end of the day."

Fiona swung her feet to the floor and stood. "You're up to something, Jay," she said, giving her a narrowed look. "I can feel it."

Jaycee's first instinct was to panic. The last thing she needed was for Rick or Dane to find out about her little sideline with Simon. She attempted to maintain a bland expression to throw her friend off the scent. "Your powers are slipping, Fiona. I'm just busy and promised to get these reports done for Rick. That's it."

Fiona wagged her finger. "Something's going on, and I'll find out, you know."

The grin she gave Fiona was weak. Truth be told, Jaycee was plenty worried. Because Fiona Goldwyn had the instincts of a bloodhound.

SIMON SWIPED the newspapers off the round dining table and dumped them in the garbage can, then rushed into the living room to pluck the half-empty soda can from the coffee table. He opened the center drawer on the square end table and slid the remote control, television guide and crossword puzzle magazine inside, then shoved it closed.

He checked his watch. Three minutes until Jaycee arrived.

His gaze darted around the apartment. He hadn't meant to be so late getting home, but he'd done more of a major number on those quarterly reports than he'd initially thought. By the time he repaired the damage caused by his daydreaming, it was quarter after seven, leaving him forty-five minutes to stop at the liquor store for a bottle of wine, get home and tidy the apartment before she arrived.

He would have made it, too, with plenty of time to spare, if it hadn't been for the phone call from his widowed father "just to say hello." It'd taken a promise to come for dinner the next night before his dad had finally bid him goodbye.

The doorbell sounded.

With the blue plastic kitchen garbage can still clutched in his hand, he quickly scanned the living room. A thin layer of dust covered the oblong coffee table. Bending low, he swiped his forearm along the top of the pine.

The bell rang again.

"Just a minute," he called, wiping the dust from his forearm. The trash can still gripped in his hand, he rushed to the door and swung it open, and nearly swallowed his tongue.

Considering where his mind had been all afternoon, the fierce longing that raced through him shouldn't have taken him by surprise. It nearly flattened him. He had a hard time believing his fantasies could possibly pale in comparison to the reality of Jaycee standing on his doorstep.

A hesitant smile curved her full, wide mouth. He dropped his gaze to her long, luscious legs. The desire to smooth his hands over those limbs was strong, urging him to peek and see for himself if the dove-gray satin garter he'd been dreaming of all afternoon held her hose in place, or if his forbidden musings were nothing more than a product of his overactive, highly lustful imagination.

Slowly, he tore his gaze from her legs and moved it upward, over the gray linen skirt and the gentle swell of her hips, to her slender waist, and farther up and over the deep charcoal silk blouse tucked into the waistband. He continued onward, along the seductive outline of her full breasts, not stopping until he scanned the length of her lovely throat and the delicate gold chain resting against the pulse beating there. He once again scanned the fullness of her kissable-looking mouth, and then found himself gazing directly into her narrowed, pale blue eyes.

Simon swallowed and resisted the urge to ease his suddenly nooselike tie from around his neck. Admiring a woman was one thing. Getting caught was another.

Conscious of the heat inching up his neck and scorching his cheeks, he cleared his throat and stood back, inviting her into his apartment.

She looked behind her at the brick walkway, then at him as if weighing her chances for a quick getaway. He really wasn't an oversexed geek, just an extremely convincing facsimile.

"Come in," he said. Something fluttered against his ankle when he swept his arm back in a grand welcoming gesture. He looked down at his hand

and the half-tipped trash can still clutched in his grasp, newspapers fluttering to the floor around his feet.

Simon stared at her in horror as she bit back a grin and stepped inside his apartment before stooping to pick up the fallen newspapers. He doubted she'd ever seen a guy blush before, at least not one over the age of twelve. She probably thought he was a freak.

"I hope I'm not too early," she said calmly, a hint of amusement in her husky voice. She stuffed the paper into the garbage can he was reluctant to part with for some reason.

"No. I...I'm, uh, running late," he stammered.

His nervousness was more embarrassing than being caught tidying up the apartment or gawking at her like a sailor on a weekend pass. To a woman as sleek and professional as Jaycee, who was more adorable and sexier than any woman he'd ever embarrassed himself in front of, he was merely an image in desperate need of improvement. If he could remember that instead of stuttering and blushing like an adolescent whenever they came in contact, he'd be better off.

"Why don't I take that?" She tugged the can from his reluctant fingers and set it outside the open door.

He pulled in a deep breath and let it out slowly.

By the time she closed the door behind her and turned to face him, he managed to convince himself he was calm and ready to concentrate on her reason for coming to his apartment. They had a job to do, and they couldn't do it if he continued to cloud the issue with thoughts of satin garters and her wide, kissable mouth.

Professionalism. His new buzz word.

Her mouth eased into a smile. "Where would you like me?"

A dozen thoughts jockeyed for position.

"Would you like to do this on that table over there?" she asked innocently, pointing toward the round oak dining table.

The most erotic thought trampled his new buzz word and stole center stage.

She looked over her shoulder at him. "Or do you think we'd be more comfortable on the sofa?"

His libido gave the thought hogging center stage a standing ovation.

Moving past her so she wouldn't notice his uncomfortable state, he walked toward the table in the small alcove he used for a dining room. "In here would probably be best," he said, stopping behind one of the oak ladder-back chairs. Physical distance would *really* be the best if he was going to maintain his sanity.

She set a large black bag on the table and pulled

out a file along with a small stack of thin letter-size pieces of cardboard secured by a rubber band. "You sit here," she instructed, pulling out the chair closest to her.

He did as she ordered, then watched as she slipped the rubber band off the sheets of cardboard before bending over the table to arrange them. Her skirt inched upward as she leaned across the table, giving him a teasing and far from professional glimpse of the lace tops securing her hose around her slim thighs.

He let out a slow, even breath, feeling about as professional as a fourteen-year-old peeping into the girls' locker room.

"There," she announced, and turned to face him. Her lightning-bright smile robbed him of any remnants of common sense remaining in his sex-starved mind. "Simon Hawthorne, prepare to have your socks blown off."

3

"ELIZA DOOLITTLE may have started out as nothing more ambitious than a flower peddler," Jaycee said, holding up the first of her makeshift storyboards for Simon's inspection, "but by the time Professor Higgins and Colonel Pickering were finished, Eliza was as refined as any English lady, and even able to pass for a grand duchess." Thanks to the Internet, a color printer, glue sticks and some cardboard from the Better Images supply closet, she'd managed to put together what she hoped was a convincing, if makeshift, pitch.

The nervousness she'd sensed in Simon upon arriving had waned, and he leaned back casually in the oak chair with his arms folded and his long legs stretching under the table. The earlier blush that had stained his masculine complexion had faded, too, and she couldn't help but find his shyness absolutely endearing. She'd lived her entire life in the shadow of self-assured chauvinists. Simon was like a breath of fresh air after being locked away without the benefits of daylight. His head was cocked slightly to the side, his deep green eyes filled with curiosity. She definitely had his attention.

She set the *My Fair Lady* example on the table and showed him her next board. "Norma Jean Baker wasn't a natural-born Marilyn Monroe," she continued, revealing a picture of both personalities. "The breathy voice, bombshell body and platinum locks were all created by the wholesome Norma Jean as part of her new knockout persona."

"I might be stating the obvious," he said dryly, "but Eliza Doolittle is a fictional character and Marilyn was an unstable neurotic who committed suicide. And they're both women."

"No one knows for certain exactly what happened to Marilyn," she argued, then grinned when he rolled his eyes. She suspected he might balk at the two transformation examples and was prepared to throw a little testosterone his way. "Reginald Dwight was once a quiet, unassuming lad with a remarkable talent for the piano."

Simon shrugged. "Who's Reginald Dwight?"

Jaycee tossed the Marilyn-Norma Jean example aside to reveal an outrageous picture of Elton John in his role as the pinball wizard from the movie version of the rock opera, "Tommy."

Simon frowned and shook his head. "You want

me to wear diamond-studded glasses, platform shoes and green coveralls?''

''This is a really old picture. I'm thinking of something a little more conservative for you.''

He made a noise that sounded strangely like a grunt. Whether in disapproval or relief, she couldn't be sure, but she continued with the pitch she'd hastily put together after the rest of the support staff had cleared the office for the weekend. After a couple more masculine examples, she laid the last two images on the table and indicated for Simon to rise. One of the final boards contained a collage of cutouts from mens' clothing catalogues. The last board was from the cover of *GQ* magazine, sporting a gorgeous hunk who had Simon's body structure—when he stood straight.

''So what do you think?'' she asked, unable to keep the excitement out of her voice. ''If I'd had more time I could've come up with something a lot more professional.''

Simon lifted the cardboard with the cover model and tipped it toward the light for a closer look. A deep wrinkle creased the space between his eyes, and his thick frames slid down a fraction. He did that thing with his nose to push them back in place.

He tapped the cardboard with his finger. ''You think you can make me look like this?'' he asked incredulously. "Ms. Richmond, I don't think anyone has *that* much money."

She chuckled, took the storyboard from him and tossed it on the table with the others. "Now that you've brought it up, perhaps we should discuss our terms." She propped her backside against the edge of the table and faced him. This was where things got just a wee bit tricky. On the drive to his apartment, she'd decided it was best that he believe she really was a full-fledged image consultant, not just some wannabe held back by her chauvinistic brothers. He needed to believe not just in her, but in what she could do for him. If Simon suspected she was anything but the real thing, then the confidence necessary for a complete transformation would be lost. Although not completely without principals, she'd decided not to accept money from him. At least not for her services.

She crossed her feet at the ankles and curled her fingers around the edge of the table. "I don't want your money," she said. "But I really could use some sound financial advice once we're finished."

He rubbed the back of his neck, his attention still on the last two storyboards. "I'm an accountant," he said, glancing at her cautiously, "not a financial adviser."

"Then perhaps you can recommend someone."

She couldn't blame him for eyeing her skeptically, but she hoped he'd accept her offer.

"You don't want me to pay you," he clarified, "but to give you financial advice instead?"

She attempted a casual shrug. "I'm looking to do a little investing and I'd like to learn to play the stock market. I figured since you're an accountant you might know a few things and could teach me."

He shoved his hands in the front pockets of his navy trousers and gave her a stern look. "No one *plays* the stock market, Ms. Richmond. Investing is serious business, and anyone who thinks other—"

"It's Jaycee," she interrupted.

He blinked at her from behind the heavy lenses of his eyeglasses. When his sable eyebrows pulled together in a frown, she added, "Call me Jaycee."

He nodded and turned away, as if embarrassed by something. With his gaze clearly focused on the discarded storyboards, he asked, "Jaycee? Is that short for something?"

She leaned over the table to collect her presentation, her hand brushing his arm. That same funny tingling she'd felt when they'd shook hands earlier traveled up her arm then swooped down to the pit of her belly.

Hunger pangs, she reasoned. Had to be. She hadn't eaten since lunch. "Jocelyn Camille."

He picked up the *GQ* cover and held it out to her. "That's pretty," he said quietly.

Now it was her turn to blush. Surely she'd imagined that Simon's voice had gone all deep and rich on her. "Thank you." She kept her gaze averted and concentrated on slipping the rubber band around the presentation boards. "I've never really been fond of it."

One corner of his mouth tipped into a lopsided grin, and her gaze was drawn to his full lower lip. "Try being named after a couple of chipmunks."

At her questioning frown, he said, "Simon Theodore."

The grin tugging his lips widened into a full-fledged smile, and she couldn't help returning it with one of her own. She'd been in his company for a total of less than one hour, and she hadn't seen a glimpse of the non-user-friendly accountant he'd been accused of being. He wasn't rude, brusque or even withdrawn. He was just very intense when the discussion shifted to anything numerical. If someone was asking her, she'd have to say that Simon was just plain cute, and adorably shy.

"Would you like some wine?" he asked suddenly, standing just a tad straighter for all of two seconds.

Until his shoulders slumped forward again. "I bought…" His hands eased into the front pockets of his navy trousers. "I thought…I mean…" He looked at the floor. "I figured we could…"

"Have a drink to seal the deal?" she finished when he seemed incapable of doing so himself. "I'd love a glass."

His relief was so obvious when his gaze lifted to hers, she couldn't help but smile. His shoulders straightened and his hands returned to view. Simon went into the kitchen to take care of the wine, and she used the opportunity to look around his apartment.

"Have you lived here long?" she called from the living room.

"About six years," he replied.

Well, that was certainly a surprise. Other than a bookcase with a few books on stamp collecting, there wasn't much in the apartment to give her a feel for who Simon really was beneath his nerdlike exterior. A quick perusal of his compact discs revealed his taste in music was as varied as her own, running from classical to country. Her place was crammed full of things from her youth, from places she'd visited throughout the years and homemade gifts from her two great-aunts. Simon's place was almost impersonal, like one of those condos the big image consulting firms owned and offered to their clients as a perk.

He returned a few minutes later and handed her a glass of blush wine. "I'm not much of a connoisseur, but the salesman said this was a good after-dinner wine. I took a chance that you've had dinner."

She sipped the wine. "It's fine," she said, reminding herself she hadn't had dinner. "May I see your closet?"

His free hand went into his pocket and he hunched forward again. "Why?"

"For an inventory. I need to see if there's anything in there we can salvage."

His brow puckered, then he did that thing when his glasses slid down the slope of his nose again. "How much is this going to cost me?"

"Let's see what we've got to work with first."

Why she felt uncomfortable following Simon into his bedroom, she couldn't rightly say, and shaking off the feeling wasn't as simple as she might have thought. It wasn't like she'd never been in a bedroom alone with a man before, just not very often, as Fiona would take great delight in reminding her.

She was a professional. Being in the same room with a man and a very large four-poster bed that dominated the intimate space didn't mean she wasn't operating in a professional capacity. Lots of people worked in their bedrooms, and not all of them charged by the hour.

"I prefer to keep things simple," she heard him say. She couldn't seem to get her eyes off the four-poster bed or the odd framed print hanging above it.

"How do you like it?" he asked.

A dozen thoughts flew through her mind, and not one of them held even the slightest hint of professionalism. "I'm not sure. What's it called?" she asked, praying he was referring to the print.

"Erotic."

Okay, now she really was uncomfortable. "Erotic?"

The smile he'd shown her earlier returned when he shook his head. *"Etudes,"* he clarified. "It's from Picasso's modern collection."

She smiled weakly. "Fan or collector?" She'd suspected he was a stamp collector based on the books she'd found in his living room. A collection of butterflies she might have also expected. Or bugs, for that matter. But art? Simon just didn't strike her as the artsy type.

He shrugged. "Neither, really. This stuff, that reproduction included, all belonged to my grandmother. Here's the closet," he said, sliding open the mirrored door.

"Well, let's see what we have to work with...." Her voice trailed off as she looked inside the perfectly organized closet. At least a dozen short-sleeve white dress shirts hung in a neat row. Next came two long-sleeve shirts, not surprisingly also white. On the rack below the shirts hung pairs of slacks—three black, three gray and two navy blue. She glanced over her shoulder at Simon. He wore the third navy pair.

"Not much," she muttered, then slid the door closed. "If you have plans for tomorrow, cancel them. We're going shopping."

"Shopping?" He shook his head vehemently, and his eyes filled with panic. "I don't like shopping."

What man does?

"I can see that," she countered. "Simon, your wardrobe is in serious trouble. You want a new image, right?"

He looked at himself, then at her. The panic she'd detected was unchanged. "What's wrong with my clothes? They're perfectly..."

Perfectly boring.

"There's nothing *wrong* with them," she explained, "it's just that they're...they're not..." She hated to be rude, but he was, in essence, pay-

ing her to perform a service. What kind of professional would she be if she continued to worry
about hurting his feelings every time she had to
explain something to him? "Simon, your taste in
clothes isn't very flattering."

He set his wineglass on the antique bureau,
planted his hands on his hips and turned to face
her. "I've been wearing this stuff for years."

"Exactly my point." Snagging his hand, she
tugged until he was standing in front of the full-
length mirrored sliding doors of his closet. "Tell
me what you see."

Surprisingly, he didn't pull the slumped-
shoulder, hand-in-pocket routine. Instead, he gave
himself a once-over before looking at her. "Me?"

She shook her head. "No. Look beyond that."

"The new lead character for *Revenge of the
Nerds Four*?"

She let out a sigh. The man was impossibly obtuse. "You want to know what I see?" She
reached up to pull the thick black frames from his
face. Taking a step back, she tipped her head to
look into the clearest, greenest gaze she'd ever
seen. He returned her gaze, and her breath stilled.
The heavy frames hid a handsomely chiseled face
with high angular cheekbones, a straight nose and
a strong, square jaw she hadn't noticed until now.

"I see a whole lot of untapped potential," she whispered.

Simon squinted and leaned past her to peer into the mirror. "You want to know what I see?"

"What?"

He moved back and looked at her. "Very little without my glasses."

Jaycee sipped her wine. "What about contacts?" It really was a shame to hide those chiseled features behind such ugly glasses that did absolutely nothing to enhance his natural good looks.

"No, thanks. I'd end up sticking my finger in my eye."

She ignored his complaining and handed him his eyeglasses. "New frames, then. Something wireless."

He really was a fount of potential. Her own very special lump of coal, and it was up to her to make him shine like the most brilliant of gems. Tapping her foot, she waited while he slipped on his glasses, her attention on the play of muscle and sinew in his forearms.

"Hold this," she said, thrusting her wineglass at him. She slipped behind him, grabbed a handful of his plain white shirt and pulled it tight until she could see the outline of his torso. "Very impressive," she murmured, then yanked his shirttails from his trousers.

"What are you doing?" The tenor of his voice rose a notch.

She started with the top button and worked her way down, wanting to see exactly what she had to work with...and if it was as promising as she suspected. "Shh, I'm thinking."

He tried unsuccessfully to pull away from her. She hadn't spent years holding her own against two overbearing brothers for nothing.

"You're undressing me!"

She ignored his outrage and let out a sigh. "This isn't going to work." An equally loose T-shirt blocked her view of his torso.

"I could have told you that," he muttered, then said something she didn't quite catch.

Ignoring him, she slid open the closet door and searched the shelves. Stacked neatly in wire baskets were more white T-shirts along with a few sweaters in his stock colors of navy blue, black and gray.

"Jaycee, what are you looking for?"

"I saw something...aha!" She pulled a black sweater from the basket, then reached toward the top shelf for a pair of jeans that had snagged her attention. "Can you reach those for me?"

The toe of her shoe slipped slightly on the hardwood floor. She took a step to steady herself, then felt two things simultaneously—her finger catching on a wire basket and very large pieces of confetti fluttering around her.

Cool liquid poured down her back.

She squealed, tried to jump away from the cold and slammed right into Simon's wide chest.

He swore and grabbed her, his arms banding her waist and lifting her off her feet. The small oval rug slipped beneath his feet, and he pulled her tight against him, using his big body to cushion the fall.

They landed together on the hardwood floor. Stunned into silence, she watched as small bits of paper fluttered over her and stuck to her damp blouse and skirt.

She tried to move, but something rock-hard and solid was pressed against her backside. A low moan she couldn't claim as entirely professional escaped as she realized it was Simon's thighs cradling her bottom.

And despite that Simon was strictly a client, the sensations rippling along her spine were far from professional.

4

JAYCEE STARED at the sculpted ceiling in Simon's bedroom, wondering what on earth had gone wrong. One minute she was reaching high on a shelf for a pair of jeans and the next she had a warm male body cradling her in his arms.

"Are you all right?"

Simon's deep voice, combined with his warm breath teasing the side of her neck, had flutters leaping down her spine and launching into frenetic flight inside her empty stomach. A not altogether unpleasant feeling, but one that made Jaycee distinctly aware of her bottom pressing against some very interesting masculine parts.

"I think so," she said. But the chill of the wine against her back told her the blouse was history. The front of her clothes confirmed that fact, considering she was covered in stamps that now stuck to the wine stains.

"What went wrong?" she asked. All she knew for certain was that her back was plastered against solid male—and she liked it.

"Foot slipped," he murmured, his firm, wide chest rumbling against her soaked back.

Her flutters got flutters of their own.

She made an attempt to scoot off him.

Simon's arm banded her waist. "Don't move," he said, his voice tight as if he was gritting his teeth.

She lowered her head to his shoulder. "What do you suggest we do? We can't stay like this forever you know."

Pity.

His chest rose and fell, and Jaycee with it. "You're right," he said after a moment. "Okay. You can move, but you gotta do it slow. Some of those stamps could be worth a lot of money."

She resisted the urge to roll her eyes and tell him if they were that important, then they shouldn't be lying around loose where something like this could happen. Instead, she concentrated on carefully scooting her bottom across Simon's thigh.

Her care was rewarded by him sucking in a sharp breath she thought had less to do with fear she'd injure his precious stamp collection and more to do with the electric contact of their bodies and the friction her movements against those interesting masculine parts was causing.

Stamps were the least of their worries, she

thought, when another electrical current skittered along the surface of her skin the second his big, warm hands grasped her hips.

Her breath caught.

His fingers gently lifted her bottom, his touch singeing her through her clothes.

Her temperature skyrocketed.

"What are you doing?" she squeaked.

"Saving us both a lot of embarrassment," he said, his voice tight with tension.

It took two heartbeats for his meaning to register.

"Oh." It was all she could muster as he raised her up and away from him and set her onto the cool, smooth hardwood floor. The rest of her followed, except her head, which was cushioned by a thick bicep.

A very nice feeling, indeed.

She let out a little sigh of pleasure as she looked up and admired Simon's square jaw, lightly peppered with five o'clock shadow.

Before she managed to collect herself enough to ease away from him and stand, he leaned over her, his gaze clear and bright even behind those bulky eyeglasses—and filled with an intensity that had her struggling to maintain a normal breathing pattern.

"Are you sure you're all right?" he asked, his voice low and sensual.

Her heart was pounding at a frantic pace. Did that count? she wondered.

"I think so." She kept waiting for the awkwardness of their position to hit her. When it didn't, she reached down and plucked a stamp from her blouse. "This belong to you?" she quipped.

He took the stamp from her and held it gingerly between his fingers. "This was a mistake," he said softly.

"Accidents happen," she whispered, wondering why she had the sudden urge to sneak her hand around his neck and shock him clear to the toes of his argyle socks by pulling him down for a hot, openmouthed kiss.

He shook his head. "I meant this." He turned the stamp so she could see the face. "What's wrong with this picture?"

Gee, where did she start? Maybe with lying on the floor in Simon's bedroom? Or how about with the sizzling awareness she couldn't help but notice?

What was wrong with her? She was supposed to be his image consultant, not his...regular Friday night gal.

"Take a look at the traffic light," he prompted

when she continued to stare at him instead of the stamp.

Okay. She could play along. She peered closer at the stamp in his fingertips. "The red light is on the bottom, not the top." She grinned at him. "Does that make it valuable?"

He eased them into a sitting position, then stood. With his hand still holding hers, he helped her to her feet then led her over to the four-poster bed and urged her to sit.

As if hypnotized, Jaycee moved, sat, then stared into Simon's handsomely chiseled face, into those eyes she could easily lose herself in if she let it happen.

Boy, was it ever happening.

He leaned over her and gently plucked another stamp from her blouse. "Not in this case," he said, lifting his gaze to her mouth.

Jaycee swallowed and tried like the devil to follow the conversation.

Not in what case?

Stamps!

They were talking about stamps.

"This 1947 Italian stamp is just unusual," he explained, carefully removing another stamp stuck dangerously close to her breast.

She pulled in a deep breath.

"There's a 1952 French stamp that's similar and extremely valuable."

Another stamp fell from her blouse and fluttered somewhere on the floor. Neither of them paid it any attention.

"There are only three known to be in existence," he said. His gaze locked on hers like a heat-seeking missile.

Breathe, Jaycee. Just breathe.

"Three?" Something was happening here. A tension that, if she pushed it, she could consider image-related, in a very roundabout sort of way. The only problem was the images filtering through her mind had more to do with Simon and sharing a horizontal position.

What was wrong with her? Richmond women didn't lust after men. *She* didn't lust after men. She had goals, and they didn't include panting after the client she planned to provide to her brothers as proof she was equal partnership material despite her gender.

Too bad the only partnering on her mind was the kind that required good old-fashioned coupling...with her off-limits client.

There was definitely something happening to her, something that had do with awareness and curiosity. And kisses. The deep, tempting, toe-curling kind. The kind hotter than the sidewalks in Las Vegas on a hot summer night.

"And French," he said.

Her lusty thoughts zeroed in on that one innocent word and shoved her professionalism and goal-oriented arguments right out the window.

"French?" she said, her voice barely above a whisper.

He nodded. "French." His gaze shifted to her eyes, then to her mouth.

Self-consciously, she moistened her bottom lip. She hadn't meant it as an invitation, but when Simon slowly dipped his head, she ignored all the warnings she should've paid heed to and opted to lift her lips toward his and satisfy her curiosity instead.

Keeping his gaze locked with hers, he removed his glasses and set them on the mattress. "Very French," he added, his voice as soft and smooth as the most luxurious cashmere, and just as tempting.

His lips were warm, coaxing and gentle. His tongue tasted lightly of the wine he'd had earlier, only twice as intoxicating.

Jaycee was no rookie when it came to kissing, but Simon Hawthorne gave the term French kissing a whole new meaning. Wild, head-spinning sensations rippled through her body and skimmed just beneath the surface of her skin.

He deepened the kiss, and she moaned. When his fingertips brushed gently down her cheek to slip into her hair and he cupped the back of her head in his large, warm palm, she wreathed her arms around his neck and held on tight.

Simon obviously had no qualms about complying with her wishes. He eased her onto the bed and covered her with his body. While the heat of his chest pressed enticingly against her ultrasensitive breasts, she responded to the gentle demands of his mouth, then, like a brazen hussy, she rocked her hips forward against the hard length of his erection pressing against her thigh.

Simon Hawthorne was no nerd. He was one-hundred-percent man, a man who was making her want and need to the point of no return. If they were engaged in a battle, she'd be more than happy to call for a complete and total surrender, so long as he kept making her feel so…sensual.

Sensation after sensation caught her attention for the flash of an instant before the next one clamored to the top of the ever-growing stack, never giving her the opportunity to properly savor each luscious, sensuous feeling. A tightness caught in her belly then gathered energy before practically exploding to spread throughout her limbs, making her feel hot and cold all at the same time.

They couldn't do this.

But Simon's mouth on hers was absolute heaven.

She had to stop him. Deep, tongue-tangling kisses were hardly considered professional.

Snagging hold of a tenuous thread of common sense, she used her palms and pushed gently at Simon's shoulders. He lifted his head and looked at her, confusion and something much more telling and interesting in his gaze—lust.

"Is something wrong?" he asked.

Stunned into silence by the branding-iron-hot desire in his eyes, she could only manage a nod.

"What?" he finally asked when she couldn't find her voice with two hands, a flashlight and a road map.

Pulling in a deep breath, she let it out very slowly. It didn't work. In fact she doubted an effective coolant existed against her rising temperature. Except the stall tactic did allow her valuable seconds to attempt to pull herself together.

A grin tugged his lips. "You've got to come up with something better than that," he said, a teasing note in his voice. He dipped his head to skim his lips along her throat.

A deep moan was as close to a denial as she could manage.

He nipped at her throat then soothed the spot with his tongue.

She toed off her pumps and traced her foot along his calf, her feet coming in direct contact with rough, nubby polyester.

What was she doing? She was behaving like a professional, all right, but one that expected a generous tip left on the nightstand. And it was not the kind of profession found in any telephone directory, either.

"Simon," she said in a breathless whisper. "We have to stop."

Oh, that was convincing, Richmond. You might as well shout, "Take me now, stud!"

When it came to the opposite sex, why did her conscience always sound like Fiona?

"Hmm. I know," he murmured against her skin.

"This isn't the kind of image I want to portray."

At the moment, she couldn't think of a damn thing wrong with Simon's image. Ditch the polyester, and the man was pure perfection!

You're sexually depraved.

Maybe so, but yowza, can Simon ever kiss!

He nuzzled the spot below her ear and she trembled in his arms like the sex-starved nymph she was starting to believe was the real Jaycee Richmond.

"I kinda like this image," he whispered seductively in her ear, his warm breath fanning her cheek.

Oh, heaven help her, she was really loving *his* image.

"I was speaking as a professional image consultant," she said, in what she hoped was a prim voice.

If anyone had told her the accountant in need of a more hip, user-friendly appearance would have her insides melting and liquefy her resolve just as easily, she wouldn't have believed it for a second.

Her fingertips teased the hair at the base of his neck, then danced along the collar of his T-shirt. Maybe her conscience was right. Maybe she was just a sexually depraved woman. Good grief, she couldn't remember the last time she'd even had a date.

But then, with Simon creating such delicious distractions, who cared?

Before she could stop herself, she dipped her hand beneath the cotton fabric of his T-shirt to tentatively explore the muscle and sinew hidden beneath. She groaned softly and pushed the fingers of her free hand into his hair...and they just kept on going!

She rubbed her fingertips together. They were coated in... Good grief, she didn't know what!

"Simon. Stop."

He let out a huff of breath. "Are you sure?"

No.

She rubbed her fingertips together again. "I'm sure."

Reluctantly, he eased away from her and sat.

She pushed off the bed and stood, grabbed a tissue from the nightstand and wiped her hands. Then she concentrated on plucking the last of the stamps from her clothes, while trying to ignore the way her body still hummed from the intense pleasure of Simon's unexpectedly erotic kisses.

After setting the stamps on the dresser, she came to the bed and looked at him and the hopeful expression in his eyes. Her insides twisted into more knots. Before her common sense escaped again, she grabbed Simon's hand, pulled him away from the temptation of the four-poster bed and led him into the bathroom.

"I need my glasses," he told her. His voice sounded as shaky as her insides.

No matter how unprofessional that kiss, the thought that he was equally shaken gave her feminine pride a thrill.

"Not where we're going, you don't," she told him, and flipped on the overhead light.

"What *are* you planning?"

She didn't say a word, but stopped at the bath-tub. He had one of those showerheads with a de-tachable sprayer, which would make her job a whole lot easier. She turned on the faucet, then waited for the water to heat.

"On your knees, Hawthorne."

The instant grin that tugged his lips was nothing short of wicked. Before he could guess her intent or continue with the wrong impression, she put her hand on the back of his head and pushed him over the side of the bathtub.

"What are you doing?" he sputtered when she turned on the sprayer and proceeded to rinse the goop out of his hair.

"It's time to change more than your image, Simon."

She grabbed the shampoo bottle and started scrubbing, ignoring her client's sputtering protests. "I'd say you're way overdue for an oil change."

5

SIMON COULD THINK of lots of places on his body he'd just love to see Jaycee's hands. Or better yet, places he'd beg to feel the tips of her fingers gently massaging. Shoving his head under running water, then shampooing his hair failed to make the list. Especially after the mind-blowing kiss they'd shared not five minutes ago.

Maybe she had a shampoo fetish.

In fact, now that he thought about it, he wasn't sure what he expected since he'd kissed Jaycee. Or had she kissed him first? It didn't matter. All that mattered was that they did it some more. A whole lot more.

He felt the cool tingle of the conditioner from a fancy bottle his secretary had given him for Christmas that he never used, followed by the sensuous feel of Jaycee's hands sliding over his head, her fingers gliding through his hair, teasing his scalp.

Suddenly, he was glad to be bent over the tub, where she couldn't get an eyeful of just how much he was enjoying the pleasure her hands were giving him.

He might be what the partners at Eaton and Simms labeled a nerd, but he'd never qualify as a monk, although he was beginning to feel like one. Could anyone but a monk be turned on just because a woman was washing his hair?

Okay, so he didn't get laid half as much as the jocks in high school and college, but he had managed to garner *some* experience with the opposite sex. Those other women might not have been half as beautiful and alluring as Jaycee, nor had they ever washed his hair, but that didn't mean they qualified as moon howlers, either. The only difference between the scant number of women in his past and Jaycee was that none of those other women had ever shaken him up with so much as a simple kiss.

Simple? There was nothing simple about it.

She held the sprayer away from his head. "Did you say something?" she asked.

"Yummy," he answered, keeping his head down and his gaze on the white porcelain bathtub. *Oh, that was intelligent.*

"What's yummy?" she asked, dousing his head with water again.

You. "That stuff smells good," he answered lamely, cataloging the cool cucumber fragrance of the conditioner before zeroing in on the subtle floral aroma of Jaycee's more intoxicating scent.

The water stopped, and she dropped a towel over his head.

"Turn slowly toward me," she instructed, urging him with her hands on his shoulders. She guided him to the commode, lowered the lid and urged him to sit down.

She spoke as she towel dried his hair, but he couldn't make out her words as they faded in and out. The scene brought back a distant memory from long ago, resurrected from a forgotten past. He caught a fragmented glimpse of his mother, Elena, her voice filled with laughter and the same disjointed words while she towel dried his hair. A memory from a happier time, before the disappointment settled in...before her departure shattered a little boy's heart.

Jaycee had a lot in common with Elena Hawthorne, he realized. Outgoing, strong-willed, vivacious, as well as beautiful. Jaycee was everything he wasn't, just like his mother was everything his old man, Steven Hawthorne, wasn't. And everything Simon had learned a long time ago *he* could never be, despite his promising gene pool.

What did he think? Just because he and Jaycee had experienced one very intense, mega-hot, bone-melting kiss they were destined to walk down the aisle, raise a half dozen kids? Were they supposed to live happily ever after in one of Seattle's better suburban neighborhoods just because they'd locked lips?

Hardly.

Jaycee was his image consultant. She might be creating one hell of an image in his fantasies, but that's where it had to end. Reality differed greatly from the more interesting fantasies.

She pulled the towel off his head and tossed it over the shower curtain rod. "I hope you understand," she was saying, as she bent and looked under the sink for something.

He understood she had one curvy bottom he didn't think he'd ever grow tired of admiring.

His gaze lingered on the bottom in question, and he suppressed a moan as her lovely posterior pressed seductively against the soiled linen of her skirt. It took every ounce of willpower he possessed, and then some, to remain silent.

"It's nothing personal. That kiss…"

Qualified as a religious experience.

"Aha!" she exclaimed, not finishing her sentence. She stood, the blow-dryer he never used clasped in her hand. With her lips pursed, she attempted to rid the dryer of accumulated dust, then realized it was futile and snagged a washcloth from the holder to wipe away the remaining dust.

"It was...well," she said, rifling through the drawer and producing a brush, "that kiss was a distraction, and that's something neither one of us needs right now."

He didn't know about her, but he could use a few more distractions if they were anywhere near as intoxicating as the last diversion.

She found the plug then turned the dryer on low. "We each have goals," she continued, loud enough to be heard over the noise as she dried his hair. The subject of her lecture didn't hold much value. Not when the view in front of him was one that any red-blooded male would be enjoying.

Jaycee pulled in a deep breath.

Simon's heart nearly stopped.

Her full breasts, the same ones he'd felt pressing seductively against his chest before she'd dragged him into the bathroom and doused him with water and shampoo, lifted and pressed enticingly against the material of her ruined silk blouse. He had every intention of replacing the blouse, considering his stamps had ruined it, but for now, he was prepared to let her lecture away so long as she continued to stand and breathe in front of him.

"I mean you have a goal," she said, gently tugging on his hair and applying the heat from the blow-dryer to the strands. "You need the partners in your firm to see you as a hip, user-friendly kind of guy. And that's my goal, too, but..."

She paused, gathered more of his hair with the brush and moved the blow-dryer around his head. "We got caught up in the moment," she continued. "The moment. Nothing more."

That caught his attention.

"The moment?" he repeated, wondering why he had the sudden impression she was trying to convince herself more than him that their kiss was anything less than a mind-blowing, bone-melting experience.

She turned off the dryer and set it on the counter before reaching into the drawer for a comb. "You know what I mean."

He looked at her. Even without his glasses he could see the adorable blush staining her cheeks. "I don't think I do," he told her. Oh, he knew exactly what she meant, but darned if he didn't think watching her try to explain it to him would be tons more fun. "You mean the *heat* of the moment, don't you?"

He stood and shoved his hands through his hair, liking the way Jaycee had made it feel, lighter and much softer. Since he had a tendency toward ignoring the alarm clock in the morning, the slicked-back look had become more of a necessity than a fashion option.

His glasses were in the bedroom, where he'd left them on the bed, so he leaned closer to peer at Jaycee in hopes of gauging her reaction to her styling techniques.

"What do you think?" he asked.

He heard her quick intake of breath. Male satisfaction edged aside his usual discomfort around women like Jaycee.

"Of the heat?" she asked, her voice sounding hushed and strident at the same time.

"Well, yeah," he lied. "Isn't that what you're trying to say?"

"I think so," she whispered, turning her head slightly to the side so those silken, chestnut strands fell away from her face. Something in her gaze flickered, and she straightened before taking a step back. "That's not important, Simon. We're both professionals. That's what we have to remember."

"Jaycee, there was nothing professional about that kiss. That kiss was—"

"A mistake," she said quickly. She unplugged the dryer and started wrapping the cord around the handle.

He let out a breath. "I was going to say hot." So much for the great pep talk about keeping their relationship based in reality. One catch of feminine breath, one hesitant look filled with a wealth of sexual anticipation, and he was ready to shove reality out the window and let it suffer a violent death.

She set the dryer on the counter and turned. "Hot?"

He nodded slowly and closed the short distance between them. Reality? Forget reality. He was about to dive straight into fantasy again for one more taste of her sweet mouth.

"Very," he said, easing his hand around the base of her neck, reveling in the contrasting sensations of warm skin and the coolness of downy-soft chestnut hair cascading over his fingers.

"Oh." The professional tone she'd been striving for slid away, and her voice quieted with hushed anticipation.

"Can you honestly deny it?"

She closed her eyes, and that part of him that wasn't completely lost in polyester hoped she wouldn't dare deny either of them another round of erotic sensations. He wanted her staunch self-control, which she so piously attempted to keep erect between them, to crumble like an ancient ruin.

"Of course not," she said. "I was merely attempting to make a point."

He pushed the hair away from her neck, tempted to dip his head for a taste of her skin.

"And what point is that?" he asked, thinking

that getting Jaycee to lose control in his arms was something worthy of further experimentation.

Jaycee couldn't believe she was falling for this a second time in the same night. For crying out loud, Simon was her client, not her… "Sexual attraction," she blurted.

"You're sexually attracted to me?"

His voice had gone all husky and deep.

"No," she lied.

And oh, how wonderfully sexy he sounded.

How beautifully distracting his thumb smoothing back and forth just below her earlobe.

How powerful was the pull, the need to feel more and more of that incredibly delicious thrum of anticipation pulsing in her veins as she envisioned Simon's mouth moving sensuously over hers.

"Yes," she blurted, unable to tell a lie. She'd thought he was cute before. Now that she'd manage to peel away a few layers, she'd found drop-dead gorgeous, one-hundred-percent hunk beneath the unflattering clothes and that awful wet look.

"I mean, not to me," she amended, trading complete honesty for a quasi fib. "What I mean is—" she attempted to explain without tripping over her tongue "—women will find you sexually attractive, and that's what I was trying to prove."

It didn't seem possible, but he narrowed the distance between them. "By kissing me?" he asked.

His question sounded very much like a sensual demand. One her body begged her to respond to regardless of her mind's stern lecture to the contrary. "That's one way," she told him, looking into those deep green eyes.

"There's more?"

She couldn't find an ounce of insincerity or mockery in his gaze, yet despite the honesty she detected, she couldn't stop thinking this could just be a ploy to…what? Get closer? If they got any closer they'd be cited!

"Of course there's more," she said, sidestepping him before she did something really stupid, like wreathe her arms around his neck and pull him down for another one of those wet and wild kisses.

"Not that we'll be doing anything about it," she reminded him firmly, effectively smoothing out the smile that had started to ease across his incredibly seductive mouth.

His hand fell to his side. "That's too bad." He stuffed his hands in the front pockets of his trousers. Despite the gorgeous male specimen she was slowly uncovering, his shoulders still slumped forward, which enhanced his lack of confidence.

Doing the smart thing, she walked out of the bathroom. Following that up by something completely stupid, she stopped and stared longingly at the foot of his bed, still mussed from their enticing tumble across the comforter.

"Simon," she said, easing her way toward the door and into the neutral territory of his living room, "sex appeal is more than just knowing how to kiss a woman so you turn her insides to butter."

She plucked her bag from the table where she'd left it and slung it over her shoulder. Her clothes were probably ruined, and while her feminine pride was definitely reaching untold heights, her professionalism was a breath away from being trampled to death. Time to make haste and maintain at least a little of her dignity.

"*I* turned your insides to butter?"

Did he ever!

"Yes."

Simon grinned and slipped on his black-framed glasses.

"No." She pulled in a deep breath and let it out slowly before she continued. "What I mean is, you not only have to look the part of the smooth, polished professional, but you have to live it, as well."

His grin deepened. That was *not* the reaction she wanted. "Will turning your insides to butter again make me closer to living the part?"

She held firm. "That can't be an option, Simon."

The grin was erased, and his dark, sable eyebrows tugged together into a frown. "Why not?"

Because you're a means to an end.

Because if I let you distract me, it'll only prove to my brothers that I am a mere woman whose emotions overrule her good business sense.

Regardless of the reminder to keep her relationship within ethical business boundaries, the urge to cross the room, press her lips to his and reassure him he really did turn her insides to butter nearly overwhelmed her.

This was not good.

Even if it could be real good.

"Because it isn't professional," she answered and headed toward the door. If she didn't get out of there, she just might do what her body was screaming at her to do...wrap her arms around Simon and never let go.

"I'll pick you up at noon tomorrow," she said, reaching for the door. "Bring your credit cards, because we'll be doing some serious shopping."

He stuffed his hands into his pockets again and slumped forward. "Do we have to?" he asked, reminding her of the next generation of Richmonds when they were attempting to garner some treat or another out of her parents.

She bit back a grin. "Yes. We do. You have to look the part, remember. When I'm finished with you, you're not only going to be very user-friendly, but the term *nerd* will never be synonymous with Simon Hawthorne again."

She slipped through the door and pulled it firmly shut behind her. Not even a deep, calming breath of cool, sea-scented air, nor the firm command to her heart to stop beating erratically in her chest, could lessen the truth that had caught her completely off guard tonight.

When she'd agreed to take on the task of changing Simon's image, the last thing she expected was that her client would turn out to be nothing short of a drop-dead-gorgeous gem of a man who, with just a little polishing, would turn into some lucky woman's Mr. Right.

6

JAYCEE THUMBED through a women's magazine and waited for Simon to emerge from the dressing room. This was their fourth store in as many hours and, thankfully, their last. Irritation generously described Simon's mood when he'd walked into the dressing room of the upscale men's clothing store ten minutes ago. He'd grumbled something about his credit-card bills rivaling the national debt. She'd smiled sweetly at the sales clerk and pretended to ignore Simon's complaining.

When she'd picked him up precisely at noon, a part of her had expected him to return to his status-quo look. Change didn't happen overnight, but Simon was obviously determined and had heeded her advice. The other part of her, the one consistently ignoring her internal professionalism lectures, had felt a distinct feminine thrill at the sight of the tall hunk of man answering the door. He might have been dressed in the same boring attire she'd scouted in his closet the night before, but he'd forgone the solid-colored tie and the slicked-back look. He'd surprised the heck out of her when he'd told her he'd spent time with his neglected blow-dryer that morning. His rich sable hair had looked silky and smooth, and she'd had the almost irresistible urge to run her fingers through the thick, goo-free strands.

Instead she'd forced herself to concentrate on Simon the client and not Simon the man.

Simon the man had kept her up half the night tossing and turning with an achiness she couldn't recall feeling before. Every time she'd closed her eyes, her traitorous mind had replayed that kiss. All night long she'd recounted the seconds before his lips had touched hers, when he'd looked at her as if he treasured her more than his precious stamp collection.

A silly notion, anyway. They'd just met. They didn't even *know* each other.

Better for her to concentrate on Simon the client, so she could keep her head out of the clouds and away from absurd notions that would deter her from her two goals—to be taken seriously by her brothers, and to ensure continued employment for Simon.

She had to maintain her focus, keep her emotions locked away, or she'd end up diluting her goals, she thought, peering at a body-lotion ad promising younger, healthier skin. How could she expect Dane and Rick to take her seriously otherwise? She couldn't, and she knew they'd blow her off in a heartbeat if she revealed Simon was her own personal client, and oh-by-the-way-we're-involved.

She had to find a way to darken the professional line so she wouldn't continue stepping over it and plastering her mouth all over Simon.

Retaining her focus on her goals might have been a heck of a lot simpler if she hadn't insisted on their first stop being the one-hour-or-less vision store. With the heavy black frames keeping his handsome features hidden, categorizing him in the off-limits clientele section had been so much easier. Following that up with a stop at the hairdresser had intensified her inability to think of Simon in only professional terms. Not when every time she looked at him she wanted to run her fingers through his newly styled hair.

She let out a sigh and tossed the magazine she hadn't really been reading on the glass-topped table. Arguments be damned. She couldn't help herself. Simon the man was slowly changing into one sexy specimen. Neither she nor her senses had been prepared for the impact of his very tempting metamorphosis.

Without the hindrance of the thick glasses, his

eyes were an even darker, more intense shade of green. For as up close and personal as they'd been last night, she was finding it tough to handle the truth—that Simon's jaw really was breathtakingly square and strong. And those cheekbones she'd considered angular and sharp had been softened by the more flattering frames and his newly styled hair.

Unfortunately, her fascination with Simon the man didn't stop there. Maybe *she* was the one who needed glasses, but she could swear that after each stop on their shopping excursion, a different Simon emerged from every exclusive menswear store. And with each new look, her big ideals of staunch professionalism blurred faster than the five-fifteen ferry crossing Puget Sound to Bremerton.

Moments later, a movement caught her attention. She shook her head as if she couldn't quite believe the man coming out of the dressing room was really her client—a client who made her temperature rise, her pulse leap and her body crave a whole lot more than just his luscious kisses.

"I dunno," he muttered, a frown pulling his sable brows together. "This is an awful lot of money for something I might not ever use."

"Simon?"

Just because he looked over his shoulder at her with that emerald-forest gaze was no excuse for her tummy to tighten, but it did, and her pulse leaped, and an enticing chill skirted her skin.

"Tell me again why I need a tuxedo," he complained, then scowled deeper as he pointedly shifted his attention to the price tag he'd eased from the sleeve.

Stunned at the sight of the absolutely gorgeous hunk speaking to her, she crossed the thick blue carpeting to stand beside him and peer closer. She stared in disbelief at the reflection in the angled mirrors. It really was Simon.

"Wow," she whispered unprofessionally. "Simon, you look…wow!"

A corner of his mouth lifted into a lopsided grin with enough sex appeal to have her insides doing a series of pirouettes. "That doesn't exactly answer my question."

Shaking her head, she slowly walked around him, looking him up and down in utter amazement. The rare moments when he wasn't stuffing his hands in his pockets, hunching his shoulders and slouching forward, she'd suspected Simon kept a great body hidden beneath boring ties, polyester slacks and ill-fitting starched white shirts. Yet the pleasant discovery of his physical attributes in no way prepared her for the heart-stopping, breathtaking man standing in front of her.

"It's just so amazing," she whispered, then

closed the distance between them to straighten his bow tie a notch. "They say the clothes don't make the man, so I guess it's really you doing one heck of a number on this tux."

And an even bigger one on her.

"And I need this...why?" he asked, looking away.

She hid a smile at the sight of a blush darkening his skin. Dusting an invisible fleck of lint from his wide shoulder, she looked into his eyes and said, "User-friendly. Isn't that what you told me?"

"Not at these prices." He balked, dangling the hefty price tag between them. "I'm an accountant, Jaycee. I don't think I'll be needing a tux."

"If your accounting firm is changing their image from the staunch and staid, stereotypical stuffy accountants, the chances of you having to pucker up for the clients is a very real possibility. By that I mean schmoozing, which could very well include fancy formal affairs that require more than just a suit."

His frown returned, deeper than before. "Too bad," he said, and gave her a pointed look. "Since I now have a half dozen new suits locked in the trunk of your car."

"Oh, stop complaining," she chastised him, ignoring his sarcasm. She slid her hand down his arm—to smooth a wrinkle from the sleeve and not because she enjoyed the play of muscle and sinew beneath the elegant fabric. "You look gorgeous."

His brows lifted, and he gave her one of those lopsided grins again. The one she was beginning to find far too attractive and distracting. "Gorgeous, huh?"

A knock on the door to the private dressing area saved her from making more of a fool of herself than she had already. "We're taking the tuxedo," she told the clerk when he rushed into the room.

She gave a quick tug to the hem of her shirt and turned away once Simon disappeared behind the door to the changing area. The clerk waited for the tuxedo then gathered the other discarded garments and accessories before discreetly disappearing again.

"You know, looks aren't everything, Jaycee," Simon said, stepping out of the dressing room. A pair of dark olive trousers and a tan shirt with a dark-olive and slate-gray plaid replaced the starched and ill-fitting white short-sleeve shirt and black polyester pants he'd worn earlier. Instead of his standard basic black wing tips, he wore new tan loafers, which completed the casual, relaxed look.

"Meaning?" she asked.

He propped his foot on the seat of the chair next to her and adjusted the hem of his pant leg.

"Meaning you can dress me up like one of Barbie's dates, but that's not going to change the fact that I'm no Ken doll."

He had a point, she thought, watching him straighten. With a sense of pride in her usually suppressed talent, she realized she had more than replaced the clothes on the man, she'd actually replaced the man. Instead of the cute but definite geek who'd come to her looking for a new image twenty-four hours ago, she stood facing a very sexy and attractive man. But she'd made a drastic error in judgment. Clothes *didn't* make the man, as she'd told him earlier. What about his ability to communicate with others? To charm and sway potential clients? Weren't those as foreign to Simon as equal rights were to the chauvinist members of her family?

She grinned suddenly. She knew just the place to take Simon so he could watch and learn—the pet-loss support group her grandmother's veterinarian had suggested Margo Richmond join following the loss of her beloved canary, Pietro. Jaycee had started out driving her grandmother to the monthly meetings. After four months, Margo had declared her loss resolved and stopped attending. For reasons Jaycee didn't look into too deeply, she'd continued to attend the meetings. She told herself it was because she enjoyed the company of the eclectic group and found them endearing and definitely more accepting of her ambitions. Aside from Fiona, the members of LOLA—Loss Of a Loving Animal—were the only ones to take her academic achievements seriously.

She shook off the dark thoughts and crossed the space separating her from Simon to adjust the collar of his shirt. "I have an idea," she said, leading him out of the private dressing room. "I have a support group that meets tonight. Why don't you come with me?"

"And do what?"

"Listen. Observe," she said as they approached the counter.

Simon automatically pulled his credit card from his wallet and waited for the clerk to ring up the sale of the tuxedo he was convinced he'd never wear. Jaycee's reaction when he'd walked out of the dressing room, however, almost made the purchase worth the enormous price tag.

"You can watch and see how the LOLA members interact with one another," she continued, moving to examine a rack with silk ties. "You'd be surprised what you can discover about human nature when it's stripped down that way."

She slipped a chocolate and blue paisley tie from the rack and held it up for inspection, then flashed him a high-wattage grin and set it on the counter.

"It'll go great with that blue suit we bought today."

By store number two on the trek this afternoon, he'd learned not to argue with her when it came to clothing purchases. Not only did she have excellent taste, but when she cast those pale blue eyes at him in steely determination, he found her completely irresistible.

"So what do you say?" she asked.

He shrugged. "I guess it can't hurt." At least it'd be no more painful than the hefty withdrawal he'd be making from his savings account to pay the balances on his credit cards next month.

He had no clue what LOLA stood for. Lots of Lovers Anonymous? Some kind of line-dancing addiction group? Maybe if he possessed one iota of Jaycee's confidence, he would've asked her. Instead, he took the credit slip from the clerk and sighed when he glanced at the total.

"THE LAST SIX MONTHS have been difficult. The house is too quiet." The elderly woman dabbed at the corner of her soft gray eyes with an embroidered handkerchief. "Moses and I were together nearly sixteen years before he was taken from me. After Harold, I didn't think I'd find another, but the good Lord saw fit to offer me another blessing."

Despite the constant urge to slip from the room and escape from the intimacy of the group, Simon felt a distinct tug near the vicinity of his heart at the soulful mourning still evident in Catherine Lincoln's voice six months after losing her husband. Two things kept him in his seat—the fact that he wasn't being asked to participate and the way Jaycee's eyes had sparkled with delight when he walked into the semicrowded room.

"I'm so sorry about Moses, Catherine," Lida, the group's leader, offered in a calm tone that would make any funeral director proud. "But remember, good things often come in threes. I'm sure you'll find happiness again."

"There'll never be another Moses," Catherine countered, her voice catching with emotion. "Not after the operation."

Before leaving the exclusive men's store, Jaycee had given him directions and told him to meet her at the community center by seven. Dinner with his old man had run longer than anticipated but was no less than he'd expected. Lately his father had been reluctant to let him leave, which surprised Simon, considering Steven Hawthorne had always stressed independence to his only son.

By the time Simon was able to leave, he'd been thirty minutes late and the meeting was already in session. Since there were no seats available near

Jaycee, he found a place to the side of the group and observed. Observed not just the group, but the woman he hadn't been able to stop thinking about since meeting her.

All afternoon and into the evening he'd been wondering what someone like Jaycee would be doing with a support group, but ten minutes after hearing Catherine Lincoln go on about her dear departed Moses, understanding dawned, and his discomfort rose in spite of Jaycee's personal need of the group. LOLA was a support group for people attempting to cope with the loss of a loved one.

"No, there probably won't," Lida told Catherine consolingly. "But that doesn't mean you can't find happiness again, or that you shouldn't expect it, either."

"We all deserve to be happy," an elderly gentleman said, and received agreeing nods from the rest of the group.

"Duke's right," Lida added, then reached over to squeeze Catherine's hand.

Jaycee stood quietly and discreetly slipped to the back of the room. Simon watched her walk away, enjoying the gentle sway of her hips. She eased behind the refreshment table, opened a large pink bakery box and began setting slices of cake on paper plates while the group continued.

"It was such a comfort to roll over and find

Moses's head on the pillow beside mine in the middle of the night,'' Catherine said in a wistful tone, drawing Simon's attention from Jaycee. ''I think that's what I miss most. That, and how he'd wrap himself around me when I came home from my quilting bee or my weekly canasta game with the Seattle Sisters League. Moses just hated being left alone.''

Simon knew all about being alone, and until this moment he hadn't believed it mattered one way or another. He wasn't exactly lonely, but listening to the members of LOLA, he realized he wasn't really content, either. He had a handful of buddies he hung out with occasionally. They weren't cigar-smoking, whiskey-swilling, poker-playing types, but a small group of intellectual single guys with similar interests. But those were friendships, and none of them garnered the kind of emotional attachment Catherine Lincoln referred to when she spoke of her beloved Moses.

''My Prissy was the same way,'' Duke said. ''That old girl would give me hell when I left her alone for too long.''

Rupert, an extremely tall and lanky younger man, giggled, then shifted his long body toward Prissy's surviving spouse. ''That's nothin', honey,'' he said, slicing his hand through the air before settling his fingers near his breastbone.

"Mr. Jones would curl his big ol' body up on the sofa to sleep, and heaven help me if I tried to wake him. He'd nearly take my hand off."

The older man's bushy salt-and-pepper brows shifted into a frown. "You should've corrected him for that, Rupert," he said, shaking his head and drawing his lips into a thin, disapproving line.

"Duke's right. You can't let 'em walk all over you," a middle-aged woman added in a barely audible voice.

Mr. Jones's significant other giggled again. "Give them an inch..."

"Of course," Catherine affirmed with a brisk, knowing nod. "But love makes it so hard sometimes."

For some reason, Rupert thought that humorous and giggled one last time before Lida regained control. "Georgia, we haven't heard from you lately. How are you doing?" she asked a young woman Simon estimated to be around eighteen or nineteen.

He shifted his attention to Jaycee, half listening to Georgia's account of losing her best friend, Hildy. Was Jaycee ever lonely? he wondered.

His old man had always said there was a difference between being alone and being lonely. Simon's mother died when he was only six, and Steven Hawthorne chose never to remarry. Lately, however, Simon began to wonder if his old man wasn't really lonely, after all. Surely now that his golden years had arrived he regretted his decision to remain a widower all those years. That would certainly explain his dad's reluctance to let him leave tonight.

Just because his dad chose to remain alone, it didn't mean Simon had to, as well, did it? No, he thought, shifting his gaze from the group to Jaycee again. Simon didn't want to make the same mistakes as his father. He would have to make sure that when he found that special someone, she was more suited to his quiet way of life. Unfortunately, that excluded vivacious and spontaneous types no matter how high a particular woman of that type spiked his temperature.

Jaycee set plastic utensils and paper napkins on the refreshment table, then checked the large urn of coffee before looking in his direction. His gaze caught hers and held it. Even across the room he could see her eyes darken.

Was she remembering the kiss they shared last night? Was she hoping he'd kiss her again? Had she been wondering what making love to him would be like?

He'd been thinking about that kiss. He'd been hoping to kiss her again. He'd thought about making love to her. *A lot.*

He considered moving to the rear of the room to be near her. His only task tonight was to observe the interaction between the members of the group, and he'd heard enough. In fact, he didn't quite see how a group of grieving spouses, significant others and friends was supposed to help him improve his people skills. Wouldn't a little interaction have been more in line with his needs?

"Ichabod had always made a funny little noise in the back of his throat," Carlotta, a high-powered newspaper owner was saying. "I had no idea it was a splintered chicken bone."

Simon winced. He'd choked on a hot dog once when he was a kid and recalled it hurt like the devil. He couldn't imagine what a chicken bone would feel like lodged in his throat.

"Didn't the doctor tell you not to feed him chicken bones?" Catherine asked, her tight expression reflecting her disapproval. "Especially at his age?"

"I didn't *feed* them to him," Carlotta answered hotly. "He'd sneak them from the garbage when I wasn't looking."

"You let your husband eat out of the trash can?" Simon blurted. He ignored the stares from the group and, in particular, the giggles from Rupert. "It's no wonder he died if he was eating food from the garbage can!"

Carlotta glared at him. "How dare you make assumptions?"

Jaycee shot out from behind the refreshment table. "Simon, it's not what you're thinking."

Simon heard the crispness in Jaycee's voice and ignored it. There was something inherently wrong with a woman whose husband had to sneak food from the trash. That she came looking for comfort and understanding from a nice group of people attempting to cope with their own losses was more than Simon could understand.

Assumptions?

Not what he was thinking?

His skin heated seconds before complete realization struck and left him mortified. Mr. Jones wasn't Rupert's lover, as he'd assumed. Mr. Jones was Rupert's *pet!*

"Forgive me," he said to the group, then headed toward the door, knowing he could never be the man Jaycee intended.

7

SIMON PUSHED through the doors to step outside into the sultry night air. He considered getting into his car and driving away, calling Jaycee tomorrow to tell her thanks, but no thanks. What she was asking was too much, or more accurately, what he was asking her to perform was too much like a miracle.

Only he wasn't a coward. He'd wait and tell her when she left the meeting.

Regardless of the transformation his sexy image maker believed him capable of, he'd still made a fool of himself tonight. The worst of it was, he wasn't bothered so much by his asinine reaction in front of the group, or even by his disappointment that he couldn't be what Jaycee wanted. No, what drove him from the room was the embarrassment he'd seen in her eyes when she watched in horror as he opened his mouth and inserted his foot. Couple that with his disappointment brought on by wishful thinking that for a few brief hours, he'd believed Jaycee could help him become a new man.

Memories of the day his mother died hit him. His father hadn't lied to him about where his mother had gone. He hadn't attempted to create an easy-to-swallow reference that a young boy could understand. Elena Hawthorne had died, and she wasn't coming back.

His parents had loved each other in their own way, but not all Simon's memories were filled with sunshine and flowers. The child he'd been hadn't understood the arguments. The man he'd become understood that his parents were wrong for each other and the best thing they could've done for themselves and their only son was divorce. They would have eventually, of that he was sure, but fate had intervened and left a workaholic man a widower and a six-year-old boy without a softer, gentler influence in his life.

The memories of his mother were few, but he recalled her as strong-willed with an outgoing personality. Elena Hawthorne was a vivacious woman with heavenly, lyrical laughter who wove fantastic tales of knights and dragons for a young boy eager for adventure. A woman who bitterly resented staying home night after night while her husband worked long hours building his accounting and tax-consulting business. Her husband, while not exactly a recluse, preferred home and hearth to the nightlife Seattle had to offer, something a social butterfly of a wife couldn't tolerate for long.

What happened to that little boy? he wondered. The one who listened with rapt attention to the tales, who begged for the silly adventures where mother and child pretended the blanket cave held a hidden treasure or the mulberry tree in the backyard of their small white-frame house was a castle wall to be scaled by the mighty knight, Sir Simon. That little boy had chattered incessantly, nor had he feared anything. Not the fire-breathing dragon found on the other side of the castle wall or the pirates guarding the treasure. That little boy had tackled the obstacles to save the fairy mommy princess.

Except the fairy mommy princess had been taken away, and everything changed. She'd left her tales and magical excursions into caves and over castle walls with no one to weave them. She'd left them behind just as she'd left her little boy's heart behind.

Simon let out a sigh. The past was the past, and it couldn't be changed. Maybe if his mother had survived the breast cancer, he might have garnered a little of her desire for socializing. Being raised by his workaholic father and a part-time housekeeper, he learned that hard work was rewarded and as his father drilled into him, that the only person he should ever depend on was himself. Something he'd forgotten until tonight, reinforcing the fact that hiring Jaycee to perform miracles was useless.

Coward or not, he searched the parking lot for his car and turned toward the concrete steps to leave, stopping when he heard Jaycee's sweet, husky voice.

"Please don't leave."

With a sensual woman like her asking him to stay, what man in his right mind could leave? In spite of reality, not even himself.

He turned in time to see her hurry to him across the concrete landing of the community center. She wore the same banana-colored, double-breasted, sleeveless shorts outfit she'd worn shopping, and looked just as fresh as she had when she'd picked him up at noon. The salty sea breeze caught the ends of her rich, chestnut hair, which teased her cheek. She slipped the strands behind her ear and looked at him with disappointment filling her gaze. "It's my fault," she said. "I just assumed…"

"That I'd know LOLA was a support group for people coping with the loss of their pets, not human loved ones?" he finished for her. He stuffed his hands in the front pockets of his trousers and shook his head. "That was embarrassing."

"I know. I can't tell you how sorry I am about that," she said, resting her hand on his forearm. "I didn't think."

He was having a hard time thinking, too, but it had nothing to do with assumptions and misunderstandings and everything to do with her fingers running over his skin.

"How was bringing me here supposed to improve my people skills?" he asked, a trace of irritation in his voice. "Unless it was to give me a crash course in humility, I'm at a loss, because about all I managed to do in there was make a fool of myself."

"I am so sorry about that, Simon." She slipped her hand from his arm. "These are some of the most accepting people I know. With the exception of one or two, they don't judge. They don't make assumptions. I thought they'd be the perfect mix for you to mingle with, and I'd hoped you'd feel comfortable with them, as well."

He let out a sound he'd thought would be a chuckle, but it fell drastically short. With a rough sigh, he propped his shoulder against the concrete Doric column and looked at her. "You should have explained it to me. You told me to observe, and I did. I got nothing out of this tonight other than looking like a fool."

Tell her it won't work, his conscience prodded. *Tell her that her services are no longer required.*

He should put an end to their association, but for the life of him, he couldn't bring himself to say the words. If he said the words his conscience demanded, he knew he'd never see her again, and that wasn't something he was willing to do yet. Even the old argument that women like her didn't go out with guys like him failed to shake the words from him that would bring their association to its logical conclusion.

As he gazed into her light blue eyes, taking in the soft, floral scent of her perfume and the way her chestnut hair shone in the moonlight, he realized about the only thing he was seriously considering doing was kissing her again.

Instead of pulling her into his arms and making them both senseless with need, he stuffed his hands in the front pockets of his trousers. "Forget about it," he said, not sure whether he was referring to kissing her again or her apology. "You can't take all the blame. I should've asked you about it if I wasn't completely sure."

A slight grin tugged her mouth, and she visibly relaxed.

"So now that I know what LOLA stands for, care to tell me what brings you to the group?" he asked.

"My grandmother's vet referred her here when her canary, Pietro, died," she explained. She moved to the retaining wall and sat, bracing her hands next to her hips, her fingers wrapping around the concrete ledge. "Grandfather doesn't believe in things like support groups, so she asked me to bring her to the meetings."

"I didn't know your grandmother was in there," he said. Of course he hadn't given her a chance to introduce him to anyone, considering his abrupt departure.

She turned her head and looked toward the Sound. "She wasn't. Grandmother stopped coming a few months ago."

"Were you close to your grandmother's canary?"

She shook her head and smiled. "No," she said, looking at him. "I come for the group members."

"I see," he said, but he really didn't.

Her smile never wavered. "I know it's weird to come to a group that I don't really belong to, but these people are important to me. Thank you for not judging me."

"Me? Judge you?"

She shrugged. "Anything's possible."

Tell her it won't work, his conscience prodded again. *Tell her that her services are no longer re-*

quired and get back to what you know best. Solitude.

"So tell me," he said, moving to sit beside her. "What's next on the agenda?"

"I've been thinking about that," she said.

She swung her legs, drawing his attention to those long, luscious limbs. The urge to smooth his hand over her silky-looking skin was strong.

"A social situation with more interaction rather than observation would have been more in line with your needs," she said. "Tomorrow afternoon we can resolve that. A friend of mine is having a barbecue at her place. Just an informal gathering, small and intimate, a perfect way for you to polish your social skills."

Alarm bells rang in his head. This was what he'd been dreading. In one-on-one situations with Jaycee, he was fine. Put him in a group setting where he was required to participate, and disaster would be the end result.

Panic had him shaking his head and standing. He started to pace. "It won't work."

"Of course it will."

"How can I polish something when I don't even know if I have the right tools for the job?"

That flare of light was in her eyes again, and her luscious mouth eased into a full, wide grin. "Be at my place at eleven. By the time we leave for Fiona's, you'll be ready. I promise."

"How can you be so sure?" he asked, certain they were headed straight into disaster.

"Just leave it to me," she said.

"TELL ME AGAIN how knowing the top ten dating no-nos are going to help me polish my social skills, because I seriously doubt that's something I'll be discussing with potential clients."

Jaycee ignored the sarcasm in Simon's voice, recognizing it for what it was, a front to hide his anxiety that he was going to make a fool of himself. Her plan was to replace his apprehension with confidence, something she wasn't altogether certain she could accomplish.

A variety of magazines lay scattered across the glass-topped table in her dining room. She'd picked them up last night on her way home from the community center in hopes that they would provide a crash course of well-rounded knowledge for Simon to use in social situations. She'd bought the latest issues of *Good Housekeeping*, as well as *Time, Newsweek* and *U.S. News and Reports, Popular Science, Sports Illustrated* and *Outdoor Life*. She'd picked up a copy of *Cosmo* that had caught her attention, and not because of the article claiming to share secrets on how to please a man in bed tonight and every night. Although she did find the piece quite enlightening, the research was probably suspect.

Her gaze caught Simon's, and she couldn't help wondering what he'd think about cherry Popsicles in the bedroom.

She let out a sigh and forced her mind to business and away from things like silk scarves and whipped-cream bikinis. "By the time we leave for Fiona's this afternoon, you're going to have enough knowledge to participate in just about any topic, from current events to the latest scientific discoveries to where the bigmouth bass are biting this time of year."

"It's better than dating no-nos," he grumbled, lifting the sports magazine from the pile.

"But just as important. This article on the Seattle Mariners' position in the draft," she said, tapping the page he'd opened to, "would make a great icebreaker."

"I'm not much of a sports fan," he said, looking over the article.

"What about this little tidbit on the reason the Senate voted down the White House's latest health care bill?" she asked, flipping open the copy of *Newsweek*. "Business is more than just business, Simon. It's knowing your clients and finding a common ground, something to break the ice or to talk about when you're finished with the task at hand.''

He leaned back in the white vinyl chair and crossed his arms over his chest. The navy blue short-sleeved shirt with tan pinstripes emphasized his lean torso, while khaki trousers covered his long legs. He looked handsome and relaxed, like a guy ready to spend a casual day in a casual setting with friends. Gone was the geek with slicked-back hair, thick glasses and polyester who walked into her office mistakenly thinking Better Images was a personal image consulting firm. She'd thought he was kinda cute then. He was a knockout now.

During their shopping trip, after watching Simon attempt to match clothes, she'd discovered he'd have trouble dressing unless he was able to match colors in one way or another. As he'd explained to her, white shirts went with everything, and his ties and trousers matched because it was easier to remember what tie to wear with what trousers. She'd made certain everything they'd purchased yesterday had a corresponding color, and obviously her idea worked, because he'd taken her breath away when he'd knocked on her door at five minutes to eleven.

A frown pulled his eyebrows together. ''What's wrong with talking business?''

She dropped into the chair across from him.

"There's nothing wrong with talking business, so long as that isn't all you're talking. That's what these magazines are for——to help you learn that life isn't always about business, plus provide you with some basic common knowledge that will enable you to communicate effectively and sound reasonably intelligent."

His frown deepened. "I sound reasonably intelligent," he said defensively.

She let out a sigh and stood. "What I mean is there's more going on in the world than balance sheets and profit-and-loss statements. Hungry?"

At his nod, she crossed the dining room into the kitchen. She'd made chicken Caesar salads and iced tea, keeping it light since they'd be eating later at Fiona's.

"This is harder than I thought it'd be," he admitted.

She ladled Caesar dressing over the salads, then sprinkled Parmesan cheese over the top. The doorbell rang. She frowned, then wiped her hands on a dish towel. "When you're finished with the health-care article, try the one about which lures work best for catching freshwater trout."

She wasn't expecting anyone and couldn't have been more stunned to find Dane on the other side of the peephole. "Just a minute," she called when her brother rang the doorbell a second time.

She hurried to the dining room. "It's my brother," she said, slapping the magazine in front of Simon closed.

He looked at Jaycee with amazement. She couldn't blame him. Panic made a person behave irrationally, and slapping magazines and pacing certainly qualified.

"You're not supposed to have men over or what?"

"Simon, please," she begged, not the least amused by his ill-timed humor. "Don't ask questions. Not now. Just..."

God, what was she going to do with Simon? She couldn't let her brother see him, not without explaining the truth, and the truth wasn't an option. Lying was equally out of the question, since she was a terrible liar.

"Hide," she blurted.

He looked at her as if she was nuts. He was closer to the truth than she cared to admit.

"Hide?"

She tugged his hand and pulled him toward the kitchen. "You have to hide." Frantic, she looked around. "There!"

"You want me to hide under the sink?" he asked, his tone incredulous.

She dropped his hand and then snapped her fingers. "I know. Pretend you're looking at the plumbing."

She tried to push him toward the sink, but he resisted. "I don't know anything about plumbing," he argued.

She let out an exasperated sigh. "That's not the point."

"Jaycee? You in there?"

If she hid him in her bedroom... No. She didn't want to think about what her brother would say if he happened to find a man lurking in her bedroom. Or worse, what he'd tell her parents!

"Just a minute," she called, then made a noise that sounded a lot like a frustrated wail filled with way too much panic. "Please, Simon. Don't come out until I tell you to, okay?"

He gave her a look that said he planned to demand an explanation, and she supposed she owed him one, but that would have to wait until after she'd dealt with Dane.

She waited until Simon crouched in front of the cabinet doors muttering something about preferring to be the phone guy before she rushed to the door and swung it open.

"Dane!" she said, plastering what she hoped was a pleasant smile on her face. "What a surprise. What brings you by this morning?"

"When Mother didn't see you at church," he

said, brushing past her, "she asked me to stop by and check on you."

"Well," she said, slapping her hands together, "as you can see, I'm just fine. I had a late night so I slept in this morning."

Dane shrugged. "Got any coffee?"

"No!" But it was too late. Dane had turned the corner and stopped at the entrance to her kitchen.

"Who's that?" he asked in that demanding big-brother voice.

Her plastered-on smile wavered as she peered around Dane toward the sink. Simon lay on his back, the upper half of his torso under her sink, his khaki-covered legs stretched out over the white linoleum. "The plumber?"

Dane tossed one of his worried looks at her as she moved around him to the sink.

"Why didn't you call me?" he asked, moving into the kitchen. He helped himself to a mug from the metal tree and poured himself a cup from the carafe warming on the hot plate of the coffee-maker. "I would have fixed your sink for you. Do you know what these guys charge for working weekends?"

"Not enough."

With the edge of her sandal, she pressed her foot firmly against Simon's upper thigh, smiling when he muttered a muffled, "Ow."

"The homeowners' association pays for it," she told Dane.

"And they pass the cost on to you and the other tenants. Jaycee, if you need something fixed, call me or Rick. You know we'll take care of it for you."

She let out a sigh. "And shall I sit outside under my pretty pink parasol while you fix whatever is broken for helpless little ol' me?"

"We care about you. That's all."

"Did it ever occur to you that I like taking care of myself?"

"I don't know why when you have a family that's more than willing to take on the task."

"Have you looked at a calendar lately, Dane? Do you understand what century it is? Women have been taking care of themselves for a very long time now."

He shot her a brotherly scowl and set his mug on the pristine white ceramic tile counter. "I just stopped by because Mother wanted to be sure you were okay and to remind you about the family meeting tomorrow night. You'll be there, right?"

She felt instantly contrite, something she always did no matter how irritated her brothers made her. "To discuss the plans for Dad's birthday party next month?" At his nod, she added, "Of course I'll be there."

"I'll see you then," he said briskly, and headed toward the front door of her condo.

He really did care about her. She knew that, and he was the least chauvinistic of her family, but that wasn't saying much.

"Dane," she called, as he pulled opened the front door. "Thanks for stopping by."

His eyes softened as he looked at her. "No problem. Oh, and that plumber is hosing you, Jay. Everyone knows it's easier to unclog pipes if you use actual tools."

He gave her a wink, then promised to see her at the office the next morning and closed the door.

Great, she thought, watching her brother saunter down the brick path toward the parking lot. Dane would report to her family that the reason she missed Sunday morning services followed by breakfast at their favorite home-style diner was because she had a—gasp—*man* in her home. In addition to the planning of her dad's sixtieth birthday celebration, tomorrow night the hot topic would be speculation about the man hiding out under her sink.

The man in question rounded the corner and looked at her expectantly.

"You want an explanation, don't you?" she asked. At his nod, she headed toward the dining room. "Let's eat, because this isn't something I relish discussing on an empty stomach."

8

"REMEMBER when I said that *I* could help you and not Better Images?"

Simon nodded slowly. How could he forget? Her chasing him into the elevator remained at the top of his list of fantasies. Of course the proposition in those fantasies was a lot more interesting than the one she'd given him in reality.

"That's because I'm not..." She closed her eyes briefly. When she opened them again, he detected an uncertainty that had him wanting to reach across the glass-topped table and settle his hand over hers reassuringly.

"I'm a secretary for my brothers," she admitted, "not an image consultant. I'm qualified, but the title isn't mine. At least not yet."

"I take it this is something you've wanted for a while." He suspected her answer before she nodded. The trace of steel in her voice was a strong indicator. The one-step-shy-of-condescending way her brother had spoken to her completed more of the picture Jaycee was painting for him now.

"That's where you come in," she continued. She pushed her half-eaten salad away and looked at him over the silk rose centerpiece, frustration evident in her pale eyes.

"I've tried before," she said, "and they've always taken the client away without giving me a chance to prove myself to them. I figure if I can show Rick and Dane I can transform a person, they'll know I'd be more than capable of doing the same for a company. So they'd have to promote me.

"That's why I'm not charging you a fee, Simon. *I'm* handling you, not Better Images, and I apologize for not telling you everything up front."

He waved away her apology. She hadn't told him anything he didn't already know, other than that her job title wasn't quite what he'd been led to believe. The day he'd gone to Better Images, the receptionist had said that Jaycee's office was the first door on the right. The office was no bigger than a cubicle with floor-to-ceiling walls, but he'd assumed she was a junior consultant. His conclusion hadn't been the result of any fabrication Jaycee had created, just his own assumptions.

None of that explained why she'd shoved him under the sink.

"Why make me hide?" he asked.

She let out a sigh and toyed with the silk foliage.

"If I told them you were a client, Dane would have insisted on taking over your account. They always do whenever I try to take on a client. Forget that Better Images doesn't even handle individuals, which would have ended your association with the firm anyway."

He eyed her speculatively. "Somehow I get the impression making me pretend to be your plumber didn't go quite as planned."

"No," she admitted with a hint of contrition. "I saw the look in Dane's eyes. He assumed my plumber was more than just a plumber. If he'd seen you, when the time came to make my presentation to them and I revealed the guy Dane thought I was having an affair with, they'd never take me seriously. They'd conveniently blame my feminine instincts, or emotions, or whatever got in the way and kept me from making sound business decisions. An inability to separate emotions from business is why women don't belong in the male-dominated positions, according to the Richmond men."

He understood why she'd felt forced to go to such lengths to prove herself, especially with her family's antiquated philosophies about women. Even a columns-and-numbers guy like him understood and appreciated the concept of the women's movement.

"So by keeping me secret," he reasoned, "you can remake my image, use me to make your presentation to your brothers and then sit back and wait for the accolades on your brilliance."

"Something like that."

He probably should have been miffed, maybe even mildly irritated. But he knew what it was like to be taken at face value, and he'd never been much of a hypocrite.

What he wanted to know was where that left them. He wasn't officially a Better Images client. She wasn't officially acting in the capacity of a Better Images employee. Did that mean they were just a man and a woman doing each other a favor? If that was the case, then her arguments about professional boundaries were moot—which, in his opinion, left open some very interesting possibilities.

He wasn't completely obtuse. He understood her arguments about them not kissing didn't have so much to do with a lack of professionalism as an excess of feeling. Just as he couldn't deny that what he was feeling for her went beyond sexual attraction, even if he wasn't exactly ready to pin an emotional label on it.

He pushed his salad plate forward and braced his forearms on the table. "What happens if they still refuse to see the real you?"

"I haven't thought that far ahead." She took a sip of her iced tea then looked at him. One delicately arched eyebrow shot upward. "What do you mean, the real me?" she asked, setting her glass on the rose-patterned place mat.

"Someone intelligent, with business savvy," he said. "Someone with a lot of drive and ambition to succeed despite the obstacles thrown in her way. Someone capable of doing more than sitting from nine to five in a five-by-five space typing and filing documents for a couple of candidates for the Neanderthal Award."

She let out another sigh, propped her elbow on the table and dropped her head in her hand. Picking up her fork, she pushed a piece of chicken breast through the Caesar dressing left on her plate. "I have days when I think I'd be happy if they just saw me as something other than their little sister."

She continued to torture the piece of chicken. He was content to sit quietly and watch her. Watch the way her chestnut hair glistened in the sunlight streaming through the sliding glass doors of the small dining room. The way her eyes flared with determination when she straightened and leveled her gaze on him.

God, she was so beautiful, he thought.

Beautiful and maybe not as off-limits as he'd believed two days ago. One thing was perfectly clear. Jaycee Richmond excited him, and he'd wager his continued employment with Eaton and Simms that she returned the sentiment.

Now all he had to do was figure out how in the world to convince the woman in question.

JAYCEE SMILED despite Fiona's smug look. The only thing missing was an "I told you so." "I knew you were talking to a hunk the other day on the phone."

"He's not a hunk," Jaycee claimed for the third time during the afternoon barbecue. Okay, so she was lying. Probably the worst lie she'd ever told, too, because the Simon she'd introduced as her friend was every inch the hunk.

She gazed at him and realized with a stab of some unidentifiable emotion that he wasn't doing so badly in the charming department. He might have started out the afternoon shy and reserved, but after thirty minutes in Fiona's company, even sweet, gentle Simon opened up—and, she noted, he wasn't completely unaffected by her friend's exotic beauty.

Unaware of their conversation he nodded and said something to Fiona's foot-model neighbor, Hattie. Probably another one of the model's diatribes on the fashion industry, or lack thereof, in the Seattle area. Jaycee might have believed his attention was focused solely on his conversation with Hattie, except he'd been casting surreptitious glances in her direction for the past ten minutes.

Unfortunately, Fiona had noticed, as well.

"Come on, Jay. What gives?" Fiona nudged Jaycee with her elbow. "Who is he?"

Jaycee sighed then took a sip of her iced tea. "I told you. He's just a friend."

"Then he's available?" Her friend's almond-shaped eyes zeroed in on Simon, who stood with a cool drink in one hand, his other in the front pocket of his trousers. He didn't slump his wide shoulders forward, but stood straight. He looked like a man comfortable in his own skin, and Jaycee couldn't help but be proud that she'd been the one to help him find a little of that confidence he'd kept buried beneath the nerd gear.

"I guess he is," she said, not at all surprised that she had to force out the words that would lay Simon before Fiona's sacrificial altar.

A slow grin spread across Fiona's wide mouth, and her eyes took on that huntress gleam Jaycee had seen all too often in the years she'd known Fiona. "Interesting," the other woman said, almost purring.

As much as Jaycee adored her friend, she understood that, when it came to the opposite sex, Fiona really was a viper. After a heartbreaking relationship five years ago that left her devastated, Fiona had adopted the philosophy when dealing with the opposite sex to hunt them down, toy with them awhile and then forget about them first. Fiona would chew Simon up for dinner and spit him out by dessert without a hint of indigestion. Simon was far too sweet and gentle, and definitely not Fiona's type.

"He's…" Jaycee made a mental note to visit a shrink the next morning, because she most certainly needed her head examined for telling Fiona the truth about Simon. "He's my client."

Two perfectly arched raven eyebrows shot upward. "He's your what?"

"Shh," she ordered, then grabbed Fiona's arm and pulled her toward the sliding glass door into the lushly furnished den.

"Are you nuts?" Fiona demanded once they were alone.

I am if I'm seriously considering telling you, my bigmouth friend.

"Simon is my client," Jaycee admitted. She gave her friend a hard look. "I swear, Fiona, if you breathe a word of this to Rick or Dane I'll strangle you myself."

Fiona dropped onto the white leather sofa facing the enormous hearth that took up the northern wall. She'd inherited the elegant home from her parents when they'd died tragically during a trip to Ireland. They were supposed to have been at the airport on their way home for a huge celebration for Fiona's twenty-first birthday. Fate had other plans, and a late departure had kept them at the hotel, making them one of over a dozen victims of a terrorist bomb that had ripped through the lobby.

"What do think you're doing?" Fiona asked. "You are nuts, aren't you?"

"Undoubtedly," she admitted. "It was the only thing I could think of to prove to my hardheaded, backward-thinking brothers that I *am* executive material."

This wasn't the first time Jaycee had shared her frustration with Fiona, and Fiona's advice was always the same. If she didn't like the way things were, then she should go elsewhere. Fiona was remarkably silent while Jaycee explained how Simon had come to the firm for help, then she described what she'd accomplished thus far and her plans for the next few days. When she finished, Fiona shook her head.

Jaycee sat on the stone hearth. "What?" she asked, smoothing the folds of her floral sundress over her bare legs.

"It'll never work."

"Yes, it will." It had to work. How many people with a master's degree in business administration with an emphasis on publicity and advertising spent their careers typing and filing? She frowned at her friend. "Why won't it work?"

Fiona kicked off her loafers and pulled her feet beneath her on the sofa. "Because no matter what you do, you'll always be their little sister. They think they're protecting you."

"I don't need protecting," she said with determination.

"After pulling a stunt like this, they're going to think you need protection from yourself. Are you certifiable? Who is this guy? Do you even know him?"

"A minute ago you were ready to swallow him whole," she reminded Fiona.

"That was before I found out you don't know him from Adam."

"Simon is perfectly safe." So long as she kept her heart out of the deal. "Besides, it'll all be over by next week. Once I make my presentation to Rick and Dane, that'll be the end of my association with Simon."

For reasons she was afraid to analyze, that statement filled her with something she could only describe as sadness, an emotion that took her completely by surprise. Sad? Because she wouldn't see Simon again? The truth startled her.

"I think you're crazy, but your secret is safe with me so long as you promise me one thing."

"What's that?"

"That I get to attend this little presentation of yours."

"Because?"

"Because it is going to be the most memorable presentation Better Images has ever seen."

SIMON PULLED INTO the visitors' parking lot outside Jaycee's condominium complex and killed the engine of his sensible Ford Taurus. Maybe he should get a new car, he thought. Something updated and hip to go with the new updated and hip image Jaycee had created for him. Nothing too fancy or ridiculously expensive like a Porsche, but one of those sport utility vehicles would be a nice change. At least it was a little more trendy than the staid and dependable model he drove.

The warmth of the early-summer day had faded when the winds from the Pacific had blown across the Sound, bringing with them scattered showers and a premature end to the barbecue. Other than the steady patter of rain on the car and the ticks of the warm engine as it cooled, silence pervaded the vehicle.

"I had a nice time today," he told Jaycee quietly, breaking the suddenly uncomfortable silence. "Thank you for taking me."

"It's all part of the package," she said brightly. Too brightly, in his opinion. "You did a great job."

"Come on, I'll walk you to the door." He slid from the vehicle, but before he could circle the car to her side, she was on the sidewalk heading toward her condo. Her steps were hurried, but that didn't reduce the sway of her hips beneath the floral sundress, or his appreciation of the movement.

"You think I'm getting the hang of this social stuff?" he asked when he caught up with her.

"You're off to a great start," she said, digging through her purse for her key. "If you do like you did today, then I'm sure you're going to be fine tomorrow."

Alarm shot down his spine, and his steps faltered. "Tomorrow?"

She pulled her keys from her purse as they reached the small framed porch of her unit. "Tomorrow at your office," she said, wrapping her hand around the wooden post. She gazed at him and smiled with a confidence he wasn't buying.

"Considering these are people that know you," she continued, "you're actually going to get to see how well your new and improved exterior affects the people around you."

He swallowed. "They'll talk to me?"

"Probably. And they're going to notice you, too. Some will even stare. Don't let them unsettle you."

No one ever talked to him. No one but Stella. Even the partners preferred to speak to Stella, and rarely spoke to him. He'd never felt very comfortable communicating with people on a level that wasn't business-related. He knew numbers and columns, assets and liabilities, profit-and-loss statements and balance sheets. Receivables, payables and general ledger balances only changed when he provided the information necessary for the new balance. There was a control, a constant about the numbers and columns and spreadsheets that made him feel…safe, he realized suddenly. He felt in control because he knew that one and one would always add up to two.

People changed. There was nothing constant or consistent about people. Their attitudes and ideals altered with life experience, and they moved on or they died.

God, had his life been so chaotic as a child that he'd withdrawn to the point of closing himself off from humanity? Was he so incapable of communication with a living, breathing person that the one thing that had been his entire world—his work— was in jeopardy?

Obviously, he thought with distaste. Thankfully he'd come to his senses and had gone to seek help. Help in the form of the beautiful woman with pale blue eyes and skin as smooth as satin gazing at him under the dim glow of the porch light.

With sudden clarity, he realized if he continued as he had been, he'd have lost not only his job, but a chance at gaining something even more treasurable.

Jaycee.

He shoved his hands into the pockets of his trousers. The action gave him a modicum of comfort. "For a minute there, I was thinking of calling in sick tomorrow."

She reached out and pressed her hand against his cheek. Her touch was cool, gentle, yet he felt branded.

"You're going to be fine," she said quietly.

"It won't be easy. Not at first," he admitted. He turned his lips toward her palm, and she trembled.

"You'll be fine. I have all the confidence in the world in you, and you should, too. You had it today."

He tugged his hand from his pocket and slipped his fingers over hers, which still cupped his cheek. "I didn't know those people," he said, bringing her hand to his mouth. With feather-light precision, he brushed his lips over each of her knuckles.

Her pale eyes darkened. "It's even tougher to exude confidence with strangers, and you did it. Stop worrying about tomorrow."

"You were there today." He turned her hand over and pressed his lips against her wrist, touching his tongue to the pulse point. "Maybe that's why it worked."

She sucked in a sharp breath but didn't pull away. "I'll be with you tomorrow," she said, her voice as soft as the skin beneath his lips, "in spirit if not the flesh."

He grinned, then tugged her wrist, pulling her into his arms. "Flesh is definitely better," he said, then settled his mouth over hers in what had to be the hottest, most erotic kiss of his life.

9

JAYCEE was convinced she'd died and gone to heaven, because nothing on earth could feel as wonderful as Simon's mouth over hers. If she wasn't dying, then she was positive her insides were melting. There wasn't a thing she could do about it, or worse, wanted to do about it, except enjoy every single second of the sensual exploration.

The feel of his hands smoothing down her back to rest just above her bottom heightened her need. The way her sensitized breasts rubbed against the lace of her bra when she wreathed her arms around his neck made her tremble in his arms. The way her body came alive when she pressed against him made her dizzy with desire.

Professional or not, she *liked* kissing Simon. And she wanted more than just to kiss him, too. She wanted Simon.

Her body craved. Her heart yearned. Her soul reached out to touch the man who so effortlessly made her knees weak and her breath catch with his touch, his mouth, his scent. The look in his eyes seconds before his mouth descended upon hers had been filled with a sultry heat. A look that wasn't practiced, she knew, but raw and honest. Something she'd never before experienced. He was like a breath of fresh air after being locked away in a dank and dark place, and she felt she'd never be able to get enough of his refreshing brand of sex appeal.

His mouth left hers and trailed a path along her cheek, over her jaw and down her throat. She couldn't keep the soft moan from escaping any more than she could stop the delightful shimmer dancing down her spine when his hand swept up her back to cup her head in his warm palm. He guided her mouth to his in another hot, demanding, tongue-tangling kiss, and she moaned again.

She wanted. He offered.

She needed. He gave selflessly.

She craved. He responded and made her body ache for more than just his hot and wet kisses.

Simon was dangerous. Dangerous to her peace of mind, to her goals, to the way of life she'd been struggling to carve out for herself. She wanted a successful career, while her family believed home, hearth and babies were enough. It wasn't that she didn't one day hope to have a family of her own, but it would be on her terms and not based upon the dictates of her family.

The thought of babies and life choices startled her, but not enough to have her pulling out of Simon's warm embrace. She breathed in the fresh citrus scent of his aftershave and caught the hint of something more…something much more alluring and so very male.

A car door slammed in the distance, intruding upon the enticing, sensual spell Simon had so effortlessly cast over her. Maybe her brothers weren't too far off base after all, she thought, letting her arms fall to her sides. She took a much needed step back from the man who, if she let him, held the power to make her forget about her goals.

She turned away from the look of male satisfaction glowing in his gorgeous green eyes and climbed the three steps to her front door.

"Good night, Simon," she said in a surprisingly steady voice. Without looking at him, she slipped the key into the lock and grabbed the knob with her other hand.

"Wait!"

She closed her eyes. All she had to do was twist the knob, push the door open and slip through into the safety of her home. A place where she'd be alone, with only her thoughts for company. She suspected she had a very restless night ahead.

"It's been a long day," she said, opening her eyes.

She twisted the knob.

"I want to see you again."

She didn't have to turn around to know he'd moved directly behind her. Not only was her body still humming from that sensational kiss, but her Simon radar was in full working order.

"You will," she said, keeping her hand firmly on the knob. If she let go, she'd turn around. If she turned around and saw her own hunger mirrored in his eyes, she'd charge straight across every single ethical line she'd tried so valiantly to keep drawn between them. "The Chamber of Commerce is having a mixer tomorrow evening. I thought it'd be good for you to attend."

"I was thinking of something a little more..." His fingers gently traced a line across her shoulder, making her shiver. "Intimate," he said, his voice dipping low.

Phone-sex voice be damned, she had to resist him. If she was weak, she'd lose sight of what was important. "Simon, you know—"

"I know you want me as much as I want you."

She struggled for breath. Since when had he developed mind-reading capabilities? "You've got the wrong idea," she lied.

The fingers tracing a pattern over her shoulder

moved to the back of her neck. "Do I?" He brushed aside her hair and placed a kiss just below her ear.

God help her, she trembled.

"Do I, Jaycee?"

She closed her eyes again. Why? Why did the one person who could actually help her reach her goal have to be the one who set her soul on fire? Life just wasn't fair.

"No," she admitted. "No, you don't have the wrong idea."

She opened her eyes. Summoning every ounce of willpower, courage and whatever else it took in her rapidly depleting arsenal to protect herself against the need clawing inside her, she turned to face him. The struggle to ignore the heat in his gaze, the desire emanating from him and her own need was more powerful than anything she'd ever imagined.

She had to remain strong. They could not and would not have a personal relationship. If she gave in, then the only thing she'd prove to her brothers was that they were right. A woman couldn't possibly keep business matters and matters of the heart separate.

"Forget the mixer," he said. "Let's have a real date tomorrow night."

"We can't," she told him. What she really

wanted to do was take him up on his very tempting offer.

"Yes, we can. Tell you what, I'll go to the mixer with you, but Tuesday, it's no business. It'll be just us. Deal?"

She shook her head regretfully. As much as she wanted otherwise, they had to keep their relationship on a professional plane. Her future at Better Images was at stake. "Simon, you know that's impossible."

"All right," he said easily, slipping his hand into his trouser pocket to retrieve his car keys. "I'll let you off the hook for now."

Without another word, he grinned, then turned and walked toward his car.

Although he hadn't said it, Jaycee distinctly heard a *but* in that statement. And that made her *very* nervous.

THE NEXT MORNING, dressed in one of the new suits he and Jaycee had purchased, Simon stepped off the elevator and turned toward the double doors of Eaton and Simms. He hadn't been lying when he'd told Jaycee he'd considered calling in sick this morning.

Only he couldn't do it, not when he was trying to show the partners he had what it took to fit in with the new image of the firm. Besides, he told himself as he stood staring at the imposing double doors, all the work Jaycee had done over the weekend would have been for nothing. He valued the time they'd spent together too much to resort to his old habits of burying himself in his work and trading columns and numbers for human contact, no matter how uncomfortable the latter made him. He'd get used to his new and improved image eventually, of that he was convinced. It was the transitional period that had him worried.

He took a deep breath, then another.

He pulled his hands from his pockets and stood straight.

He considered pushing the button to call the elevator back so he could make a clean getaway.

With thoughts of Jaycee planted firmly in his mind, and how disappointed she'd be in him if he turned and pushed the down button, he walked purposefully to the door and swung it wide open.

Nothing had changed. The furniture was still the same mass-produced Victorian, arranged in the same conversational-pit style on the same plush navy carpeting. The same mauve and dusty-blue silk flower arrangement adorned the oval cherrywood table, and the same young woman sat behind the receptionist's station using a singsong voice to announce to callers they'd reached Eaton and Simms.

Leah Porter was her name. At least that's what the name plate declared. He'd never paid attention until now and felt a stab of guilt. He didn't know how long Leah had worked for the firm. No wonder the partners thought he wasn't promotion material.

"Can I help you?" she asked, her voice pleasant and professional. Her eyes told another story, and that made Simon *very* uncomfortable.

"It's me," he said. When Leah continued to look at him as if he was the main course, he added, "Simon Hawthorne."

She cocked her head, and her eyes took on a dreamy cast when she looked him up and down. "Mr. Hawthorne's not in yet."

He shook his head. "No," he told her. "It's me. *I'm* Simon Hawthorne."

She straightened abruptly. "I'm sorry, Mr. Hawthorne, I didn't recognize you," she said after snapping her gaping mouth closed. "I mean…you look absolutely diff—I…"

"It's okay," he said, liking the idea that the twenty-something receptionist had gotten flustered in his presence. The idea was a novelty. "Any messages?"

"Uh…" She shook her head slowly. "No."

"Thank you," he said, feeling a lot more confident than when he'd stepped off the elevator. He stood a little straighter, adjusted his new navy and chocolate paisley silk tie and headed through the door leading to the offices of the firm.

The large open area, filled with a maze of cubicles and called the hub, buzzed with subdued conversation. Secretaries, accounting clerks and junior accountants milled around before settling down to start their workday. The more senior staff, like Simon, had private offices on the perimeter of the hub. He followed the same path he had every morning for the past twelve years. The only difference was the sharp gasp and the whispered, "Who is that?" he heard when he strolled past a group of secretaries.

He recognized an accounting clerk and a junior accountant Stella shared lunch with on occasion, and murmured a quiet, "Good morning."

Jaycee had been right. The clerk stared at him, a sheaf of papers slipping from her fingers to flutter to the floor. Both women continued to stare at him in utter fascination when he stooped to pick up the papers.

He stood and held them out to the clerk. "Here you go," he said, hiding a grin when the young woman blushed a bright shade of crimson.

Simon wished Jaycee was with him to see the reaction of the staff. He'd never so much as garnered a first look, let alone a second, a blush, a nervous giggle and a startled gasp.

With more confidence than he recalled feeling, he walked into his office. Stella stood at his desk, arranging the stack of files on the corner in order of importance, just like she did every morning, a mug of black coffee gripped in her clawlike fingers.

She looked up and grinned, a startling sight to anyone not accustomed to Stella. Today her hair was stark white. The contrast was made more dramatic by the bright red lipstick, kohl-lined eyes and high-necked black sweater and long skirt.

She set the mug on his desk with a thump and planted her hands on her bony hips. "Good grief, boss," she exclaimed. "What happened to you over the weekend? You're looking damn good."

Despite his embarrassment over Stella's exuberant praise, he chuckled. "Thanks, Stella."

Simon took off his jacket and slipped it over the hanger on the back of his door.

"It's unbelievable," Stella said, then let out a low wolf whistle. "I'll be the envy of the lunchroom crowd."

"Okay, Stella," he said in what he hoped was a warning tone.

"If it wasn't for my Buck...boy, oh boy."

"Was I that bad before?" he asked, circling the

desk to his chair. He already knew the answer to that question. Wasn't that why he'd hired Jaycee in the first place?

"Well," Stella said, walking toward the door. "It's not that you weren't a nice guy or anything, but— Good morning, Mr. Eaton."

Simon remained standing when Jared Eaton walked into the office. He eyed Stella with a great deal of suspicion before turning his attention to Simon. "Hawthorne," he said jovially. "Good to see you this morning."

Word spread fast at Eaton and Simms, Simon thought. He couldn't remember the last time Eaton had come into his office for anything.

Stella slipped out the door and quietly closed it behind her. Eaton glanced over his shoulder at the closed door then at Simon. "New secretary?"

Simon grinned, indicated the chair across from his desk, then waited for Eaton to sit. "No. She was a redhead last week."

"Ah, yes. The skinny one with copper hair. She looked like a bullet."

"That's Stella," Simon agreed. "What can I do for you this morning, Mr. Eaton?"

"Mr. Eaton is my father," his boss said. "Call me Jared. I'm having a dinner party Wednesday night. Cocktails at six sharp. We just landed Seattle Sports Equipment as a client, and Greg and I would like for you to be there to get to know the principals. Wives and significant others are included. Can we count on you, Hawthorne?''

This was what he'd wanted, and he couldn't quite believe it was happening already. All within thirty minutes of his walking into the office. It had cost him nothing more than a hefty chunk of his savings account to dress for success and a few simple courtesies he'd been too uncomfortable to perform in the past.

"You can count on me," he told his boss.

Eaton stood. "You do have a significant other to bring along, don't you, Hawthorne?"

Simon could think of only one person who might be willing to accompany him to the dinner. "I'm sure my date will enjoy the evening," he answered, then waited until Eaton left him alone in his office before he sank into the worn chair behind his desk. Jaycee might not be his significant other, but he was fairly confident she'd agree to be his date for the night, so long as he referred to it as a business meeting.

If she had her way, their relationship would remain entirely professional.

If he had his way, their relationship would become entirely personal.

Simon figured with the way things were going this morning, the odds were definitely in *his* favor.

TWENTY MINUTES before noon, Simon walked into the offices of Better Images. The receptionist greeted him with a smile when he asked to see Jaycee. When she inquired as to the purpose of his visit, he could tell by the look of surprise on her face that the word *personal* was the last thing she expected to hear. From conversations with Jaycee, he knew she wasn't involved with anyone, but it still gave him a sense of satisfaction to know she didn't regularly have men visiting her at work.

Instead of buzzing through to let Jaycee know he was waiting, Juliana asked him to follow her. She led the way down the corridor to the tiny office. The door was closed. Juliana knocked, then pushed it open at Jaycee's quietly spoken, "Come in."

Simon walked through the door and grinned as Jaycee's eyes widened in surprise. A flare of delight followed, making his gut clench. Then those eyes of hers narrowed with suspicion. Simon opted to concentrate on her delight at seeing him.

"What are you doing here?" she demanded, her voice a harsh, panic-filled whisper.

He shrugged as if her displeasure didn't bother him in the least. With more feigned self-confidence than he'd dreamed possible when it came to the opposite sex, he moved the few feet closer to her desk. "I came to tell you about my morning.

We've got a dinner meeting with clients scheduled for Wednesday.''

"You shouldn't be here," she said, her tone low. To his ears, the quiet tone sounded sultry, possessing the kind of husky nuances he hoped to hear in a much more intimate setting than her closet space of an office. "And who's *we?*"

"We," he said. "As in you and me. And why shouldn't I be here?"

She stood abruptly and skirted the desk to squeeze past him. He caught a whiff of her floral perfume and breathed in the intoxicating scent. Images of where she'd dabbed the fragrance assailed him, and he imagined pressing his lips to each intoxicating location.

"You know why not," she said, closing the door. "What if my brothers find you here?"

She leaned against the door, and it took every ounce of his rapidly dwindling willpower to remain standing by the desk and not leap across the two feet of space separating them. He wanted to slip his arms around her, to pull her against him and kiss her senseless. Instead, he shrugged as nonchalantly as possible. "Gee, Jaycee. I dunno. What if they do?"

A frown tugged at her arched chestnut eyebrows. "You have to leave."

"After I tell you about my morning."

"You can tell me tonight at the mixer."

He sat on the edge of her desk and gave her a grin he hoped was as wicked as he was feeling. "How about if I tell you tonight...after dinner and a movie?"

"We're going to the Chamber mixer after I have dinner with my parents."

"I thought a date would be much more fun."

The phone on her desk buzzed. "Jaycee?" A deep male voice came over the intercom.

Panic filled her eyes. "Yes, Rick?" she answered, keeping her gaze locked with Simon's. "You have to leave," she mouthed.

He shook his head. "Go out with me," he returned silently.

"Do you have the Templeton Products file?" Rick asked over the intercom. "I can't find it."

"It's on your credenza. Next to the lamp."

"Are you sure?"

She let out a short breath filled with frustration. "Look to the left of the lamp, Rick."

"Oh, yeah. There it is."

A click, then silence. Not so much as a thank-you, Simon noticed. He *always* thanked Stella. He might have been a bit reclusive, but he'd never been rude or thoughtless to his secretary. He knew better. Stella wouldn't have hesitated to make his life a living hell.

Jaycee looked at the monster she'd created and wondered when things had become so out of control. In particular, when had Simon gotten so out of control? On top of that, how on earth had it happened that he was able to turn her insides to butter with a kiss? And make her want things she had no business wanting? He had her right where he wanted her, between a rock and his proposition, and darned if he wasn't looking awfully smug about it, too.

"We've been over this before, Simon," she said in what she hoped was a firm voice.

Why had he come here? Just to make her even more crazy? She'd had a horrible night, tossing and turning until well past three in the morning. When she finally had fallen asleep, it had been to dreams starring her sexier-than-sin client in some very erotic situations.

He stood. "I'm not leaving until you agree to go out with me," he said with a grin filled with enough purpose to really make her nervous. "I guess that means I'll get to meet your brothers sooner than you intended."

"Okay." She relented. "You win. But not tonight."

"Tomorrow then."

She nodded reluctantly. He might think they were going on a date, but if she continued to tell herself what they were embarking upon was another exercise in socialization, then maybe, just maybe, she'd be able to keep her focus out of the bedroom.

"I had a feeling you'd see it my way," he said with a hint of arrogance she suspected was quite foreign to him regardless of how well he pulled it off.

Despite her goals, despite her arguments that they not get involved, she couldn't stop the smile from spreading across her face. He really had changed a lot in just three days. "You don't play fair, Simon."

He shrugged and stepped around her to the door. "You know what they say," he said, reaching for the handle. "All's fair in love and war."

Now why did she have a feeling war had nothing to do with what he'd just declared?

10

JAYCEE had expected nervousness, maybe even a little apprehension. What she did not expect was a confident, well-dressed, absolutely handsome man to come to her door at precisely five-thirty, exuding charm and behaving as if dinner parties and cocktail hours with clients were something he'd been doing for years.

Her physical reaction to Simon hadn't been all that much of a surprise—he still managed to take her breath away. When his hand had come to rest on the small of her back as he'd led her to his car, her breasts had tingled. The scent of his aftershave had made her dizzy. The sound of his voice had skirted along her highly sensitized nerve endings, and a pool of growing heat had settled in her belly and burned. Burned through cocktails, dinner and the after-dinner brandy she'd been nursing for the past twenty minutes.

Her emotional reaction had been a complete and total surprise.

Two things were crystal clear to Jaycee. One, regardless of her arguments to the contrary, she wanted Simon. She wanted to feel his mouth on hers, to feel his hands caress her skin, to feel his body pressed intimately against hers, flesh to flesh, man to woman.

The second was more difficult to accept. What she felt for Simon exceeded professional boundaries and headed straight to the place she couldn't afford for him to reside—her heart.

She set her barely touched brandy on the tray of a passing waiter and continued to watch Simon across the spacious living room of Jared and Kathryn Eaton's elegantly furnished home. Embroiled in a discussion with one of the executives from a sports equipment chain Eaton and Simms had recently acquired the account of, he shined. He charmed, he dazzled and he spoke with a confidence that five days ago had been foreign to him.

She felt a stab of pride that she'd been the one to help Simon, but she couldn't in good conscience take credit. The intelligence and wit he used to enchant the board of directors and their wives had been there inside him all along.

No one would believe that the drop-dead-gorgeous specimen was the same adorably clumsy guy who'd walked into her office asking her to reinvent him. But she hadn't had to reinvent anything. All she'd done was show him how to dress in a more updated style, exchange his thick glasses for sleek, modern frames and introduced him to the blow-dryer collecting dust under his bathroom sink. His new look gave him confidence. The rest was pure Simon.

And pure torture to her feminine senses.

Despite Simon's success, Jaycee couldn't help the twinge of disappointment she felt at the thought of never seeing him again. Her job here was finished. Mission accomplished. There was nothing left to do except make her presentation to Rick and Dane in two days.

Sadness washed over her at the thought of never seeing Simon again. She tried to shake it off, but the sensation lingered. Telling herself she didn't have time in her life for a relationship, especially one that would be a constant reminder to her brothers that she didn't have what it takes to make it in the business world, did nothing to loosen the sudden tightness in her chest. How could she be expected to make sound business decisions if she continued to drool over her own client?

She didn't need this. Not now. Not when she was so close to grasping her future.

She'd never been a particularly spontaneous person, but something Simon had said niggled her consciousness and made her question her future.

What if, no matter what proof she offered to Rick and Dane, despite her qualifications and education, they still refused her the upward mobility she wanted within the family business? What would she do then?

She hadn't wanted to think about the alternatives, but considering the rather spirited discussion she'd had with her father and eldest brother after dinner the other night, maybe she really did need to think about those alternatives.

One thing she did know, if she continued to work for her brothers without the benefit of moving up the ladder, she'd end up miserable and resentful. Would she better serve herself, and her relationship with her family, if she opted for moving onward and upward elsewhere? Should she continue to fight old battles that could never be won, or elect to face new challenges?

No closer to an answer, she eased out a sigh and crossed the living room toward Simon. He looked up as she neared, his green eyes holding hers, a tantalizing smile on his handsome face. That tingling sensation in her breasts started again, and the heat in her belly warmed even more.

Jaycee was unable to help prevent it—a smile teased the corners of her mouth. She joined the group and leaned close to Simon, breathing in his rich, masculine scent. "Can we get out of here?" she asked him quietly.

He nodded, then reached for her hand, lacing their fingers together while he answered a tax question.

Thirty minutes later, they were finally able to bid their hosts good-night. "Where to?" Simon asked, pulling his keys from the pocket of his charcoal suit jacket as they stepped onto the brick porch.

Maybe it was the full moon. Maybe it was the way Simon had looked at her across the room earlier. Maybe it was just that she had a serious case of lust happening, but she refused to let the evening end so soon.

Deciding it wouldn't be the end of her career if she forgot her staunch professionalism for once and did something spontaneous and fun, she slipped her arm through his and flashed him her most wicked grin.

"Come on," she said, steering him toward the car. "Let's go back to my place and be decadent."

"WHIPPED CREAM?" Jaycee squealed, her voice filled with a dizzying playfulness that was short-circuiting his senses. "That's a heck of lot more decadent than even I'd imagined."

Simon vigorously shook the chilled can of

whipped topping. "Aw, come on, Jaycee," he coaxed, pushing a soft tendril away from the side of her face. "Let's live it up a little."

She bit her lip, then nodded. "I have a feeling I'm going to regret this in the morning."

"You've come this far," he teased. "Don't stop now."

Her laughter warmed him. "Go for it," she said, dipping her finger into the dollop of whipped cream he'd served himself.

Simon held the nozzle over her caramel-covered ice cream sundae, smothering the gooey topping with even more calories while Jaycee hurried across the kitchen in her stocking feet to the pantry. She tugged open the cabinet door and peered inside.

His heart hit the floor when she bent over, her delectable backside pressing seductively against the thin fabric of her black sweater dress.

A guy just couldn't get a break these days, he decided. An invite back to her place, and what does he get? Not the hotter-than-sin kiss good-night he'd been anticipating since their last hotter-than-sin kiss, that's for sure. When she suggested something decadent, ice cream had been the last thing on his mind.

Some days life just wasn't fair.

"Nuts!" she called, and produced a half-full bag

of chopped walnuts. She returned and sprinkled a generous amount of walnuts over the twin mountains of whipped topping in their dessert dishes, then produced two spoons and handed him one.

He took the spoon, scooped his sundae off the counter and followed her into her stylishly furnished living room. The decor was cool and refreshing, like an easy spring morning. Light pastel accents kept the soft cream color dominating the room from feeling too stark or sterile. Regardless of how dreary the Seattle landscapes might be on any one of the hundred or more rainy days each year, spring reigned twenty-four-seven inside Jaycee's condo.

She sat in the corner of the sofa, curling her feet beneath her before smoothing the dress over her legs. "I thought tonight went very well," she said, running her spoon along the whipped cream threatening to spill over the scalloped edge of the sundae dish. "You were great."

He finished a mouthful of whipped cream and caramel topping before taking a seat on the center cushion of the sofa—close enough to breathe in her alluring floral scent, but far enough not to threaten. "Eaton asked me to handle the account," he said, unable to keep the pride out of his voice. "And Greg Simms invited me to spend next weekend at the firm's cabin in Mount Rainier. That's a pretty big coup for me—it's the annual partnership weekend.''

"I'm not surprised," she said between bites of sundae. "You were wonderful tonight."

He grinned. "Thanks to you."

She shook her head. "All I did was give you a few pointers. The rest was you, Simon."

"You're right, you know." He polished off his sundae and set the dish on the bleached oak coffee table. "A week ago I couldn't have said that."

She swallowed a spoonful of thick caramel and vanilla ice cream. Her tongue darted out to smooth along her lower lip, drawing his attention to her sweet, kissable mouth. "You will succeed in anything you put your mind to," she said. "I have faith in you, Simon."

It was that faith that encouraged him and allowed him to accept her praise in the spirit she'd intended. He also understood she had more to do with his success than she realized. She hadn't just given him a new and improved look. When she was by his side, he truly believed he had it in him to be the man she'd intended. She complemented him in more ways than one.

Now he had to find a way to let her know how he felt.

"I used to think I was a lot like my dad," he said, leaning against the sofa and stretching his arm along the back. "You made me realize that isn't necessarily true."

"What's your dad like?" she asked, scooping up another bite of sundae. She slicked her tongue over the drizzle of caramel that stayed on her spoon.

He nearly died.

"Reserved," he said, forcing his attention on the conversation and not the jump start to his overly responsive libido. "Dad's an accountant, retired now, but he had his own business ever since I can remember. I used to think he was this introvert and that I was just like him, but the truth is, he was a workaholic because it was easier than making the time for anyone or anything else in his life."

She leaned forward and set the empty sundae glass next to his on the coffee table. "What about your mother?" she asked.

"She passed away when I was six."

"I'm sorry, Simon." Compassion filled her eyes, and she laced her fingers with his.

He shrugged, but the truth was, as much as he loved his dad, Steven Hawthorne had been selfish, putting his fears before the needs of his son. The admission startled him but freed him at the same time.

"I know now that my dad was selfish. I used to think he avoided people because he was just really shy, but the truth is he was afraid of getting hurt. My parents' marriage wasn't the greatest, but he loved her. Don't get me wrong, I do have some great memories, laughter and singing, but not many after my mom died. Dad just wasn't that kind of parent. He not only shut out the rest of the world, but his own son, too, to a certain extent.''

Understanding edged aside the compassion in her gaze. ''Because it was easier not to let anyone close than risk getting hurt again?''

He gave her hand a gentle squeeze. ''That about sums it up. Dad wasn't a recluse. He was a work-aholic because it was safer than letting the real world in where it could hurt him. And I almost followed right in Dad's footsteps.''

''I know what it's like to be different than your family. Don't get me wrong, I love my family, but when it comes to women's issues, they're about as forward thinking as Stonewall Jackson. My point is, you don't have to be like dear old Dad to love him.''

''Exactly,'' he said. He drew his thumb over her smooth, silky skin. ''There's more to life than tax shelters and balance sheets. I don't want to end up like my dad. Forty years from now, I don't want to look back and see that life has passed me by and there's no one to share the porch swing with when I'm an old man. I want memories, Jaycee. I want memories to share with someone special.''

Jaycee pulled in a deep breath and told herself not to panic. He wasn't asking her to be that person. Or was he? ''What are you saying?'' she asked, her voice barely more than a whisper.

He shifted on the sofa and smoothed his free hand over her knee, setting off a series of sparks that ignited in her belly as he leaned closer.

She breathed in his warm, male scent. She wasn't supposed to be attracted to Simon. Too bad her body failed to recognize the warnings from her mind and chose instead to focus on the intense awareness between them.

''Be one of my memories, Jaycee,'' he murmured, his velvet-smooth voice dipping to a low, husky rumble.

''But...'' It wasn't like he was asking for forever. Just a memory. A memory that would also last her a lifetime, she realized, and couldn't threaten her goals.

Just a memory.

He moved in, narrowing the remaining distance between them, and she shifted until her back pressed against the thick padded arm of the sofa. He reached out and gently straightened her legs until they were stretched out on the sofa. With the tip of his finger, he touched her chin, looking deep into her eyes, letting her see the determination and something else there that made her heart beat a whole lot faster.

He eased closer, and she held her breath, waiting for the first tentative brush of his lips against hers. His warm breath fanned her lips, and she was positive she'd never felt anything more exciting.

She swallowed and struggled for breath. Blood roared in her ears, and her heart thundered in her chest. "Simon..."

"It's just a kiss, Jaycee," he said, bracing the flat of his palms on either side of her, framing her within his embrace. "It's just a memory."

Just a memory.

He was all man, she thought vaguely, mesmerized by the heat and emotion banked in his eyes. She lifted her hand and brushed a lock of sable from his forehead, something she'd longed to do since she'd freed those thick, rich strands from their gooey prison. "Just a memory," she whispered, moving her fingers through his hair.

"Yes," he said. His lips brushed hers in a gentle, tender kiss that made her glad she wasn't standing because her knees definitely felt weaker than they had two seconds ago.

"Simon," she whispered when he lifted his head to look into her eyes. His gaze darkened, and something she could only define as desire burned hot.

"One won't be enough. It'll never be enough," he said roughly, then slipped one hand alongside her jaw. He cupped the back of her head in his big hand, and before she could blink, he covered her mouth with his.

She wasn't sure what she expected. Maybe slow and easy, maybe gentleness, maybe tenderness. Why, she wasn't sure, because every other kiss they'd shared had been all-consuming. This one was no different and produced enough heat to reduce them both to ash.

His thumb pressed against her chin. "Open for me," he said against her mouth, his voice rough and demanding.

She did. His tongue slid across hers, and she tasted caramel and brandy and man. Tiny shivers of delight rippled through her as he teased her mouth wider, demanding her response. She obliged, slipping her arms around his neck and arching toward him until her breasts rubbed against his firm, wide chest. Her nipples beaded against the satin of her bra, the sensation adding to the heat Simon so effortlessly fanned from a low, simmering flame into an inferno of heat and desire.

She'd known Simon's kisses were filled with a sensuality that made her dizzy. She'd known kissing him filled her with an excitement she'd never experienced before. She'd known he made her *hot*. Yet she was still shocked by the impact of his kiss.

A moan escaped when his hand shifted, coming to rest on her hip. Even through the airy fabric of her mock cashmere dress, she could feel his fingertips pressing into her soft flesh. He shifted and rocked her closer, the smooth silk blend of his trousers brushing against her thighs, sending a spiral of heat through her. She moved against him, against the heaviness settling in her tummy and winding a slow, heated path down to her most intimate place.

His fingertips teased her jaw, traced lazy patterns down her arm, then moved to her waist seconds before they inched upward to settle on her rib cage. His thumb brushed rhythmically along the underside of her breast, and she trembled. He emitted a low sound deep in his throat, a hungry sound that matched her own growing hunger. Never had she felt so in tune to another human being, so warm and tingly all over, so...*alive*.

The fingers that teased her breast moved to her other hip and gently pulled her farther down on the sofa. He shifted until he was half lying beside her. She looked into his eyes, and a wealth of pleasure ribboned through her.

"What are we doing?" she asked.

He smoothed her hair from her eyes, framing her face gently between his palms. His mouth brushed across hers with aching tenderness. "We're going to create one hell of a great memory."

11

THE EFFECT of Simon's erotic promise was instant. He hadn't specifically stated they were going to make love. Just because his words implied they would was no reason for her stomach to bottom out or her pulse to career out of control. There wasn't an ounce of justification for the powerful wave of longing that took hold of her and wouldn't let go.

Apparently she was suddenly into lying to herself.

Because his eyes told the truth. His eyes told a tale of fierce passion just waiting to be unleashed and, for the life of her, Jaycee couldn't decide which surprised her more, his sexy promise or the way her insides melted at the thought of fulfilling that pledge.

Lamplight bathed the room in a soft, romantic glow. The perfect setting, except if she was going to make love to Simon, she didn't relish the idea of grappling on the sofa like a couple of teens.

Gently, she pushed his shoulder, and he eased back so she could swing her feet to the floor. She stood and faced him, extending her hand.

He slipped his fingers around hers and stood. Never had she seen anything sweeter than the care etched on Simon's handsomely chiseled face as he looked at her and smiled.

"Not here," she said, then bent to turn off the lamp. With only the cool glow of the full moon filtering through the miniblinds to guide her, she led him down the corridor to her bedroom.

He hesitated just inside the door. With a gentle tug of her hand, he brought her around to face him.

"I want you, Jaycee," he said. A slight frown marred his forehead. "And I know you want me." His voice was tinged with just enough concern and hesitation to warm her heart.

She ignored the *but* she heard in his voice and slowly pulled his starched white dress shirt free from his trousers. One by one, she opened the buttons until his bare chest was gloriously exposed for her inspection.

"Then there's nothing to stop us from making that memory for your old age, is there?" She splayed her palms over his torso, causing the muscle beneath the sleek skin to jump and flex. She bent and pressed her lips to his taut flesh. A sound, somewhere between a moan of pain and a growl, ripped from his throat, and she smiled against his skin. Her tongue snaked out and laved his nipple, heightening her awareness and his.

He clasped his hands on her shoulders and gently set her from him, giving her one last chance to change her mind before they reached the point of no return. Feminine satisfaction coursed through her at the pained look of a man caught in a sensuous web.

He held her gaze. He held her heart, and she feared possibly her soul as well. "Make love to me, Simon," she whispered, then slowly lifted her dress over her head.

Simon's mouth went dry. His fingers itched to touch her. His body craved hers with fierce, pounding need. A need to possess, to mate, to make Jaycee his...completely his.

Wearing only a black satin bra to shield her full breasts, a pair of the skimpiest matching panties he'd ever had the pleasure of seeing and thigh-high black stockings with lacy tops, she covered the short distance between them. Fire balled in his gut then exploded south, hardening him to the point of pain. He wanted to sweep her off her feet, carry her to bed and make love to her all night long.

He couldn't have moved even if it meant saving his sorry hide.

She wreathed her arms around his neck and pressed her slender, made-for-sin body to his.

He forgot to breathe.

If he didn't regain some control, all night long would last about three and a half seconds. Starting now.

She practically wound her body around his, reminding him of a black cat. The only thing missing was a low, sultry purr.

With every ounce of control, concentration and sheer willpower, he eased his hands around her slender waist and guided her toward the double bed. Gently, he eased her down to the mattress, then surrounded her with his still-clothed body.

Jaycee lifted her mouth to his, and he moaned, the sound as warm and intimate as his rich, citrus scent. She knew there would be no turning back after tonight. Tonight he would belong to her. She'd cope with tomorrow...tomorrow.

Dragging his lips from hers, he teased her with quick darting kisses along her jaw and down her throat to her breasts. His hand skimmed over her hip, slowly moving up her body to the front catch of her bra. With a skill that shocked her, he flicked the catch and freed her breasts.

She arched her back when his lips brushed against her tightened nipple with the lightness of a dampened feather. His warm palm held her, his skin hot against her sensitized flesh. Weaving her fingers through his hair, she urged him to take her in his mouth.

Sensation after sensation clamored inside her when he pulled her nipple into his mouth, grazing the sensitive flesh with his teeth. She was through fighting her emotions and let the insanity take over. His touch, his mouth, his body pressed against hers were absolute heaven. Every inch of her felt alive and starved at the same time. She'd never have enough of him, yet he touched, he kissed, he caressed her everywhere.

Her need tripled. Not only physical need, but emotional need, as well. The honesty of it should have filled her with a frosty chill. Instead, it ignited her blood.

Simon rolled away from the woman driving him to the brink of pain with her gentle, alluring brand of sensuality to finish undressing and to struggle with that all important self-control again.

"For a minute there I thought you were going to leave me...all hot," she said, as he slid over her. She wiggled closer. "All hot..."

He gritted his teeth when she pressed her lips against his chest, her tongue snaking out to circle his nipple.

"And achy."

He sucked in a sharp breath when she pulled his

flat nipple into her mouth, grazing the tip with her teeth as he'd done to her.

"Oh, God," he groaned. "Do you know what you're doing to me?"

She rocked her hips, the smooth scrap of satin covering her feminine secrets pressing enticingly against his rock-hard erection. "Hmm. I think I do."

Her cool hands chased down his back, down to his backside where she pressed her fingers into the muscle then rocked her hips to meet him again, her demand crystal clear.

Oh, man, was he ever in trouble.

Before he embarrassed himself by putting a premature end to their lovemaking, he shifted his lower body to safer territory. Determined to make her as crazy with desire as she was making him, he used tongue and hands to explore her gentle curves. He eased lower, carefully pulling her satin panties from her body. He teased the lace tops of her nylons, the back of his hand brushing against her dampening chestnut curls. When she urgently whispered his name, male satisfaction reared inside him.

As he brought his mouth to her most sensitive spot, her back bowed off the bed, and she cried his name along with a moan of pleasure so pure and raw he felt awed by it, and her.

One hand held her bottom and the other aided in the intimate exploration, urging her to fall apart. Her hands twisted in the bedspread when he lifted her higher, taking her deeper into the maelstrom. Her body tensed, and he tasted her sweet orgasm as she came in a rush of passion and heat and desire.

His blood pumped hot through his veins. He was certain he'd die from the sweet agony if he didn't make her completely his, and soon. He moved over her and smoothed the hair clinging to the side of her face.

Her eyes were half lidded, her body welcoming as he slid inside her. Tiny tremors still rippled through her, heightening his pleasure. When she rocked her hips against him and moaned, he nearly came undone.

"You are so beautiful," he said, his voice tight with emotion. He kissed her, long and hard, every inch of their lovemaking perfectly in tune.

With each stroke of their bodies, sparks ignited, then burned hot. He treasured every glorious sensation as she took him closer to the ultimate fulfillment.

He slipped his hands beneath her bottom and thrust more deeply inside her. Minds retreated and bodies took control as they lost themselves to the lovemaking. He felt her tense, then heard her cry out, his name achingly sweet on her lips. A more intoxicating sound he'd never heard, he thought, then followed her into sweet oblivion.

JAYCEE quietly slipped from the double bed and padded through the bedroom to the bath, careful not to awaken Simon. The red glow from the digital clock on her nightstand indicated it was nearly four in the morning.

She turned on the shower and waited for the water to heat before stepping beneath the spray. Struggling to keep her mind blank, she went through the routine of showering and shampooing her hair. Once done, she slipped into the soft blue chenille robe she kept on a peg behind the door, then combed her hair and brushed her teeth. After turning off the light, she slowly and silently opened the door.

She held her breath until she made certain Simon still slept. As quietly as possible, she left the bedroom and crept down the corridor to the kitchen. Using only the light from the range hood, she heated a mug of water in the microwave and made herself tea.

Not until she was settled in the pale peach armchair near the window overlooking her postage-stamp-size front yard did she allow herself to think about what she'd done.

She tucked her feet beneath her and took a sip of the sweetened, soothing liquid. What she'd done was make a monumental mistake.

Exactly as the men in her family said she, or any other woman, for that matter, would do, she'd done. She wanted a promotion. She wanted what she felt was rightfully hers, an eventual partnership in the family business. All she'd managed to do was prove the Richmond men right. By allowing her emotions to cloud her judgment, she'd jeopardized her future. She'd not only breached ethical and professional boundaries by going to bed with her client, she'd allowed her feelings for Simon to escalate to the point of distracting her from her ultimate goal.

She'd not just gone to bed with him, she thought, but practically begged him to make love to her!

She couldn't argue that the memories she and Simon had created during the night were one of a kind. No matter how wonderful, how tender or emotional their lovemaking, she couldn't, *wouldn't* let it happen again.

Her future was on the line. She was struggling to carve out her mark in the family business, and the last thing she needed was to compound the mistake she'd made.

A movement caught her attention, but she didn't

have to turn to know Simon hovered in the doorway watching her.

"Would you like some tea?" she asked him.

He walked into the living room to the sofa and sat. "No. Thanks." He leaned forward, bracing his arms on his thighs, his hands clasped between his knees. "Do you always get up so early?"

She looked at him. He'd pulled his trousers on, but his feet were bare. His dress shirt hung open, drawing her gaze to his chest. Her eyes traveled upward, and she took note of his still-mussed hair. He looked rumpled and sexy, even if his lips were set in a grim line.

He knew. He knew that her next words were going to shatter whatever hope he'd had that he wasn't the only one to have felt the incredible magic between them.

She hoped he wouldn't know her next words were also going to be a lie. The biggest, fattest lie she'd ever told.

"We made a mistake," she said quietly.

He dropped his gaze to the floor between his feet as if he couldn't bear to look at her.

Her fingers tightened around the pale pink mug in her hands, as if the heat from the ceramic could warm the horrid chill filling her up inside. "*I* made a mistake. I'm sorry, Simon. Last night shouldn't have happened."

He still wouldn't look at her. She expected he might be hurt and hoped that his newly reborn confidence wouldn't take a hit. For a moment, she wondered if he'd heard her. Then he slowly lifted his gaze to hers.

The look he gave her was hard, causing a shiver to race down her spine. Anger was the last emotion she'd expected to see firing Simon's dark green eyes.

Her heart tightened in her chest. Tension crackled like a live wire between them as he stared at her. She'd known passion in his arms. She'd seen tenderness and caring in his eyes. Now only anger remained.

She had only herself to blame.

"You're sure about this?" he asked, his tone barely hinting at the anger flashing in his gaze. "You've thought it all through? Know your next move?"

"My work is done," she said, hating herself as she spoke the words. "Your future with Eaton and Simms is secure. My objectives have been met. I'd say our business association has come to an end."

"So what was tonight?" he asked, his voice dripping with sarcasm. "A bonus?"

She shrugged, then looked away, unable to bear the hurt reflected in his gaze, or the gripping pain in her chest. A lump the size of Mount Rainier lodged in her throat, rendering her unable to speak, even if she could find the words to soothe the hurt she was causing them both.

"Why are you doing this?" he demanded heatedly. "What the hell are you so afraid of?"

She couldn't bear to look at him, so she remained facing the window. Tears welled in her eyes, blurring her vision, so she closed them. She wished she could close off the pain as easily. "Like I said, the objectives have been met—"

He swore then stood. "That's bull, and you know it, Jaycee. What the hell is going on?"

She glared at him. "I screwed up, okay? Is that what you want to hear? I've made a mess of things and did exactly what my family expects a woman to do. I let my heart overrule my head, and it won't happen again."

She waited, expecting him to say something, to fight back, to tell her she was wrong and the most wonderful night of her life hadn't been a mistake.

He didn't. She felt the coldness emanating from him and tried to take comfort in it, knowing she was righting a wrong.

Her heart wouldn't buy it for a second.

He gave her one last angry look and walked away.

She heard him in the bedroom, then moments later he returned. He scooped his tie and jacket from the back of the sofa where he'd laid them when they'd arrived.

He paused at the door, and she held her breath, willing him to leave before she did something really silly and feminine like cry in front of him.

"The only mistake is the one you just made," he said, then yanked open the door and walked out of her life.

Just as she'd intended.

"DAMN FOOL WOMAN," Simon muttered, then scraped the razor down his cheek.

He'd been uttering those same three words for a week. He'd never known a more stubborn, prideful, determined, spirited, pain-in-the-backside woman than Jaycee Richmond.

"Wouldn't know the real thing if it reached up and bit her in the— Ow!"

He swore a blue streak, then examined the nick to his jaw. After sticking a piece of toilet paper on the cut, he figured he wouldn't bleed to death, then finished shaving.

He wasn't completely clueless. He'd known what she was doing the morning she'd told him their "association" was over. She was protecting herself—from him, he guessed—but the reasons behind her actions had him completely baffled.

"Association, my—"

He sucked in a sharp breath when the razor caught his chin. Bright red blood beaded on his chin, and he dabbed at the cut with another piece of tissue. He'd better come up with a plan to get through to Jaycee soon or there'd be nothing left of his face.

It wasn't like he hadn't tried, but all his attempts had failed.

He'd called her. Twice.

She'd been cool and unresponsive. Both times.

When he'd told his father about her, his old man had surprised him by suggesting flowers. He'd sent a dozen red roses and kept his musings about Steven Hawthorne's uncharacteristic acuity with the likes and dislikes of the opposite sex to himself.

All he'd gotten from Jaycee for his trouble was an emotionless and formal thank-you note.

Stella blew his mind when she suggested he send Jaycee a book of romantic poetry, claiming Buck had won her over with such a ploy. He scoured the bookstores until he found a book of poems by Elizabeth Barrett Browning.

Jaycee had returned the gift along with a note thanking him for his consideration, but asking him to please stop sending gifts. Inappropriate considering their business relationship, she'd claimed.

"Damn fool woman."

He wasn't dense. He could take a hint. Except he *knew,* knew as well as he'd draw his next breath, that Jaycee Richmond was lying not only to him, but to herself about her feelings for him.

He hadn't imagined everything that had happened between them. The heat, the passion and the emotion weren't the product of some fantasy. Those things were as real as it got. He'd fallen in love with Jaycee.

She returned his feelings. He'd stake his career on it. Everything about her, every move, every word, every nuance of her personality told him she returned his feelings. Because no one, not even the damn fool woman intent on ruining both of their lives to prove a point, was that good an actor.

He'd tried to get through to her. He'd called, sent flowers and poetry. He'd done everything except play caveman and sling her over his shoulder and carry her away until she listened to every single word he had to say. And he had plenty if she'd give him a chance.

Barring the risk of a kidnapping charge, there was nothing left for him to do but wait. Wait, and pray that the damn fool woman came to her senses and started listening to what was in her heart.

12

JAYCEE stepped off the elevator at precisely one in the afternoon. Still playing the good girl, she returned from her lunch hour on time. Today would be the day, although much of it had passed already. But her reasons for procrastination were hardly a mystery. Prolonging the inevitable was all she was doing. Her future with the company was on the line, and unless she just got it over and done with, she'd never be able to take the next step in her career—wherever that step may take her.

With determination as her only weapon, she pushed through the door marked private, walked past her personal broom closet and headed to Dane's office. If anyone would listen to what she had to say, it would be her middle brother. Rick's door stood open, and she heard his voice as he spoke on the phone. If she wanted at least a fighting chance of getting what she wanted, Dane was her best shot.

Pasting a smile on her face, she knocked on the doorjamb. "Got a minute?" she called.

Her brother looked up from the report he was reading and waved her into the office with a welcoming smile. "For you? Always."

She closed the door, then crossed the dark beige carpeting to the black leather love seat. She perched on the arm, opting for the appearance of casualness. Sitting in one of the squat leather chairs in front of his desk would have conveyed subservience. She set her purse on the seat cushion, then smoothed the hem of her black skirt. "Dane, I think it's time—"

Dane's hand shot up to stop her. "I know what you're going to say, Jaycee."

Of that she had serious doubts. There was no way he could know what she was about to tell him. "Do you?"

Dane turned in the chair to face her and leaned back before lifting his arms and settling his hands behind his head in a relaxed pose. "It's time for a raise. I know we should have taken care of this sooner, but you know Rick's been in and out of the office with the people from Cannery Row Tuna and we haven't had a chance to discuss your next increase."

"This isn't about a raise, Dane. I was hoping for more responsibility."

Slowly, he lowered his arms. "More responsibility? Jay, you practically run the office now. What more is there?''

"A lot more," she said, unable to mask her disappointment. Dane had always been a little different than her oldest brother. He'd been more... accepting. Sure, he could be a bit overbearing, but most brothers were at one time or another. He might think he knew more than she did about most things, but she'd always believed Dane was the one Richmond who believed in her. That she could be wrong...well, it hurt. A lot.

He let out a sigh and leaned forward, bracing his elbows on his knees. "A lot more *what*, exactly?" he asked in that calm, quiet voice that was more like their mother than she was sure he realized.

She gave him a level stare. "You know what I want, Dane. You know I'm qualified."

"That may be, but you're not experienced."

"How do you expect me to gain experience if you won't give me a chance?" she replied.

"Jay, it's—"

"Is it just experience I lack?" she asked meaningfully.

"You're not being fair."

"Neither are you," she countered, frustration making her voice rise a notch. She pulled in a deep breath in an attempt to calm herself. "What if I could prove to you I can do the job? Would it make a difference?'' Deep down, she already knew the answer. She just needed to hear him say it.

"To me? Maybe. To Rick?" He shrugged.

She looked away, unable to bear the truth in Dane's eyes. No matter what she did, no matter how many degrees she earned, regardless of whether she could do the job, she'd never be allowed to grow professionally because, to the Richmond men, she was a woman. And everyone knew women weren't executive material.

At least at Better Images they weren't.

Her gaze settled on the framed diplomas on the far wall along with the cover from a local magazine that had named Rick and Dane Seattle's new up-and-coming promotional and publicity giants. If they didn't change their attitude toward women in the workplace, they wouldn't be anybody's up-and-coming anything for very long.

She looked at her brother. "Forget it," she said, her tone filled with resignation. "It won't make a difference to Rick." She knew her brother. Yes, she had successfully transformed an individual. But that wasn't the type of image consulting Better Images was known for, and the work would be categorized as a useless endeavor.

"You know that you're going to be taken care of," Dane said when she stood. "Just because Rick and Dad don't think women make good business partners doesn't mean that a percentage of the business isn't being taken care of for you.''

A flash of anger ripped through her. ''This isn't about getting a percentage of the business. Dammit, Dane.'' She shot the words at him. ''This is about what I want, what I need. And for the record, I don't *want* or *need* to be taken care of, by you, Rick or Dad. Why can't you people get that through your head?''

Her brother let out a rough sigh, a pained expression evident in his clear, blue gaze. She didn't think he was being deliberately obtuse, even if he was providing her with a convincing facsimile.

''What do you want me to do?'' he asked quietly. ''You want me to talk to Rick about making you an account rep? You know as well as I do that he'll flat-out refuse. But I'll do it if that's what's going to make you happy. Even if by some miracle he did agree to the job change, you know there's no way he'll ever consent to bringing you in as a full partner. It just won't happen, Jaycee. No matter how much you might want it, it just won't happen.''

She suppressed the urge to scream in frustration. She crossed the spacious office until she was standing in front of the desk. Placing her hands on the smooth wood surface, she leaned forward to let him see her anger and frustration. ''I don't want a full partnership given to me. But I would've liked to have known that in time I could have earned that right."

Dane stood and moved to the window overlooking the busy intersection below. "Why can't you just be content, Jay?" he asked, not looking at her. "Why isn't what you have here already good enough for you?"

"Because I learned by example, Dane," she said, lowering her voice. She pushed off the desk and dropped into the leather chair. "Believe it or not, you and Rick and Dad all taught me to want more, to reach further and to do it right each and every time. I'll do what I have to do to get there. I learned that by watching all of you."

With his hands tucked in the front pockets of his slacks, he turned to face her. There was a sadness in his eyes that pulled at her, but she couldn't, wouldn't give up the fight. Not this time. Not when she was already suffering from the regrets of letting go of the one thing—the one man—who'd stolen her heart. No more regrets.

"What you want isn't here, is it?" Dane asked,

"No," she said, struck by the honesty in that one simple response. "I want a future in publicity and advertising, and it won't ever be here for me at Better Images."

A halfhearted attempt at a grin tugged his lips. "I'm sorry, Jaycee."

She shook her head and stood. "Don't apologize. I want what the company can't give me. There's nothing left for me to do but give you my two-weeks notice. And I'm taking the rest of the day and tomorrow off, too."

"You're going to give up that easily?" he asked, a hint of surprise in his voice that she wasn't going to fight with him on the subject.

Why? she thought. Why continue to fight a losing battle? Her time would be better spent reaching for what it was she wanted.

She picked up her purse from the love seat and dug through the contents for her car keys. With the keys came a small white piece of paper, which fluttered to the floor at her feet. She stooped to pick up the paper, and her hand stilled.

"Mr. Right will walk into your life today."

Still crouching, she wrapped her fingers around the fortune from Chan's Chinese Kitchen, then looked at her brother. "This isn't about giving up," she said, rising slowly.

Simon had walked into her life that day, practically within minutes of her reading Confucius's mass-produced wisdom. She didn't believe in things like fortunes or bad karma. Fortune-tellers, psychics and horoscopes were for people without the drive to make things happen. She'd smugly believed that. At least until Simon Hawthorne had walked into her life and asked her to make him a new image. The last thing she'd expected was to lose her heart in the process.

"Then what's it about?" Dane asked.

The grin she gave her brother was genuine. Her future was a mystery, but she'd never felt more safe and secure than she did at this moment. "It's about moving on."

FRIDAY MORNING Jaycee awoke with a renewed outlook, although she was about to become unemployed. Unemployed with no prospects for gainful employment in sight.

None of that mattered. She wasn't worried. She had a plan. After several telephone calls yesterday afternoon and an extremely productive dinner with her parents, her decision had been made.

The Image Maker would officially open for business in two weeks.

Even her father, the worst of the offenders of gender bias in the Richmond clan, had agreed to back her with a start-up loan for her own business. Of course she knew he thought he was simply throwing money away on a lost cause, but no matter how placating he meant the gesture to be, Jaycee had every intention of turning the tax write-off he expected into a profitable and worthwhile investment.

The number of public relations firms in the Seattle area could be counted on one hand, which meant if she'd planned to remain in the business, relocation would have been a serious option. That would've meant selling her condo and moving away from her family. No matter how much they irritated her with their antiquated ideals, they were still her family, and she loved them.

Relocation would also have meant never seeing Simon again, a thought that had left her with an empty feeling somewhere in the vicinity of her heart. She didn't consider for a minute that the men in her family were right about women, but she couldn't deny it was her heart, not her head, that had kept her from starting the wheels spinning toward relocation.

Now all she had to do was find a way to let Simon know that she'd been stupid and stubborn and that she was ready for whatever the future might bring—as long as they faced it together. A process that would most likely include groveling.

She'd made an appointment to see Simon through his secretary, saying only that she was interviewing accountants for The Image Maker. By the time she dressed in her best business suit and drove downtown to the offices of Eaton and

Simms, some of her courage began to waver. She hadn't heard a word from him since she'd returned the book of poetry. Maybe he'd given up on her.

By the time she found an empty parking spot a half block away from the building where Eaton and Simms was located, walked the distance to the building and took the elevator to the appropriate floor, her courage not only wavered, but took flight completely.

She gave her name to the receptionist, and a moment later a reed-thin woman with hair as black as midnight and parchment-white skin led her into the heart of Eaton and Simms. Her heart pounded painfully in her chest as she followed the woman into a small conference room. Her breathing stilled, and her pounding heart stuttered behind her ribs before resuming at a maddening pace. Simon stood next to the window overlooking the Sound, looking confident and absolutely gorgeous in the dark gray pinstripe suit she'd helped him pick out a little over a week ago.

"Thank you, Stella," he said in that deep, resonant voice she'd missed hearing.

Stella closed the door on her way out, leaving them in complete privacy.

"Hello, Simon."

Simon's heart was in danger of exploding inside his chest. It took every ounce of self-control not to leap over the conference table and pull Jaycee into his arms. Just because she'd come to see him didn't mean she'd finally realized she'd been in love with him from the moment they laid eyes on each other.

His gaze flicked over her. "Why are you here?"

"I...I need an accountant."

Those weren't exactly the words he wanted to hear, but the hesitancy in her voice combined with the tenderness brimming in her eyes gave him hope. He wanted to hear, "I love you, Simon. I can't live without you, Simon."

"I would like to hire you," she said when he remained silent.

He slipped his hands into his trouser pockets and rocked back on his heels. "I don't know. I don't handle individuals as a rule," he said, using the words she'd said to him when he'd gone to her office looking for a new image.

Her mouth quirked as she fought a grin. "I'll make it worth your while," she said, slowly circling the table toward him.

Maintaining an uninterested facade was tough, especially when he was still fighting those table-leaping urges. "I'm pretty busy."

"What if I told you it was for my new company, The Image Maker?"

He shook his head. "Wouldn't make a difference."

"What would make a difference?" she asked, stopping less than a foot away. He breathed in her scent, a combination of floral and feminine that had the power to drive him to his knees.

He lifted his hand and smoothed his fingers down her satiny cheek. "A kiss might be a step in the right direction."

The blue of her eyes darkened to the color of a summer sky. "Just a kiss?"

He closed the distance between them then slid his hand beneath the fall of her hair to cup her neck in his palm. "For starters," he said, then guided her mouth to meet his in a hot, blinding kiss.

The first taste of her mouth was electrifying. The second caused a jolt of heat capable of melting the polar ice caps.

"I've missed you," she said, when his mouth left hers to taste her jaw, her throat, the lobe of her ear.

Missing him was a start, he thought. A damn good start.

Her hands pressed against his shoulders. "I owe you an apology."

He let out a sigh and looked at her. Words could

wait, couldn't they? He wanted more kisses, although he did appreciate her apology.

She dropped her gaze to her feet and pulled in a deep breath before looking at him with apprehension. He wanted to set aside her fears but decided to hear what she had to say. A man deserved to have some pride, didn't he? A little late, considering, but he'd been terribly wounded. Was it so wrong for him to want it salved just a little?

"I made a mistake, Simon," she said in a hushed tone full of contrition. "Not because we made love, but because I let my fear get in the way. I let it stop me from having what I really wanted. Not just professionally, but personally."

He bit the inside of his lip to keep his mouth shut.

"I wanted you, Simon."

Yes!

"I still do."

Life is good!

"I love you."

And it just got better.

Her hands landed on her hips, and she gave him a fierce frown. "Aren't you going to say something?"

He moved away from her and propped his backside on the oak conference table. "What do you want me to say?" he asked her.

She closed the distance between them and slipped her arms around his neck. They were eye-to-eye and the raw emotion banked in her eyes had his heart constricting in his chest. "I want you to say that it's not too late," she said softly.

A grin eased across his mouth. He'd tortured them both long enough. "It's not too late," he said, settling his hands on her hips. He rocked her closer, then kissed her again.

"God, I've missed you," he said when he lifted his head. "I love you, Jaycee. Even if you are the most stubborn, hardheaded—"

"Don't forget self-employed," she added, planting a quick, hard kiss on his lips. "I quit my job yesterday."

The news that she'd left Better Images didn't surprise him. He'd expected her to do so sooner or later, based on what she'd told him about her family. "Really?"

She nodded. "Yup."

"I thought you—"

"That I was going to further my employment in the family business? Not going to happen."

He listened while she told him about quitting her job and her father's agreement to back her business. The Image Maker would represent individuals as well as companies in need of public relations. Whatever she decided to do, she'd succeed.

She not only had the brains, but she had the confidence to make a winner out of anything she set her mind to.

"We haven't discussed my terms," he said, his hands still resting on the gentle swell of her hips.

"Terms?"

"You still need an accountant, don't you?"

"Hmm, most definitely," she said, moving closer. "How about dinner?"

"I was thinking about breakfast. Every morning."

"What will your other clients have to say about me getting such special privileges?"

"I won't be married to my other clients."

Her answer was a teary-eyed smile and an exuberant nod.

And then they sealed the deal with a kiss.

I Waxed My Legs for *This?*

HOLLY JACOBS

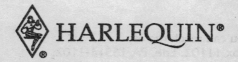

HARLEQUIN®

TORONTO • NEW YORK • LONDON
AMSTERDAM • PARIS • SYDNEY • HAMBURG
STOCKHOLM • ATHENS • TOKYO • MILAN • MADRID
PRAGUE • WARSAW • BUDAPEST • AUCKLAND

Dear Reader,

When I talk about *I Waxed My Legs for This?* I refer to it as my hairy legs book. My grandmother is scandalized! In her world, women don't talk about waxing their legs, much less write about heroines who actually do. But with too many kids, too few hours and legs that get five-o'clock shadow, well, I've learned to take romance where I can find it, both personally and in my writing!

You'll notice that Carrie and Jack live in Erie, Pennsylvania—my hometown. I like to feature Erie in my writing because I think it's a little bit of heaven right here in Pennsylvania. We've got some of the nicest non-ocean beaches around, and of course, when talking about beaches, a woman's mind always turns to...you've got it, non-hairy legs!

So now you know a little about me—a mother of four who tries to keep her five-o'clock shadow to a minimum, who loves her city and its beaches, and finds her inspiration in the oddest places. Now keep flipping the pages and let me introduce you to Carrie and Jack, and the hairy legs that kickstart their romance!

Warmly,

Holly

P.S. You can reach me at
P.O. Box 11102, Erie, PA 16514-1102,
or online at http://members.aol.com/hfur/.

To DJ, Jessica, Katie and Abbey:
thanks for putting up with me, and always believing
I could not only chase but catch my rainbow!

And to Kathryn Lye:
thank you for seeing that rainbow
and helping me find the pot of gold at the end of it!

1

JACK TEMPLETON bounded up the stairs that led to Carrie Delany's apartment, cursing her Bohemian spirit—the one that led her to lease a fifth-story loft in a building that had no elevator.

"Carrie." He beat his worry onto the door with a quick succession of raps. When she called, Carrie had just told him she was in trouble and to hurry. For the entire fifteen-minute race through traffic he agonized about what type of *trouble* she could have gotten into this time.

"Coming," a female voice called. The door slid open. Half of Carrie's blond hair was in a ponytail, the other half trailed wisps down her neck. She was wearing a disreputable robe, peeking out beneath it his old football jersey—a shirt she'd borrowed back in high school and never returned.

Whenever Jack asked for the jersey, Carrie told him it was dirty; that she'd get it back to him as soon as she'd laundered it. It had been over a decade, and either Carrie had the worst hygienic habits on record, or she intended to keep the jersey.

She looked fine. Relief flooded Jack's body. Carrie looked a little nervous, but fine. After all the grisly possibilities he'd been imagining, a stolen high school jersey wasn't much of a concern.

"Are you okay?" Jack waltzed through the door and slammed it shut. He made himself at home, tossing his jacket on a chair and settling on the couch. He patted the cushion next to him. "You look a little green."

"I really did it this time," she said with quiet resignation in her voice. "Why do I keep getting myself in these messes? I mean, I'm almost in my thirties. I have gainful employment. I got the okay on that dress for Jaycee Smith—you know, for the awards in Tennessee? It's my first major commission. Eloise was almost more excited than I was. I was going to call you tonight and tell you. Maybe even invite you to a celebration."

She shook her head and sank awkwardly next to him on the couch. "I just don't know how these things happen. I take my vitamins every day and run five miles on Sundays."

Jack lifted his eyebrow at that statement. He'd been with Carrie on more than one of her *runs.*

She grinned. "Okay, I walk fast—"

"And stop at every hot dog stand, doughnut shop, candy store on the way."

"But I'm walking at least. And that's not the point. The point is, I'm not dumb, I take care of myself, but I still—"

"What is it this time?" She'd get to the point. Eventually. Sometimes Jack would allow her to meander her way around her trouble, but he was curious and not feeling particularly patient. Carrie's predicaments were always interesting, and inventive.

"This," she said, pulling her robe aside with flourish, and plopped her legs onto the coffee table. They were covered in…something.

"What the h—" Jack cut himself off just in time.

Carrie heard the potential swearword and frowned.

He substituted, "Heck. What the heck have you done now?"

He could see the tears gathering in her eyes and felt a wave of sympathy.

"I'm going to the beach this weekend to work on my tan," she offered, as if the statement explained the goop on her legs.

"And?"

"And I didn't want hairy legs. I mean, I'm a blonde, for goodness' sakes. You'd think the hair on my legs would be as light and as fine as the hair on my head. Unfortunately it's thick and black. I shave them in the morning and by dinner I have five-o'clock shadow. It's embarrassing. So I decided to wax them."

She stopped and began to dig in the pockets of her robe, sniffing dramatically.

Jack reached in his pocket and pulled out his handkerchief. It wasn't fashionable to carry them, he knew that. But his mother had always been tucking one in his pocket when he was younger, and the habit stuck. It was a handy habit with a friend like Carrie.

He handed the cotton square to her and she gave a very unladylike honk into it.

"So you decided to wax your legs. What's the problem?"

She gave a muffled sob from the depths of his once pristine handkerchief. "It hurts." She hiccuped—a side effect whenever Carrie cried. "I pulled the first section off and it hurt like crazy. Now I can't make myself pull the rest off. I've sat here most of the afternoon trying, but I just can't do it."

"And you want me to do it?" Any residual worry evaporated. Jack's lips twitched as he dutifully tried to avoid smiling. He knew Carrie would see the humor in the situation, but not until the moment had passed.

"I didn't think it would be as bad as the time I asked you to get my class ring for me," she offered.

"Nothing could be that bad." The memory surfaced, though he'd tried to bury it deep. Carrie's puppy, Muffin, had eaten the ring and the vet had told them it would eventually come out. Jack had spent the better part of a week sifting through...byproducts searching for it. Carrie had claimed the duty made her squeamish and her parents refused to oblige her by doing it.

"You finally did find it," she said in a triumphant voice. The smile she shot him almost made up for the task. Almost. "You even cleaned it up for me."

"But you never wore it again."

"Would you?" Her sobs turned to laughter.

That was the thing about Carrie; she never could make up her mind just what mood she was in. And when he was with her, Jack's moods shifted just as rapidly.

Carrie got herself into ridiculous situations and expected Jack to get her out. Then she somehow made him feel like a cross between a white knight and a court jester.

"So you think me pulling wax off your legs will be easier than digging through Muffin's muffins?"

"For you, not for me. It really does hurt." She shifted on the couch and placed her right leg onto his lap. "I think it would be easier if we just talk and you pull when I least expect...ow!" She yanked her leg off his lap and began massaging it. "That hurt," she said, looking at him as if it was his fault.

He tossed the piece of waxed and hair covered paper on the coffee table. "You said I should pull it off when you weren't expecting it."

"But I want you to do it when I'm expecting not to expect it." She rubbed the injured limb a moment and then placed it back on Jack's lap.

He rubbed the slightly red area. "Do you remember when you were ten and decided you could slam-dunk?"

Carrie groaned and threw her head back against

the pillow in the corner of the couch. "It could have worked."

"If you had let go. Jumping off the ladder and grabbing the rim was a decent idea, but hanging there—"

"I didn't want to fall and hurt something."

"So you screamed for me to help you down," Jack explained and pulled another strip.

"Ow! I should have kicked you harder." She rubbed the offended area.

"You kicked me hard enough to break my glasses." He pulled another sheet.

"Hey! That was too fast. You didn't let me recover from the last one."

"Sorry. But we're almost done with this leg." Jack rubbed the exposed skin for her.

"So, what's new?"

"Since we talked yesterday?" She paused for a moment. "I dumped Ted."

Jack had never liked the guy. He had shifty eyes and a habit of toying with Carrie's hair. Jack had no rational explanation for why, but Ted's habit set his teeth on edge. Trying to forget the fact that he wouldn't miss Ted a bit, Jack tried to sound sympathetic. "I'm sorry. You've been seeing him almost a year. What happened?"

"Well, last night, while we were at dinner I decided he'd never do."

Jack pulled another sheet, but Carrie didn't even yelp this time, just glared at him and rubbed.

"Because?" Jack inquired.

"We both ordered the fettuccine."

Jack should have been used to Carrie's twists and turns. He was a lawyer, used to sorting through mountains of information to get to the truth. But with Carrie the twists left him lost in the muddle of her weird brand of logic. "And?"

"And I realized if I was with you, you would have ordered the shrimp," she replied.

He smiled encouragingly, because she was right, he would have ordered shrimp. But that didn't explain why she'd dumped Ted.

Carrie smiled right back at him and nodded her head.

Jack frowned. "I don't get it."

Slowly, as if he was just a bit dim, she explained. "When you order shrimp I always steal some. That way I get the best of both worlds—my fettuccine and your shrimp. I mean it's just like when we go to the movies. He never got the jujube candies and I'd have to buy my own along with the licorice and it'd be too much. I looked like a pig."

Jack ripped off two more sheets in quick succession.

"Ow!" Carrie glared. "You're enjoying this."

"One leg down, one to go." He grabbed her left leg and pulled it onto his lap with the right one. "So you dumped him because he ordered the wrong food?"

Carrie shook her head and blushed. Jack

stopped. He'd seen many things in the years they'd been friends, but her blushing wasn't one of them.

"No." She shrugged. "I dumped him because while he was kissing me good-night—a rather sloppy, pathetic kind of kiss, I might add—I realized that you weren't a sloppy kisser. Not that I'm asking you to kiss me," she hastily added. "It's just that I want to find a man someday who can kiss as good as you and knows how to order the proper food and all."

Jack stopped, midrip.

"Hey, finish it off, that's even worse, making me worry about when you're going to finish... Ow." She jerked her leg off his lap and rubbed the hairless strip of skin. "Doggone it. Men don't have to have hairless legs. It's not fair. Maybe I'll move to Europe where women can go hairy."

"When did you kiss me?" Jack asked, ignoring her grumbles. He didn't remember kissing Carrie. He'd been kicked by her, and there was the time she set him on fire, the time she locked him in a locker for an entire health period, the time... No, Jack was sure he'd never kissed her. Looking at her lips he was equally sure he'd remember it if he had.

"Why, Jack, I'm hurt. Chemistry class, I was a junior, you were a senior?"

He waited, still unable to remember a kiss.

"I was mixing chemicals and they blew up. I passed out. There I was, lying on the floor and you leaned over and gave me the most wonderful kiss

I've ever experienced. You quite ruined me for other men. I worried you didn't kiss me again because I didn't kiss good enough. When you went away to college, I spent my senior year practicing. I hoped the next time you were home, we could try again.''

Jack took her leg back and ripped three sheets off, one after another, out of sheer frustration.

"Hey, that wasn't nice," she protested.

"And that wasn't a kiss." He kept his voice low and tried to relax the tension in his jaw. "I was giving you mouth-to-mouth resuscitation."

It was insulting, having Carrie think that his rescue attempt was the best kiss he could give. Memories of the boys she dated her senior year; how he'd hated hearing his parents talk about each and every one of them. Never hearing Carrie mention one of them when they talked, and all the while she'd practiced kissing them in hopes she'd get better.

Carrie stared at him a moment before the giggles started. Moments before she'd been sobbing into his handkerchief, now she wiped her eyes again, but this time mirth was the reason. "You mean, I spent my senior year practicing so I'd be a good kisser next time you gave me mouth-to-mouth?"

"Carrie," he started, but she cut him off.

"I thought I must have been horrible, but then Ben Thaker told me I was the best he'd ever kissed. You remember Ben, he kissed a lot of girls. So, I finally figured that you'd always called me kid because that's how you saw me, just the kid next door. Your almost little sister. Plus by then you had Patti, and then Lynda," she paused a moment, and then smiled. "Yeah, then it was Amy, then that first year at the firm you met Julie, and then Sandy—" She cut off the sentence and shot him a look of sympathy.

"Sorry. Anyway, I finally gave up." Her smile slipped a fraction, but reappeared instantly. "In the end, I'm glad I gave up chasing you. You're the best friend a girl could want. I mean, we go to movies, hang out together. You even go on my Sunday runs with me."

"Eating orgies," he corrected. He pulled the last sheet.

"Boy, that hurt," Carrie said, massaging her newly liberated left leg. "It better last for six weeks like the box said or I'll be…"

Jack watched her, momentarily tuning out her chatter.

She had chased him? He didn't quite remember it that way. When she'd moved in next door they'd been too young for him to think of her as a girl, she was just a neighbor. As they grew older they moved from neighbors to friends.

Friends.

Of course that's what they were. Friends. If she'd chased him, it hadn't been very far. She'd always been there; ready to listen, needing to be rescued, rescuing him, though Jack doubted she knew how many times her generous heart had

soothed him, especially over the last few months
since Sandy—

He shut off all thoughts of Sandy. He didn't
want to face them. Didn't want to face his failure.
Carrie's litany of names proved what he'd begun
to suspect—he was a failure with the opposite sex.
Five serious romances since college and not one
of them had lasted. He'd thought he'd finally found
the right woman with Sandy, thought they'd eventually marry and have a family. Those dreams had
died with Sandy's accident. It wasn't long after the
incident that they decided to go their separate
ways.

"Jack," Carrie said, pulling him from his
thoughts.

She rose on her dehaired legs and smiled as Jack
tuned back in. "Jack, I was just going to make
dinner." There was an unspoken invitation in that
one statement, or maybe it was a warning.

Jack resisted groaning and thought fast. *Carrie*
and *cooking* were two words that didn't go well
together. *Carrie* and *indigestion* were words that
went together better.

"Since your legs are so smooth, why don't I
take them, and the rest of you, out for something.
I'll promise to order shrimp."

A look of relief swept over her face. Carrie
wasn't any more fond of cooking than he was of
eating her attempts. "I was counting on you asking. Now that I'm once again between boyfriends

there will be too many nights of my cooking. I look at it as incentive to find another."

"Cook?"

"Boyfriend." She rose from the couch. Her robe parted revealing her hairless leg. Though Jack had just waxed them, watching them peek through her robe emphasized what shapely legs they were. Not that he was looking. Carrie was a buddy, and no one eyed up a buddy's legs.

She knotted the robe. "Guess I better change. I can't go out in this."

"Ah, Carrie, isn't that my jersey?" Now that she'd recovered from her mishap, he didn't feel bad about teasing her. Actually, teasing about the jersey had almost become a ritual. Both of them knew Jack would never get it back.

Right on cue, Carrie looked down and her eyes widened. "Why now that you mention it, it is. I'd give it to you now, but it's dirty. Let me launder it, and I'll get it back to you next week."

She walked into the bathroom to change and Jack stared after her, unable to resist watching the sway of her robe. She was a nicely packaged woman.

He put the thought away. They'd been friends for so many years, that he was just sort of used to her.

Carrington Rose Delany, his friend, his almost sister.

Carrie was lucky she'd never pursued her girl-hood infatuation. If she had, Jack would have surely wrecked whatever relationship they built. He certainly had a track record for messing up where women were concerned.

No, they were both lucky the infatuation hadn't gone any further than one mouth-to-mouth experience.

CARRIE RUMMAGED THROUGH the dresser she kept in the bathroom. Dinner with Jack never meant hamburgers and fries, so jeans wouldn't do. That was okay with Carrie. She loved dressing up. It was sort of an occupational hazard.

Working in a vintage dress shop gave Carrie far too many opportunities to indulge her weakness. And she'd certainly indulged it this week. She'd bought the perfect dress for tonight's ruse. It had come into the shop last week. It was just the thing for a night out with Jack; just the thing to put her plan into action.

It was antique-white, a color that should have made it look almost virginal, and it did look that way, at least on the hanger. But when she had it on... Carrie smiled. She slipped the deceptively simple design over her head and gazed at her reflection in the full-length mirror at the other end of the room.

Yes, the flapper era dress might look virginal on the hanger, but when worn it was pure temptation. And, tonight she needed to play the role of temptress to the hilt in order to trick Jack.

She felt a bit guilty about the ruse she was about

to employ, but she recognized the need for the sub-
terfuge. Jack was too stubborn for his own good.
And it was his own good she had in mind. She
couldn't help but notice the dark circles that had
become a permanent fixture under his eyes these
past few months. And today she'd noticed he
looked like he'd lost some weight. He was still
mourning the loss of his last relationship.

Carrie pushed aside any residual guilt and concentrated on her plan. It might be slightly under-
handed, but it was in Jack's best interest. He was
too stubborn to realize how much he needed to get
away. But he wouldn't be able to resist playing the
hero, and he'd never know that she was really rescuing him.

She fished at the bottom of the closet and found
her off-white pumps and slipped them on. She
wrapped her hair in a simple little chignon and,
with a light hand, applied a bit of makeup. Jewelry
and perfume were added and she was done. Just
fifteen minutes. Not too bad, she congratulated herself as she went out to meet Jack.

"Ready," she called cheerfully.

He whistled and she pirouetted. "Like?" she
asked, needing to hear him say the words.

"Not quite the word I'd use. What did I do to
warrant a dress like that?"

He was falling right into her plan. Playing her
role, Carrie shrugged her shoulders. "Not you. If
you're taking me out, I want to look my best. After
all, I'm currently footloose and fancy-free. Maybe

the man of my dreams will show up tonight. I certainly want to be ready if he does."

Jack's smile slipped a bit. "Ready for what?"

"For anything. You can never tell what's waiting for you when you walk out the door." So saying, she moved toward the door. Her stomach was growling, something that might embarrass her if it made noises in front of anyone besides Jack.

"I'll agree with you there. But, Carrie honey, I don't know if you should advertise as heavily as that dress does."

"What do you mean? It's perfectly decent." She rummaged in the coat closet and found a shawl that accented the dress perfectly.

Jack hadn't moved. He stood there, arms crossed and frowning in a very lawyerish way. "*Decent* isn't the word I'd choose to describe that dress."

"Jack, I'm wearing the dress. Just think, if I don't manage to collect a date or two tonight I'll have to eat my own cooking. You wouldn't really want that, would you?"

He sighed and walked out the door.

Carrie trailed after him, locking the door behind her. "Is there something the matter, I mean, other than my dress?" Carrie had her suspicions. There had only been one thing wrong with Jack for months. "Sandy?"

He turned, his expression was odd. Carrie knew for sure that something was the matter, but Jack just shook his head and continued down the stairs. "No, I'm fine. Just a bit tired."

"Well, of course you are." She pasted a smile on her face, determined to hide her concern. She had her plan, after all. "You've been working too hard. We haven't done anything together in weeks."

"You were pretty wrapped up in your boyfriend," he reminded her.

She gripped the railing as she started down the stairs. The only time she regretted her loft was when she was wearing heels. "He's gone now." Carrie placed her hand on Jack's shoulder. "When you're ready to talk about Sandy, I'm here."

For him there was work, and then there was work. At least, that's how it had been ever since Sandy had left him. Actually his work at Ericson and Roberts law firm had always been a priority. During the five years he'd worked there he'd found his niche and endeavored to secure it.

But since the breakup with Sandy, he hadn't just worked hard, he'd worked as if there was nothing else in life but work. Carrie had watched helplessly, unsure how to comfort him and how to get him to ease back on his workload. Working was his way of dealing with losing Sandy.

Sandy.

The breakup was one of the few topics that kept Jack silent. Carrie was sure he was still grieving. It was her job to see to it that he left his office long enough to recover.

Jack was a thirty-year-old heart attack waiting to happen.

Carrie had decided that she was the twenty-eight-year-old antidote.

"COME ON, BIG GUY, I'm awfully hungry." She let herself into his car and settled in.

"You're always hungry."

"Right. So you'd think you would have figured out you need to feed me regularly, but here we are, when all the food is somewhere else."

"You're absolutely right, my lady. Let's go."

They drove in companionable silence. Carrie smiled as they pulled into Bayside Country Club, Jack's club. The first time he'd brought her, Carrie had felt out of place, but that had lasted only until the food was served. Carrie felt at home wherever there was a plate of good food, and Bayside had some of the best in Erie, Pennsylvania.

"Hi, Martin," she said to the maître d'.

"Ah, Mr. Templeton and Carrie, what a pleasure."

Carrie allowed Martin to take her hand and give it a light kiss. "We don't have a reservation, Martin, and it's all my fault. I offered to cook for Jack and positively scared the man into bringing me here."

"There's always a seat for you both here." Martin ushered them toward the tables.

Martin seated her. "Would you like to start with something to drink?"

"Food, Martin. Just food. It's the only thing to salvage my broken heart."

"Another boyfriend bit the dust?" the maître d' asked Jack.

"Rumor has it he wasn't much of a kisser," Jack explained.

Carrie glared at Jack, and answered Martin herself. "Well, kissing is important. And, even worse than that, the man had absolutely no idea how to order good food."

"Ah, now that is a crime. And speaking of good food, it just so happens that Felix has this new pasta dish that will make you forget all your troubles."

"Well, I'm so upset, it will be hard to do it justice, but for your sake, I'll try."

"I'll have the shrimp," Jack tossed out.

Martin gave him a brief nod. "I'll hurry the food along," he told Carrie.

As he departed, Carrie stuck her tongue out at Jack. "See, someone realizes that I've suffered a huge loss."

"Carrie, you broke it off with him."

Leave it to Jack to try to make a breakup logical. What he didn't understand was that the heart wasn't logical. There was no way to push it in a direction it wouldn't go.

Carrie had learned that particular lesson in high school, after Jack's kiss had awoken her heart to the fact that to her he was more than just her neighbor and friend. Unfortunately his heart hadn't noticed a thing. He'd gone off to college and discovered pom-pom perfect Patti, and then her long line of successors.

She'd watched Jack try to analyze his split with Sandy for months, to no avail. If she could have talked to him about it, she would have tried to tell him that Sandy had never been right for him. But Jack wouldn't talk about the breakup. And Carrie knew that he had to figure it out for himself. He needed time and distance, not her lectures.

That's where her plan came into play.

"I might have done the breaking, but it's still a loss. And that brings me to another little problem."

"Problem?"

Sensing the game had begun, Carrie made the first move. "Forget I said anything. I'm sure some other man will be willing to help me out. After all, you said this dress was a knockout."

"I didn't say that," Jack, always the literal lawyer, argued.

Literal, but predictable. She wanted to grin, but maintained her annoyed look instead. "Fine, you implied it. Maybe I'll go see for myself if it's a knockout or not. I could go scout the bar while we're waiting for our dinners. Maybe someone there would be willing to help me out with my little problem."

As a sure sign of resignation, Jack sighed. "Carrie, honey, you know I'll help you if I can."

"No," she said, quite firmly. "I'm sure I can handle this on my own. You know how I hate to bother you with my little problems."

"Carrie," Jack said, with a note of warning in his voice.

"Why, you act as if I was perfectly helpless. I'm a big girl, have been for years, I'm sure I can figure out a way to handle this as well."

"Carrie..."

She was on a roll, unwilling to slow down. "Why I could have figured out a way to get that wax off without you, you know. I'll just make sure I don't bother you with my trivial little problems anymore."

"Carrie, what is the problem?" he asked, his voice sharp with frustration.

"You don't have to yell at me."

"Honey, I'm sorry I yelled," he said, his voice lower, but still tinged with frustration.

"Never mind, it's okay," Carrie said, and sniffed for good measure.

He leaned toward her and steepled his fingers under his chin in a very lawyerish way. "Now, tell me what the problem is."

"Well, remember when you showed up and I said I was waxing my legs because I was going to the beach this weekend to get some sun?"

Jack nodded and Carrie gave another delicate sniff. "Well, you see, that's the problem."

"But we got the wax off your legs," Jack protested.

"Not the wax, but the beach."

"The beach?" he asked, becoming more confused by the minute.

Erie was blessed with some of the most wonderful nonocean beaches around. Presque Isle, a peninsula that curled into Lake Erie, housed beaches on its lakeside and created a sheltered bay on the other. It was only minutes from town. Carrie loved to haunt it during the summer and she frequently bullied Jack into joining her. But this time she had something more in mind.

"I need a man to go with me," she said. "I was hoping you knew someone."

"Why do you need a man?"

"Because," she spoke slowly, "They only let couples on the beach."

He chuckled. "Honey, where did you hear that? Anyone can go to Presque Isle. It's a state park, after all."

"Not the peninsula, Amore Island. Remember? I told you about it. It's off the Carolina coast. Jodi's Travel Agency was having a special on the tickets, and Ted and I were going to go. Well, now there's no Ted and I'm in a bind."

"I'm not following you?"

For a lawyer, he could be pretty dense. He seemed to do well enough with his contracts, but didn't seem to be able to follow a simple conversation. Slowly, as if speaking to a very small child, Carrie said, "It's a couples' resort. I'm no longer a couple, so they won't let me on the island, much less on the beach."

"And you want me to introduce you around to my friends and help you find a replacement?"

Carrie shook her head and felt part of her chignon fall out. Sighing, she pulled the rest out and let it fall to her shoulders. It was baby fine and never stayed in any style for long. "No, silly," she said. "I want you…"

2

JACK SNORTED A HUGE quantity of his water through his nose, and inelegantly began choking on it, which earned him evil looks from the other diners.

"What?" he gasped when he was able to breathe again.

"*I want you* to come with me and pretend we're a couple. I can't go without a man, and I thought you might be—"

He wiped his chin and looked more annoyed, if that was possible. "You thought I might be a man?"

"No, I thought you might be the man to come with me and pretend to be *my* man while we have a great vacation on Ted."

"You mean Ted paid for the tickets and you kept them."

This was the part of the plan that made Carrie feel slightly guilty. Tricking Jack for his own good, was one thing, lying was another. To be on the safe side, she crossed her fingers under the table. "He said he didn't want them, and I should keep

them. We didn't fight, we just broke off, friendly-
like.''

Jack studied her, looking just like Perry Mason
used to look as he tried to figure out a maddening
case. "Let me see if I have all this straight. You've
been dating this Ted for months, but dumped him
last night because he ordered fettuccine and didn't
kiss as good as I do."

Carrie nodded encouragingly.

"And, because you broke off friendly-like, he
let you keep some tickets to a couples-only resort.
And you thought I might do for the other half of
your nonexistent couple?"

She unclenched her crossed fingers hidden under
the table. "You forgot the wax. I waxed my legs
for the beach and one way or another I'm going to
show off their hairless state."

"And the resort's beach is better than our own
Presque Isle's beaches?"

"Not better, just away. There are boardwalks,
and theaters, and clubs and... Jack, it's a play-
ground for grown-ups. There's an ocean between
us and reality. Who could ask for more?"

Here came the easy part, not a lie in sight.
"You've been working so hard, I thought you
could use the time to relax. I can always use the
time to tan and sip piña coladas. I want to have
fun."

Jack shook his head and she could hear the ex-
cuses before he even started saying, "Honey, you
know I'd do anything for you, but I don't know if

I can get the time off, especially on such short notice.''

Carrie forced herself to laugh. "You and I both know that you haven't had a decent vacation in years.''

Jack started to protest, "But—"

Carrie cut him off. "And we both also know that you're more accustomed to contracts than court, and yet court's where you've been. The stress from that, and—" she almost said Sandy, but didn't want to remind him of the woman he'd lost "—and the fact you haven't had fun in the longest time are all reasons for you to go with me.''

"But, Carrie..." he tried again.

She smiled and talked over his protests. "But nothing, Jack. I'm not making you go or anything. I'm sure I can find any number of men willing to take me to a resort for a week.''

"A week, you didn't say anything about it being a week. I thought it was just a weekend.''

Martin himself brought a tray with their dinners and set them down. "Now, Carrie, you just sit back and eat, and forget about last night.''

She leaned over and inhaled deeply. "Thank you.''

"A week," Jack snarled as Martin retreated. He automatically handed her a shrimp.

Carrie took it and bit off the end. She set the tail on the edge of her plate as she sighed with satisfaction. "A week. And, as I was saying, I'm sure I can find any number of men willing to take me.

I mean, everything's paid for and all there is to do is sit on the beach and sip frosty, fruity drinks.''

"Honey, you don't drink."

The trouble with lawyers was that the were so very literal. "Ah, maybe not here, but on some tropical island paradise, I might. Now, since you don't want to take me, let's see if maybe you can help me figure out who I might invite."

"Carrie," Jack said in a fit of exasperation. He didn't know why he bothered to get into this with her. Carrie always won.

"I mean, Martin likes me. He might like to get away. Do you think there's a Mrs. Martin?" She shook her head, her loose blond hair flying. "No, he'd have said something if there was, we're friends after all." She mused a bit about it. "Yes, maybe he'd like to go with me."

"Martin won't be going with you," Jack said with certainty.

"No?"

"No, the members here would be crushed without Martin to greet them," he reminded her.

"You're right. They might never forgive me. Okay, well, who might be available from your office?" she asked gaily. She took a bite of her pasta. She chewed, her eyes closed and a look of sheer joy on her face.

Something twisted in the pit of Jack's stomach. Something that shouldn't stir when watching a friend. It must be her dress, a dress designed to make a man think of sin. And following through on those thoughts with Carrie—his little sister, his best friend—would be nothing less than a sin.

"Who's available at my office?" he asked rhetorically. "No one."

Her eyes flew open and she swallowed. "You know, you are not being very helpful."

"I know." He speared a shrimp and bit it viciously.

"Well, if there's no one you know, I guess I'm going to have to go trolling. The problem with working at a dress shop is that we don't see a lot of men come through the doors, and the few that do visit tend to have a significant other already."

"Trolling?" Jack asked, not liking the way the word sounded on his tongue, or the images it planted in his mind.

"Trolling. Where do you think I met Ted, for Pete's sake. Certainly not at work. I answered his ad in the personals."

"Like hell you did." He'd learned over the years to expect the unconventional from Carrie, but answering personal ads...well, that went beyond unconventional.

"Like hell I didn't," she said with a sweet smile. "There are tons of guys writing to the paper every week. I'm sure one of them might want a trip to a tropical resort. Although, sharing a bedroom with a man I hardly know is a bit uncomfortable."

"Ah, *moi petite*, I know you usually don't partake, but I thought this wine would complement the pasta and lift your spirits as well. We all worry about you," Martin said in a little French, big Pittsburgh accent.

Carrie beamed at him. "My spirits are already lifting. Tell Felix that when I'm done I'll come back and let him know just how much."

Martin poured a bit of the wine in a glass and passed it to Jack who nodded without taking a sip. "Shall I pour?"

"We're fine," Jack bit out. He took the bottle and slopped the wine into their glasses.

Carrie lifted another forkful of pasta to her mouth and sighed. "Oh, my gosh, Jack. I'm in heaven, right here in Erie, PA."

"Yes."

"But you haven't even tried it." She offered him what was on her fork.

He shook his head and with resignation stated, "I said, yes, I'll go away with you."

Carrie just shook her head in turn. "Oh, Jack, I've changed my mind. It wouldn't be fair. I forgot how important your work is and how busy you are. Working in a vintage dress shop isn't nearly as demanding as working to protect and serve the public."

"That's the police."

"Well, they do a bit of protecting and serving, too, but you're the one who actually puts the bad guys in jail. I can't be the one to deny the citizens of Erie of your protection." She slipped another bite into her mouth and sighed. "I'm sure I can find someone."

"Carrie, that's the D.A., the only thing I protect is corporate liability." He felt a headache coming on with a vengeance. Carrie could do that to him as easily as she could lift one. "And you won't be finding anyone." He gulped some wine.

"Jack, I said, thank you, but my answer is no. Now, eat your dinner. That last case took a lot out of you. You're looking a bit peaked." She speared one of his shrimp and plopped it into her mouth.

"I am not. And there will be no other man taking you anywhere." Jack obliged her by taking a bite of his dinner. "I'm telling you, Carrington Rose Delany, that there will be no other man going with you on this trip."

"Jack."

"Please," he said, pulling out the big guns.

"Okay," she said brightly.

How the hell did she do it? How did she always get him to do what she wanted, practically beg to have the honor of doing it. Jack stabbed at his dinner. Damned if he could figure out women in general, Carrie specifically. Most of the time he forgot she was a woman—she was just Carrie. But times like this, he remembered her femininity with a vengeance.

"You're sure you can get the time off?"

"No, but it doesn't look like I have much choice," he said through a mouthful of food.

"Oh, you're wrong, Jack, there are always choices."

"Not for me."

"Listen, I'm a big girl. I don't need you to come along because you feel you have to. I can take care of myself and I'm sure I can find a man who would like to come on a trip with me."

"I said I'd go," Jack said again.

"Yeah, and I once showed more enthusiasm when I had to go to the doctor's and have a plantar's wart removed. Just forget it, Jack." She had that look in her eye, the one that said he might be pulling his handkerchief out of his pocket again.

"Carrie, let's get this straight here and now, I'm going."

"You really want to?" she asked, her eyes bright. "You won't mind sharing a bedroom with me? I thought we'd take turns in the bed. One night I'm in the bed and you're on the floor, next night we switch. I know pretending to be a couple might not be fun, but the beach will be."

"You don't have to convince me. I said yes."

"You're sure?"

"I'm sure."

"Well, if you're sure, then that's okay. I've been saying practically forever that you need some time off. This will be perfect. I'll work on my tan and you can read something other than a court brief."

"I thought I'd take along some paperwork and play catch-up."

She shook her finger at him. "Oh, no, not on

your life. This is a vacation, not some excuse to do paperwork. You're going to relax and maybe I can remind you of how to play."

"What do you mean remind me?"

"When's the last time you did something just because it was fun?"

"What's fun?

"I don't know, you tell me. What do you think is fun these days? You used to love to play basketball, but you don't anymore—"

"I don't have time," he protested, but Carrie just ignored him.

"You don't have time to go to any games anymore, either. You don't hang out with buddies at the bar. You don't go lie on the beach and watch the clouds. You don't take a walk in the middle of the rain, just because it's fun."

"I don't find getting soaked fun. I can get anywhere I want in my car and stay dry."

"You're hopeless," Carrie lamented.

"And you just don't understand the demands my job makes on me," he said. People counted on him, clients counted on him. He couldn't just throw things over and go play in the rain. He didn't have time to play.

At least not in recent months. Neither of them had mentioned that Jack's lack of fun coincided with his breakup with Sandy. Somehow, his ex always factored into their conversations, though neither of them ever mentioned her.

"Then change jobs," Carrie said with a careless shrug.

"What?"

"If your job is so demanding you can't afford to have fun, change it. Can you really tell me that you enjoy what you're doing? Do you get up in the morning and say, *Wow, I can't wait to get to work today?*"

"Carrie, no one likes their job that much," Jack said.

Years ago he'd had that kind of innocence, but too many dry contracts and equally dry meetings had robbed him of the idea of really making a difference. What he made was money for Ericson and Roberts. And the more money he made for them, the more cases they threw at him so he could make more money for them. It was a merry-go-round, one he couldn't seem to slow down.

"I do," she said in a small voice. "Selling, and occasionally designing dresses might not be as glamorous as being an attorney, but I love what I do." She shook her head again. "Never mind. Forget I said anything. Let's just concentrate on getting you out of town for a week without you bringing the office along with you."

"Fine," he said.

"Fine," she said, a smile on her face.

Jack watched her attack her food and felt as if he'd somehow lost a fight he hadn't even known he was waging.

SHE'D WON ROUND ONE!

Carrie burst through Encore's door, dying to tell someone what she'd done. For once she was thankful the shop was devoid of customers, as she ran to the back office and found her boss, Eloise Summit, hard at work.

"Eloise, I did it." Carrie flopped into the chair opposite Eloise's and grinned. "Oh, I so did it this time."

The tiny brunette looked up from the papers on her desk. "He fell for it?"

"Of course he fell for it. We're leaving tomorrow for a week, and Jack still doesn't have a clue how it happened."

"Carrie, someday he's going to figure out how blatantly you manipulate him."

"Never. I've been at it since we were kids. He's never known what hit him." She tipped a little farther back in her chair. She felt good. More than that, she felt great. She'd convinced Jack to take a break—a break he desperately needed. The tiny little lie she'd told was worth it.

"Someday you might push him too far."

Carrie chuckled at the idea. "Never. Jack's so busy rescuing me from myself that he never figures out how tricky I am. And never will unless you or I tell him. And of course, we're not going to tell him, right?"

Eloise sighed and pushed the pile of papers she'd been working on back. "Right."

"Geesh. I get one of you to take a break and

the other one starts to break down. So, what's got you so stressed?"

"I hate paperwork." Eloise took the pen that was tucked behind her ear and tossed it on top of the pile of paper.

"Leave it then. I'll take care of it when I come back."

Carrie didn't exactly love paperwork, but it didn't bother her nearly as much as it bothered Eloise, so she took care of most of the small shop's book-work.

"Actually it's done." Eloise picked up a sheet of paper and handed it to Carrie. "You better enjoy this vacation because your workload just picked up."

Carrie's hands trembled as she stared at the paper. "Do you mean it?"

A small rose stood delicately next to her name. Carrington Rose.

A Carrington Rose Original. Her own line of dresses.

It was a dream come true. She hadn't lied when she told Jack that she loved what she did and looked forward to going to work. She liked people, enjoyed working with them one-on-one at Encore, making them happy, dressing them beautifully. But she had bigger dreams.

Her own designs.

Creating her own line of dresses was a dream that fit neatly into the life she'd carved for herself here at Encore, working for Eloise.

Encore was a rather eclectic store, with a loyal, ever-growing, circle of clients. Not only did they sell vintage dresses and gowns, but they sold reproductions and up until now they only occasionally carried one of Carrie's originals. But now her occasional creations would be her own line with her own label.

She'd tried college, tried about a dozen jobs and then stumbled on an ad Eloise had run. Someone who could sew and sell. Well, she'd learned to do both and under Eloise's tutelage, she'd learned to do both well.

She stared at the label logo. This was the culmination of all that work and a lot of dreaming.

"You're sure it won't flop?" Carrie asked. The idea of failure was a scary part of realizing a dream.

"Carrie, you know how people rave about your work. Look at the trouble Jaycee Smith has gone to just so she can wear one of your designs to the award banquet in her honor at Tennessee State. She's in the WNBA and could have picked any number of designers. But she chose you."

"My own label," she whispered. Then louder, as the news really sunk in she sprang from the chair. "My own label!"

"Your labels will be waiting for you when you get home in a week. And it might be tough, but forget your own label." Eloise stood. "Right now, we have to do some shopping."

"For what?" Carrie asked as Eloise herded her out of the office.

"You're going to a romantic island with a man, and you have to ask? You need new clothes."

"It's just Jack."

Eloise shot Carrie a strange look she couldn't quite define.

"Yes. It's just Jack and you alone for a week."

"But—"

"Consider this a chance to advertise Encore. Because this is a special vacation package, there will be a lot of Erie-ites on that beach."

Before Carrie knew what had happened, Eloise was thrusting clothes at her in a dressing room and she was trying them on.

"You're going to be flying high," Eloise promised.

CARRIE MIGHT BE FLYING high, but she wanted nothing more than to set her feet back on solid ground.

"Oh, Jack, I forgot how bad flying is for me."

"Honey you've never flown before."

"And I never want to again." She clutched the armrests of her seat. She was sure her knuckles were almost as white as her face must be.

She'd won. She'd left Jack no time to back out of the trip, and here they were, on a plane, flying to their doom. But at the moment she didn't feel like much of a winner.

"Really, Care, it's just some turbulence."

"I don't believe you, and I don't believe Captain Dave, either. We've probably lost an engine or a wing, or something else that's equally important when flying in a plane."

"It's just turbulence," Jack said again.

"Yeah, you and Captain Dave keep saying that. And what kind of name is Captain Dave?"

"I'm sure he's competent or they wouldn't have him flying the plane." Jack rubbed her shoulders.

Carrie was too worried to enjoy his touch. "Competent, shmompetent. The man is flying us to our doom."

"Lighten up, Carrie. This was your idea," Jack said in his normal, confident way.

Carrie hated that confident, self-assured part of him at this moment. "Sure, remind me that I've driven you to your death. Yeah, that's going to make me feel better." Jack was such a man, no compassion hidden beneath that hard exterior.

He'd never realize the effort she'd made to get him to relax before he worked himself into an ulcer or worse. He'd never know how much she ached every time she saw that look in his eyes; the look that said he was thinking about Sandy. He'd never know because she'd never tell him.

And, she'd never tell him because they were obviously flying to their doom—she wouldn't have time.

He raised his dark brows in what might have been his attempt at sympathy and patted her shoulders again. "We're going to be just fine."

"Uh-huh," she managed to say.

Jack sighed. When Carrie got like this there was no reasoning with her. She once refused to leave the house on a Friday the thirteenth because a black cat had crossed her path the day before. She was convinced it was an omen and had tried to talk Jack into staying home for the day, too. He wouldn't, and laughed at her for being so superstitious.

She ended up having the last laugh because Jack had wrecked his Ferrari, totaling it. Only Carrie didn't laugh. She was relieved that just the car was wrecked and not him.

Jack reached over and pried one of her hands off the armrest and held her trembling hand in his own. "It will be just fine."

Carrie nodded her head stiffly and Jack watched for the flight attendant. "Could we have a drink when you have a moment?"

"Sure. What would you like?" the flight attendant asked with a smile.

"Fruit juice," Carrie said.

"With a bunch of vodka," Jack added.

"I don't drink," Carrie told him.

"Today you do. Remember you thought piña coladas were perfect for the beach? Well, vodka is the perfect drink for a turbulent plane."

When the drinks came, Jack handed Carrie hers and said, "Drink it."

"I don't want—"

"You'll never even taste the vodka, and it will relax you. Drink it."

With a slight grimace, Carrie took the drink and took a sip. "It's not bad."

"Finish it off."

Ten minutes later they had a second round.

After that, a third.

Within half an hour Carrie was no longer white-knuckling her seat. Instead she was giggling.

"What's so funny?" Jack asked. He was used to seeing Carrie in the middle of mishaps, and she was always sunny, but he'd never seen her silly.

He grinned as she giggled again. He kind of liked it. "Come on, what's so funny?"

"You," she said.

"Me?"

"You." She laughed as if it was the best joke she'd ever heard.

"Why am I so funny?" He smiled indulgently. A drunk Carrie was preferable to a nervous, airsick one.

"Oh, you're a man, and that makes you funny. You didn't even realize you'd been tricked into coming on this trip with me."

"I realized it." He'd realized she didn't want someone else on this trip, that she'd wanted him on this vacation right from the start.

Carrie enjoyed thinking she was manipulating him, and he was just friend enough to allow her to believe it. Most of the time he just put up resistance for the show. This time...well, a vacation wasn't what he'd had in mind, but he'd decided that maybe Carrie was right. Maybe he needed to get away from Erie, and the memories. Sandy was gone. It was time he rebuilt his life. In fact it was well past time.

"No, you didn't. I fooled you." She let out a delicate little hiccup and continued. "You know Ted didn't buy those tickets, don't you."

"He didn't?" While he might have known she'd manipulated him, he didn't know she'd out-and-out lied.

She grinned a Cheshire-catlike grin and nodded. "I did. Eloise gave me a bonus. I've been bringing in a lot of special orders. This WNBA dress is the biggest, most vis...visible one. She's making Carrington Rose Originals a sig...a sig...a signature of the store."

"Why did you lie?"

"Because you would never have let me spend that kind of money on you, even though it was a special, because you're too old...old...old-fashioned. But I knew you needed to get away. So when Eloise gave me the money and you finished your case, I knew it was a sign."

She giggled again and waggled her finger in his face. "I know you don't believe in signs, but you should. Remember, there was a time you didn't believe in Friday the thirteenth, either. But you'll never figure it out you've been tricked because you're a man and I'm a woman, that means I'm tricky."

Jack watched her giggling, she was so pleased with her trickiness, and something tightened in his chest. She'd done this for him? He thought back and couldn't remember anyone ever doing something so generous for him. Certainly not Sandy.

Carrie gave a little sigh and leaned her drunken head against his shoulder. "You're going to have a good time, you know that?"

"Sure, baby," he crooned, ready to agree with anything she said. She'd done this for him. He let the thought sink in.

"I'm going to remind you how to play. You've forgotten how. That nasty Sandy took that from you."

"Whatever you say." Jack knew as sure as he was winging along the ocean coast that he'd do whatever she wanted. She'd had him wrapped around her little finger since they were kids and this newest revelation only tightened her hold.

He was going to have fun this week...even if it killed him.

3

CARRIE WOKE UP with a groan. Someone was killing a cat somewhere, she thought in a vague, sleepy way. Why would someone want to murder a kitty, and why would they do it so noisily?

She pried open one eye, a difficult feat because the top lid appeared to be shellacked to the bottom one. Light blinded her, but the noise drove her to ignore it. She pried open the other eye.

Where was she? That was the first thing she needed to discover. And the second was who was making that horrible noise. She looked around the garish room and remembered…she was on vacation, at Amore Island…

Which meant that the horrible noise could only be one thing, actually one person—Jack. If she had to make an educated guess she'd have to guess he was singing…well, sort of.

She listened and started to make out some of the words. "Rhinestone Cowboy." That was what he was attempting to sing. Unfortunately his attempt was, well, it was pitiful.

Then she smiled. Jack singing, or at least doing his imitation of singing, could only mean one thing—he was relaxed. That's why she'd gone through her elaborate scheme, to get him away from work and help him remember how to let loose. It seemed that her plan was working.

She owed Ted, her nonfettuccine eating, bad-kissing ex-boyfriend, a debt of gratitude. He'd provided her with the excuse she needed.

She sat up, and quickly sank back down. What had Jack done to her? She vaguely recalled the plane about to crash and Jack offering her a drink and…things got fuzzy then. Hazy pictures floated through her memory, of the nice flight attendant, of Jack…and Sandy? No, she must have been hallucinating that part. She'd brought Jack to the island to forget Sandy.

Maybe the plane had really crashed and she was injured—that would explain the pounding in her head.

A concussion.

No. The pounding in her head had to be from the drinks Jack had plied her with. That would explain why her memories of their arrival at the resort were so fuzzy. She thought she remembered a lobby with a waterfall. Did they put waterfalls in lobbies or was that part of her alcoholic haze, too?

Carrie searched her memory. There was a blurry image of her being carried by Jack. His hands on her. Unbuttoning her blouse and…

Suddenly her headache increased ten thousand fold. What had she done?

Better yet, what had Jack, the man she'd tried

to save from himself, done to her while she was drunk? She peeked under the covers and felt sick to her stomach.

She sank back and buried her head in the pillow with a groan. She'd let her best friend…well, not let. And certainly not her best friend anymore if he'd—she peeked under the covers again—if he was responsible for her current lack of clothing.

The quasi-singing stopped and the object of her ire emerged from behind a door.

"You're awake," he said with a disarming grin.

"What did you do?" Carrie demanded.

Jack frowned. "What do you mean, what did I do?"

She peeked under the covers a third time just to make sure she was right. "We agreed we'd share the room, but not that we'd share the bed. Where are my clothes and what were you thinking when you…" She let the sentence trail off. The ideas of what they had done, and its implication to their friendship, were too horrible to voice.

"When I what, Carrie?"

She could feel herself blushing and couldn't do a thing to stop it. Her embarrassment fueled her anger. "When you had your way with me."

"I did no such thing," Jack protested.

"You did, too. I remember you carrying me into the room and unbuttoning my blouse…" She stopped there because things sort of faded after that.

"But you don't remember screaming, *I can undress myself* as you proceeded to do just that?"

Glaring at him, she slowly shook her head.

"Or, me leaving the room while you did?"

Again she shook.

"Or my coming back a half hour later, and taking the quilt onto the floor?"

Relief flooded through Carrie's body. He hadn't—they hadn't. She sank back into the pillows and sighed. "I'm sorry. It's just that I woke up feeling like that darn airplane had landed on my head and everything was funny. Not ha-ha funny, but surreal funny. Then I peeked under the covers and saw that there was nothing under there but me and I..." She shrugged lamely.

"You're forgiven," Jack said easily, much too easily. "Now, why don't you go take a shower and have the three aspirin I left on the counter for you and by the time you're done, breakfast should be here."

The thought of food made Carrie's stomach experience a turbulence worse than anything she'd felt yesterday. "I don't think I can eat."

"Actually you'll feel better after you have. You'll just have to trust me on this one."

Carrie doubted she would ever feel better again, but she didn't argue with Jack. "You'll have to turn your back while I run into the bathroom."

"Okay," he said, obliging her by staring at the ocean beyond the sliding glass doors.

"No peeking," she warned, wrapping the sheet around her naked body and dragging it with her.

"Cross my heart and hope to die," Jack said.

She hustled as quickly as her aching head would allow, unaware that he watched her reflection in the glass.

It probably wasn't the most gentlemanly thing he'd ever done, but Jack hadn't been able to help himself. She'd been so trusting last night. She curled in his arms as he carried her from the taxi into the hotel. She'd felt good.

She'd felt right.

Jack had many thoughts about Carrie over the years, but she'd always been a friend. A damsel he occasionally played white knight for as he rode to the rescue. He'd never thought about her as a woman, or at least not as a woman he could have a relationship with.

It had suddenly occurred to him last night that she was a woman, all woman, and since then her femaleness was all he could think of.

AN HOUR LATER THE ASPIRIN had kicked in and breakfast had slipped down quite easily. Carrie was feeling remarkably revived.

"So, what are we doing today?" Jack asked.

Carrie was sitting at the table near the window. The view from the room was wonderful. Blue skies, water beating against the sand. A paradise at their disposal. "The idea is we aren't doing anything."

Jack frowned. "You can't not do anything."

"I can, too." Carrie always felt she was a bit lacking. She had no grand aspirations, no drive to be a millionaire. She loved designing dresses, even enjoyed sewing them, but she'd never longed to be a name in New York or Paris. Establishing her own little niche in Erie was as grand as she hoped to be.

But, when she wasn't at the store, she not only managed doing nothing, but she reveled in it.

"So, where are we doing nothing at?" Jack asked, his tone suggesting he still wasn't taking her seriously.

"On the beach, of course. I mean, why come to an island paradise and do nothing in your room?" Oh, yes, she was going to teach Jack Templeton a thing or two about doing nothing. He'd practically worked himself to death since Sandy left.

Thinking of Sandy made Carrie frown. Not only was he going to relax, but he was going to laugh again. She'd see to it.

"Well, if we're on the beach doing nothing then we are in actuality doing something." Ever the lawyer, Jack was a pro at picking sentences apart. "You'll be tanning and I'll be reading—"

"You better tell me you're planning to read some novel for fun, because if you think you're going to go out there and read some thoroughly boring briefs, well, I can't be responsible for my actions." She glared. The lawyer in him wouldn't be put aside with ease. She had her work cut out for her.

"Want to give me a clue what those might be?" He grinned.

So did she. The man had no idea how hard she'd worked to pull this vacation together and he was going to enjoy himself.

"No work. I brought fun reads, just as you ordered, ma'am."

He was teasing her—grinning like a fool and picking on her as if they were still in school.

Carrie loved it. "You're lucky."

"I wouldn't have dared disobey. You had that look in your eyes when you issued your orders."

"I don't issue orders, I just make suggestions—sometimes strong ones." She paused. "What look?"

"That look that says you might very well scream if I tried to sneak my work on this vacation. Lucky for you I didn't. I brought a few books." He smiled as primly as an altar boy at mass on Sunday.

"Good for you. What kind of books?" she asked suspiciously.

"Westerns." He pointed an imaginary gun in her direction and tipped an imaginary hat.

Carrie grinned. "By who?"

"John Legg. He's always been my favorite. Even when he's writing under a pseudonym, I try to find his stuff. I haven't read anything but contracts and the like for the last few years, so I hunted up the books I'd missed.''

"There's a lot you haven't remembered to do the last few years, especially the last few months." She realized she sounded like a mother scolding a wayward child and backed off. "But we're going to change all that this week." She smiled, trying to soften the fact that she was ordering him around. Jack tended to get very defensive when he thought he'd lost control. "We're going to have fun."

"We are?"

"Oh, yeah. Consider it a course of study. Today's lesson is called, *How to do nothing and have a great time doing it.*"

He gave her a mock frown. "Sounds complicated."

"Nope. It requires a bottle of sunscreen, a couple good books and our towels."

"How about suits, or are they optional here?" he asked, a wicked gleam in his eyes.

She shook her head. "Even if they're optional, we're wearing them."

"We are?" he asked, sounding disappointed.

"We are."

"You do know how to spoil a man's good time," he groused.

"Well, I've heard that a certain amount of mystery is good. You can ogle all the other women who walk up and down the beach."

Carrie was delighted. Jack was teasing and he seemed relaxed. Her plan was working.

"So, you're going to teach me how to play and we're going to begin with me ogling women on the beach? Let me just tell you that I like the way this trip is looking."

"I said ogle, not accost. Remember, this is a couples-only resort so all those legs—and whatever else you're choosing to ogle—are not only attached to a body, but that body is attached to another body."

"Spoilsport."

"Realist." She hadn't always been a realist. There had been a time, back in high school, when she'd dreamed big dreams. But, over the years she'd learned that some dreams just weren't meant to come true, and so she'd learned to accept things the way they were.

Suddenly she thought of the small Carrington Rose label that would be waiting for her when this vacation ended. Maybe some dreams could come true. She glanced at the dark-haired man standing next to her. Maybe, just maybe when he'd healed from his break with Sandy, maybe some other dreams stood a chance.

"Ha, you're the least realistic person I've ever met," Jack insisted.

"Am, too." Realizing she was agreeing with him, she added, "A realist. I am, too, a realist."

"Carrie, you don't live in the real world, never have."

She turned her back on him. There was no use arguing. Jack had always been of the opinion that

Carrie was helpless and she doubted anything would ever change that view. To be honest she had no wish to change it. Who was she to deny Jack the joy of playing the white knight?

She *allowed* him to rescue her, he'd never understood that and she wasn't about to try to explain it at this late date. It was almost selfish. If he rescued her, he was at least in her life.

Sandy had made it clear to Carrie that she wasn't woman enough to be a threat. Carrie knew that Jack had never viewed her as a woman. She was his buddy, someone to hang around with when Sandy was on one of her frequent trips out of town. As much as his big brother attitude might annoy at times, Carrie had learned to overlook it.

Tearing herself away from serious thoughts, she pulled at his arm. "Come on. The day's a wasting."

"I thought the point was to waste the day," he said in his infuriating logical way.

"On the beach. We're wasting the day on the beach." Carrie sighed.

She had her work cut out for her.

LATER THAT EVENING, Carrie gazed in the bathroom mirror. Doing nothing was more dangerous than anything she could ever have imagined.

"Carrie, are you ever coming out of there?" Jack called through the locked bathroom door.

"No." She sat on the edge of the bathtub looking at her pile of clothes on the counter. She couldn't put them on, and she couldn't leave the room without them. Last night's nakedness was understandable, but she didn't plan on making being naked with Jack a habit.

"It can't be that bad," he called.

She gave a little sniff and grabbed a tissue. As it touched the tip of her nose, she gave up and went back to sniffing. "It's worse."

She gazed at the clothes. Pain was preferable to staying in the bathroom for the rest of the trip. She held up a scrap of silk. There was no way she was putting a bra on her sunburned skin, but she slipped the oversize T-shirt on with minimal pain. Maybe there was a reason to be pleased by her lack of endowments. No one would ever know she wasn't wearing a bra.

Deciding that underwear would be just as uncomfortable, she left her panties next to the bra, and gingerly pulled on the fleece shorts.

"Did you use that lotion they gave you at the infirmary?" Jack called.

"Sort of."

"What do you mean sort of?"

She tried moving and found that the clothes weren't quite as painful as she had thought they would be. "I couldn't reach everywhere."

"Oh." Jack paused. "Would you like some help?"

She cracked open the bathroom door. "You're not even pink," she accused him as she opened the door all the way.

"You know I never burn," he explained.

"It doesn't seem right," she said with another sniff.

"Come on, give me the lotion."

Carrie handed him the bottle and turned around. "I had problems in the center of my back. I could twist and get the top and bottom." She tugged the back of her shirt up with one hand and held the front of the shirt down with the other.

"Ah...you don't have a bra on."

"Of course not. I might have mishaps now and again, but I don't set out to torture myself. Do you have any idea how much that strap would cut into me? Getting the shirt and shorts on was hard enough."

"Oh." He squirted a hefty portion of the lotion in his hand, and held it a second until it was warm. Carrie almost purred with contentment as his hands gently massaged her tender skin. Slowly, almost sensually, his hands spread the lotion over her back, which deadened the abused skin. But it wasn't the relief that had Carrie sighing.

It was longing.

Over the years she'd learned to forget that Jack was her ideal man, but at moments like this, it was hard. She felt guilty about the feelings. Jack was grieving, working himself to death, and she was lusting. Carrie tried not to think those thoughts.

Every other man she dated was held up to Jack's standard, and every one of them failed to live up to it. She'd wanted him back in high school with a teenager's longing. But as they grew older she forgot her crush and focused on their friendship.

Except when his hands caressed her back—then she forgot to forget, and she began to feel what could only be called desire. Darn, why did she do this to herself? Why was she torturing herself like this?

"Thanks," she said, dropping her oversize T-shirt and taking the bottle. She'd had all she could stand. As she'd told Jack, torturing herself wasn't something she enjoyed.

Trying to be cheerful, she asked, "How about a movie tonight? Not only am I sore, but lying around doing nothing is exhausting. We could hit the theater and just hang out."

"We could get something on pay-for-view right here in the room," he countered.

Carrie stuck out her tongue and blew a raspberry in his direction. "You really have forgotten how to have fun," she said sadly. "Is there something about fun in the lawyer oath you took?"

Jack chuckled. "No."

"Well then?"

"Why is it more fun to go to the theater, than to stay here in the room dear old Ted paid for?" He gave her an intense, searching look.

If she didn't know better, Carrie would think he knew about her little scheme, but there was no way he could know, she assured herself.

"Ah, Jack, I've been an inattentive friend. I knew you were losing the ability to enjoy yourself, but I hadn't realized how old you'd become." She shook her head dramatically. "Well, I realize it now and before we leave you're going to remember what having fun really means. I promise you."

"You're sure you wouldn't rather stay in?" he asked, a sense of resignation in his voice.

"Come on, Jack. I'm inviting you to a movie, not to an execution. If you're a good boy, I might even buy you some candy."

He rolled his eyes. "Okay, but I'm holding you to the candy."

A vision of Jack holding *her* flitted through her mind. Jack holding her, caressing her... Carrie disregarded the thought almost immediately, but not soon enough for a little shiver of desire to climb up her spine. She ignored it, just as she'd been ignoring her feelings for years.

She'd brought Jack to the resort so he could relax, not so she could satisfy her physical itch. She thought of her back, which had settled to a dull itching, and sighed. She could handle it, she had years of experience.

"I'VE GOT THE TICKETS," Carrie called, joining Jack in the snack line.

"Good. I can't wait to see *Blood and Death*," Jack said, his eyes gleaming with a very predatory look.

"Ah, Jack, it was my turn to pick the movie."

"Was not, you had me watching that sniff and cryfest two weeks ago on television."

"But, that didn't count. We didn't go out to see it. The last time we went out to see a movie we saw one of yours."

"I can't remember the last time we went out to a movie," he said.

"Well, I can and I remember it was one of yours, so this was my pick."

They took a step forward in the line. "So what are we watching?" he asked.

Carrie held the tickets out to him. "We're going to see that one about the three sisters' wedding."

"Not a comedy. Come on, Carrie. I need blood and guts."

"I think the one sister gets in an accident, so there might be some blood."

"I'm not talking a nosebleed, I'm talking semi-automatic weapons and explosions. Sweat and testosterone, Carrie. That's what a real man wants to see in a movie."

She shook her head. "Well, next time the pick will be yours and I'll bear the sweat and testosterone. But for tonight we're watching something that will make us laugh and make us cry."

"Real men don't cry," Jack assured her.

Carrie just smiled serenely. She knew the truth about Jack Templeton, though it wouldn't do to admit it. He was man enough not to want his flaws thrown in his face. Carrie didn't see them as flaws, though. The fact that he'd be the one sniffing, not her, was decidedly cute. Not that he'd see it that way.

"Well, then you have nothing to worry about," she said. "You can do the laughing and I'll do the crying."

"Can I help you?" the girl at the snack counter asked.

"We need a big bucket of popcorn...lots of butter. A large cola and I'd like a box of licorice, please." Carrie finished her order and looked at Jack expectantly.

"Jujubes, too," he said right on cue.

The girl turned to gather their order and Carrie reached over and squeezed Jack's hand.

"What was that for?" he asked.

She smiled and thought about Ted, who didn't know how to order movie food any more than he knew how to order the right restaurant food. "Just because."

One hour and forty-seven minutes later—popcorn, soda, jujubes and licorice duly consumed—Jack and Carrie walked out of the theater.

"So, it was better than blood and guts, wasn't it?" Carrie asked.

Jack sniffed. It was a suspicious sound he'd been making for the last half hour. "No," he said gruffly.

"Liar."

"Am not. I like he-man macho films," Jack assured her.

"Oh, I'm sure you do. It's just that you don't hate funny, sentimental films as much as you'd like the world to believe."

"You're pushing it, Carrie," Jack said, all sniffing seemed a faint memory.

"Oh, I'm so scared," she taunted. She took off down the boardwalk that led to the beach.

"You should be," Jack bellowed as he gave chase.

"You can't catch me," she hollered over her shoulder.

There was no reply, which made Carrie nervous. A blustering Jack she was used to, but a silent one—that was dangerous. She glanced over her shoulders just as she was scooped up by Jack.

"Jack," she shrieked.

"When you live dangerously, sometimes you have to pay the price," he said, holding onto her despite her wriggling to get free. He laughed as she walloped his back.

That laughter…that was what had been missing for far too long. "What are you doing?" she asked, going along with the game.

"It's called getting even." He splashed into the water.

"And how are you going to do that?"

"Like this."

Carrie was no longer in Jack's arms, but flying through the air. "Jack," she screamed as she hit the surf. The water was warm, but it stung her sun-damaged skin. She came up for air. "Jack."

He was standing up to his knees in the water, laughing as she floundered in the surf. Well, two could play at the revenge game, she thought as she gave a very convincing shriek and dived under the water. Hugging the sand a couple of feet under, she swam with strong, confident strokes.

When she'd exhausted her air, she broke the water as quietly as she could and sucked in a deep breath. There he was, no longer standing knee-deep, but up to his waist, calling her name.

He dived under the water and stealthily, Carrie swam behind him.

He came up and called, "Carrie, where are you?"

"Right here," she shouted as she jumped at him, knocking him forward into the water. They both came up sputtering.

"Oh brother, Carrie. You scared about ten years off my life." He had her around the waist and dunked her into the water. She came up sputtering and he continued. "Repeat after me, I will not scare Jack ever again."

"Never," she yelled just before she was dunked again.

"Say it."

"No, you deserved it for throwing me into the water." Down she went again. "Jack," she screamed as she coughed and laughed. "I'm sorry I scared you."

"You don't look very sorry," he grumbled.

"But I am. Not that you didn't deserve it," she added.

He seemed to be considering her apology and Carrie moved in for the kill. She scooped her right leg behind him and caught the back of his left knee. As it buckled she shoved, knocking him under the water. "Threaten me, will you?" she asked as he came up for air, murder in his eyes.

"You're walking a fine line here, lady."

"Nope, I'm running," she yelled, moving as fast as the warm ocean water would allow, with Jack right on her tail.

4

THEY WERE STILL LAUGHING when they reached the room. Jack was remembering to have fun and Carrie smiled inwardly. That was the part of himself he had forgotten, the part that Sandy had stolen, the part that Carrie wanted to help him rediscover. The silly, joyful part.

Besides Sandy, for the past few years his cases at Ericson and Roberts had become more and more demanding and he'd put aside the playful part of his personality. That was the part Carrie missed.

"You really don't fight fair, do you?" Jack asked and then walked out of the bathroom, toweling his hair.

Carrie grinned. She shoved past him, slammed the bathroom door and clicked the lock in place. "I get the first shower. And to answer your question, no, I don't fight fair." She laughed as she turned the water on.

The sound of Carrie's laughter drew Jack's eyes to the door. This vacation was obviously what he needed. That Carrie knew it, and that she'd gone to such elaborate lengths to get him here... The thoughts warmed him in a way no island sun could.

He couldn't remember the last time he'd felt so...he started to think relaxed, but that wasn't it exactly. Thoughts of putting the analgesic on Carrie's braless back, of the way she looked coming out of the water, the moonlight emphasizing her features floated through his mind. He'd always regarded Carrie as a buddy, but lately the notion was becoming fainter as he realized that she was a woman—all woman. But, she also wasn't his woman.

No, *relaxed* wasn't the word he'd use to describe how he felt.

Alive.

Yes, alive, that was it.

He'd spent years trying to work things out with Sandy. He remembered thinking that love shouldn't have been so hard. If what they'd felt was real, how could she have been so content to jet around the world for months at a time, or why had he been so content to let her? Why had they kept the relationship unofficial, or not cement it in marriage?

When Sandy broke her leg, leaving her unable to travel, they both really took a look at the relationship and asked the questions that needed to be asked. They had both reached the same conclusion: What they felt for each other wasn't love, it was comfortable, familiar even, but it wasn't love.

He was with a prestigious law firm, doing work that held little interest for him. He belonged to the proper club, moved in the proper circles, behaved in a way that was appropriate for an up-and-coming lawyer. But it was all business.

It seemed that throughout his life he'd been working toward something. In college he'd worked to get into law school. In law school he'd worked to pass the bar. Then there was getting into the proper firm. Then moving up the ladder and achieving partnership.

Jack was close to that partnership. Ericson, Roberts and Templeton. It had a ring. But he was tired of working toward something. When Sandy left, he'd realized he'd paid a price for his single-minded focus.

He'd gone into law to make a difference in people's lives. He'd wanted to right wrongs, to rescue the underdog, instead he'd ended up working on endless contracts.

Now here he was on an island paradise with his best friend, but things were different between them. Now he just had to figure out what to do about it.

"KARAOKE," CARRIE SAID firmly.

"Why on earth would you want to embarrass yourself like that?" Jack asked. He wasn't going to do it, he thought stubbornly. He'd spent a second day *doing nothing*. He gave in to her little whims too often. That was the problem. Carrie didn't realize that there were limits.

Well, there were and tonight they'd reached one. Jack Templeton did not go to karaoke bars—he didn't drink in them and he certainly didn't sing in them.

"You are way too old." She grimaced sadly.

Her constant harping about his inability to have fun and his rapid aging was getting old—older than she seemed to think he was. "May I remind you I was born only two years before you were?"

"There's old as in age, and then there's old as in spirit. You've got one of the oldest spirits I've ever met. And we are going to karaoke."

"Carrie," he said. Even he could hear the exasperation in his voice. Carrie couldn't miss it. She'd back down.

Instead she pulled her hair back into a ponytail, one that would never make it through the evening, Jack knew from experience. She smiled at him and put on some silver earrings. "You can go out in shorts," she said. "These things are never formal."

"Carrington Rose Delany."

"Uh-oh. I'm always in trouble when you use my whole name." She kissed his cheek. "Why don't you tell me what I did now, while we walk over to the karaoke bar?" She slipped her feet into her sandals.

"I'm not going," he said. She never listened to him. That was the infuriating thing about Carrie. Other people jumped when he said jump, but not Carrie. Never Carrie.

"Okay." She shrugged her shoulders. "You're not going. You just stay here and have a nice quiet evening. You could probably use it, what with the work schedule you carry. A man your age can't be too careful. I mean, men in their thirties have heart attacks all the time. What with the stress you're under, and the fact that you're out of shape—''

"The hell I am," he growled.

"Well, I did outrace you last night. A man in his prime would never have allowed a woman to beat him quite so easily."

"You did no such thing. I let you win."

She patted his head. "You just make an early night of it. As a matter of fact, you take the bed again tonight. I was quite comfortable on the floor, and your old bones need all the comfort they can get."

"There's not a damn thing wrong with my bones, and I'm taking the floor."

She raised her eyebrows in that maddening way of hers, and gave him another one of those patronizing little smiles. "Well, suit yourself. You just go curl up and watch a movie on television. I'm sure there's some documentary on somewhere. I'll be quiet when I come in so I don't wake you. And if I'm not in by the time you get up in the morning, well, I'll be around later."

"Just let me get my damn shoes."

"Jack, you're so tense, and I don't understand it. You're in paradise after all. And don't bother getting your shoes. I've decided in your present mood you wouldn't be good company anyway. I'm more than capable of entertaining myself. This might be a couples' resort, but I'm sure some of the bartenders or other employees are single. And I'm betting one of them would be happy to do the karaoke thing with me.''

"I said I'm coming to the bar with you, and I'm perfectly lovely company. Now just let me get my shoes.''

Damn, she'd done it again. She always won. He'd say no to something, and she'd agree that he shouldn't do it. Then damned if he didn't do it. Jack shook his head and tried to puzzle it out, but couldn't.

Figuring out Carrington Rose Delany was going to take a smarter man than he.

Thinking of Carrie with another man did little to improve his mood. He slammed his feet into his shoes and stomped toward the door. "Are you ready?'' he bellowed.

"I'm always ready before you are,'' Carrie said. "I can't figure out where the ugly rumor developed that women were always late. From what I can see, it's generally the man who holds things up.''

She prattled on as they walked to the club. Jack half listened as he let himself relax and enjoy the cadence of her words. He felt good even though he'd lost another argument.

Being with Carrie was a roller-coaster ride. From annoyance to peace his emotions rose and fell suddenly and unexpectedly. He'd been unsettled thinking of Carrie with someone else. But walking with her, listening to her familiar chatter, he simply felt happy that she was with him, not some other, fictional, man.

Things were changing between them. And though he hadn't quite figured out what to do about the way their relationship was evolving, at this moment, walking next to her across a beach on a couples' resort, Jack Templeton was simply content.

The contentment lasted exactly one hour and three beers. "I said no," Jack yelled. He was yelling mainly to be heard; the fact that he was annoyed and that it felt good was secondary. "And," he continued, on a roll, "I think that's all the beer for you." He plucked the glass from her hand.

Carrie pouted. "I was right, you are old." Then she smiled the smile that meant things didn't bode well for Jack...not at all. "I'll switch to cola if you'll do it."

"I said..." he started.

"Otherwise," she yelled right over him. "Otherwise, I'm ordering a pitcher."

"Could I win an argument, just once?" he said more to himself than to her.

"Jack, we never fight, so there's no winner." She tugged at his arm, pulling him toward the stage.

If there was no winner, how did he manage to end up here?

Jack sighed as Carrie talked to the man running the machine. She came running back to center stage and thrust a mike in his hand.

"Come on, you know you want to." Her grin

said she believed it. She took her own microphone in hand and nodded at the man to start the music.

"Carrie, I really don't want to do this." The opening notes wafted through the speakers and Jack wanted to crawl into a hole and die. "You didn't?" he asked, though he knew she did.

"We needed a song we both knew the words to—it's too hard to just get them off the screen. And I knew you knew these from past experience." Her hips began to sway and Jack was mesmerized by the sight. She kicked him when it was his turn to jump in.

Jack grimaced every time they missed a note. As if on cue, Carrie's ponytail holder fell off and her hair whipped his shoulder as she shook her head. She shimmied and swayed, singing her heart out and by the time the song was over, Jack had forgotten they were performing for an audience.

The sight of her, the smell of her totally undid him.

They trailed off the last few notes together as a rousing round of clapping followed.

"See, you remembered," she said, beaming her approval.

How could he forget? They'd done the song, "I've Got You, Babe," after prom. Carrie had gone with Matt Barker, one of his basketball friends and he'd gone with...what was her name? He couldn't remember. All he could remember was threatening Matt if he didn't keep his hands off Carrie. She was too young, only a junior.

"Guess I'm not as old as you thought," he muttered as they wove their way through the crowd and back to their table.

"I don't know, one song can't erase your stodginess," she told him with a taunting grin.

"You enjoy this, don't you?"

"What?" she asked, the picture of innocence.

"Tormenting me."

"Tormenting you? Why, that's a fine how-do-you-do. I—"

"Jack and Carrie?" an attractive brunette asked.

Carrie looked up. "Yes?"

The brunette grinned and turned to the balding man at her side. "See, I told you, Herb," she said and then turned back to the table. "You don't remember me, do you?"

Jack shook his head and Carrie admitted, "No, I'm afraid I don't."

"Mrs. Richardson," the woman said, as if that explained it all.

Carrie, who was generally good with names, continued to draw a blank. "I'm sorry," she said with a helpless shrug.

"Chemistry at Seneca High School. Jack, you were a senior, and Carrie taking advanced classes thought you were a junior," the woman prompted.

"Mrs. Richardson? It can't be, I mean she was old." Carrie realized how that sounded and stopped herself. "I mean, she was a teacher and you don't look old enough to have taught us," she quickly backpedaled.

"I think you're both old enough to call me Emma now," Mrs. Richardson said. "And I'm not all that older than you. I was... Hmm, I must have been in my mid-twenties when the two of you were in my class."

Carrie tried to do the math and Mrs. Richardson—she would never be able to think of her former teacher as Emma—laughed.

"Which makes me forty-one," Mrs. Richardson said with a laugh. "Herb and I are here celebrating our fifteenth anniversary. We left the kids with his mom and are rekindling that old flame."

"Oh." Jack, the coward, was silent and Carrie didn't know what to say to this teacher who was no older than most of her friends.

"Would you mind if we joined you for a drink?" Mrs. Richardson asked, even as she took a seat and pulled Herb onto the neighboring one.

"So, how long are you here until?" Mrs. Richardson asked and without pausing she added, "We're here until Wednesday, aren't we, Herb?" Herb nodded. "We bought that five-day special Jodi's Travel was running. Did you as well?"

"I added a couple extra days. We're here until Friday," Carrie said. She was still trying to adjust to the idea that someone who taught her was not ancient. Her teachers should be old. They should all be white-haired and using canes by now.

Mrs. Richardson beamed. "And did you two come celebrating something significant?"

"Just a vacation," Jack said, even as Carrie said, "Well, yes, we're celebrating."

"Celebrating?" Mrs. Richardson said.

Jack kicked her, but Carrie continued, "Yes, you see Jack just finished a big case."

"Case?"

"He's a lawyer. Most of the time he's stuck in an office working on boring contracts and other boring paperwork, but this time he was in court. Anyway, he won the case and we decided to get away and celebrate."

Mrs. Richardson actually clapped her hands. "How wonderful." She turned to the silent Herb and said, "I always told you that Jack and Carrie were meant for each other, didn't I, Herb?"

Dutifully Herb silently nodded. Mrs. Richardson gave him a smile that she might have bestowed upon a well-behaved student. "Why, I knew even before I walked into the classroom and caught you two." She shook her fingers at them both, making Carrie feel as if she was back in school again. "You know, I should have given you both a detention for carrying on like that in class."

"Like what?" Jack asked.

Carrie just smiled, she knew exactly what incident Mrs. Richardson was referring to. She'd been right, and now Jack would have to admit it.

There was nothing Carrie liked more than being right.

"Why, that time you and Carrie were kissing in the chemistry class. And with everyone watching to boot. That was really quite naughty of you, you know."

"We weren't kissing," he said firmly.

"Jack, don't you think you're a little too old to lie to a teacher?" Carrie shot him a saccharine smile.

"We weren't kissing," he repeated.

Mrs. Richardson shook her finger at him again.

Jack's voice rose, as if saying it louder would make his kiss artificial respiration. "She blew up the lab, remember? I was just giving her mouth-to-mouth."

"Oh, I'll say you were giving her mouth-to-mouth. Why you had the girl flat on her back in the middle of the classroom floor, the entire class watching as you kissed her as if your life depended on it." She nudged Herb. "It was so romantic I just couldn't give them detentions."

"*Her life* did depend on it. She'd blown up the lab and I was afraid she was dead." Almost fifteen years later, Jack could still remember the wave of fear that had swept through his body when he thought Carrie was dead. He'd felt an echo of it last night when he thought he'd lost her in the ocean.

"If you say so," Mrs. Richardson commented in such a way that Jack, Carrie and even the silent Herb knew she didn't believe a word of it. "And I guess it really doesn't matter, because I knew you'd end up married and, why, here you are."

"But we aren't," Jack felt obliged to point out.

Carrie kicked him and gave him the evil eye, but he ignored it, as usual. "We're not married. We're just—"

"You're not married?" Mrs. Richardson asked. "After all these years you're still just living together?" There was censure in her look.

"No, I mean, we're not..." He gave Carrie a helpless look.

She didn't know why he would think she would save him, but his look said he did. Carrie took pity on him and supplied, "What Jack means is that we're not a couple. We're just friends traveling together. You see, I was supposed to come here with Ted, he *was* my boyfriend."

"Oh, dear," Mrs. Richardson said, patting Carrie's hand. "Men are pigs. What did he do?"

"He ordered the fettuccine," Carrie said, obviously warming to the subject. "And, he didn't kiss as good as Jack, though Jack never kissed me again after that lab incident. You know I spent a perfectly good year practicing so I'd be a better kisser next time he kissed me, not that he ever did."

Mrs. Richardson glared at him. "As I said, dear, men are pigs." Carrie nodded her agreement, and poor Herb just shot Jack a helpless look.

"It wasn't a kiss," Jack said once more, though he didn't believe either woman was listening.

"Honey, I've witnessed a lot of kisses and participated in even more, and let me tell you, it was a kiss," Mrs. Richardson said in her most teacher-like voice.

That was it, Jack thought. He was a patient man——he had to be a patient man to put up with Carrie——but even a patient man had his breaking point. "I'm telling you both, that wasn't a kiss, but this is." He reached over to the seat next to him, gave Carrie a little tug and pulled her into his arms.

5

THE MINUTE HIS LIPS touched hers, Jack realized he'd made a mistake. He hadn't kissed anyone other than Sandy for years, and when they broke up, he couldn't even imagine kissing another woman.

But, from what he remembered, it was natural to have things stirring when he kissed a woman. But what stirred this time had very little to do with sex. Okay, what was stirring had a lot to do with sex, but kissing Carrie also stirred something that felt like his heart. It was what had been missing when he kissed Sandy. Finding it while he kissed Carrie was a shock.

Jack deepened the kiss, probing, plundering, losing himself so deeply that he realized he'd never truly be free again.

When Carrie gave a little moan in the back of her throat and moved closer, wrapping her arms around his neck and hanging on for dear life, Jack knew the absolute truth of it—he wanted her.

The sound of someone clearing a throat shook Jack out of the land of possibilities and back into the karaoke bar.

"I beg your pardon, Jack. The chem lab was mouth-to-mouth," said a very humble Mrs. Richardson.

His little sister? Wanting her? Jack wasn't sure what to say, how to act.

"Wow" was Carrie's only response. She shifted out of his arms and scooted her chair as far from him as she could, until she was practically sitting in Herb's lap. "I owe you an apology, too, Jack. Mrs. Richardson was right, either the chem lab was mouth-to-mouth, or you've been doing some practicing since our lips last met." Then she said to Mrs. Richardson, "Could I borrow your husband for a dance?" Her eyes practically begged for permission to escape.

"Herb would love it," Mrs. Richardson said. As Carrie used Herb to make her escape, Mrs. Richardson leaned over and said to Jack, "I might have been wrong about the chem lab, but if you think you and Carrie are just friends, you'd better think again."

Jack watched Carrie swaying in Herb's arms on the dance floor, and couldn't have agreed more.

Carrie on the other hand, studiously practiced not looking at Jack. Dancing with the still-silent Herb was a big plus, she didn't have to make social chatter, but could use the time to think.

One of them needed to think. And because it was obvious Jack hadn't been thinking, it would have to be Carrie this once.

Only, Carrie didn't know what to think.

NOR COULD CARRIE really concentrate for the rest of the evening as she conversed with the overly talkative Mrs. Richardson. The woman was as much of a blessing as her husband was, and it was with a heavy heart that Carrie bid them both goodnight.

Jack and Carrie were silent as they walked to their room. "Carrie," Jack said while he opened the door.

"Sorry," she blurted. "When a girl's got to go, a girl's got to go." She practically ran into the bathroom and slammed the door.

"You're going to have to talk to me sometime," Jack bellowed.

Carrie just turned on the tap for a bath. "Sorry, I can't hear you over the water. We'll have to discuss it later. Why don't you just go to bed?"

Silence was her only answer. Maybe she'd manage to avoid him for tonight. There was tomorrow, of course, but she was going to let tomorrow take care of itself, and just thank her lucky stars for the reprieve, no matter how short-lived it might be.

After hearing the tub being refilled, Jack called, "I'm still waiting."

"Okay," Carrie yelled through the closed door. Okay?

Nothing was okay about this evening. He'd kissed Carrie. Not some friendly little peck on the cheek. Not some indulgent big-brother type kiss. No. The kiss was carnal and wild. A kiss he'd like to repeat…if he could repeat it with anyone but Carrie.

Carrie. His buddy. His friend.

Carrie wasn't the type of woman he fantasized over. And she certainly wasn't someone he kissed, not like that. No one kissed a friend like that.

But he had.

And even worse than that, he'd liked it.

A lot.

So now what? Did he apologize? Or did he repeat it? Jack couldn't remember the last time he'd felt so confused. And if the fact Carrie was hiding out in the bathroom was any indication, she was just as confused as he was. They had to work this out.

"Carrie, I'm not going to give up and go away so you can quit stalling."

Carrie sighed, looking very prunish. Even though the bathroom door was locked and he couldn't see a thing, she sank a little deeper in the tub. "I don't know what you're talking about," she hollered back. "I'm just taking a bath."

"Come on, Carrie. It's three o'clock in the morning. Come out here and talk to me."

"I will when I'm done," she called, then swished the tepid water with her foot. If she was lucky, when she pulled the plug to drain the water she'd go down with it. A burial at sea; it was preferable to facing Jack. She'd practically thrown herself at her best friend. It was horrible. It couldn't be any worse.

Okay, if her best friend had been a goat, it might have been worse. But the fact that he was male didn't stop it from being the most horrible moment of her life. She'd kissed her best friend with all the pent-up frustrations of a woman who wanted him in a decidedly, unfriendly sort of way. He knew now. There was no way he couldn't know.

When Sandy had walked out, Carrie watched Jack grieve, watched him throw himself into his job. He'd not only lost weight, but seemed to have lost himself as well. This trip…it had been a means to get him away from the memories, to help him start to heal.

She hadn't planned to throw herself at him.

She'd just ruined a lifelong friendship over a rampant case of hormones. She was despicable. Pathetic. Lower than a worm.

She sank farther in the tub. She'd seduced her best friend with a week in paradise.

Well, there was only one thing to do.

She jumped out of the tub, tossed on the bathrobe the resort so thoughtfully provided and opened the door. Jack was on the patio staring at the sky.

Never one to back off from an apology she knotted her belt and marched up to Jack. She patted his back. "I owe you an apology," she said.

"You're right you do. The chem lab wasn't a kiss."

She waved her hand in the air. "Oh, maybe it wasn't, but that's not what I'm apologizing for."

Jack took a step toward her. "It's not?"

Carrie shook her head, taking a step backward, needing to keep some distance between them. "I, uh…" He took another step. "Stop that," she said in what she'd intended to be a yell, but had come out a breathy sort of whisper.

"Stop what?" Jack asked. There was something in his eyes that she'd never seen before, and it would have scared Carrie out of her socks had she been wearing any. As it was, the bathrobe she'd knotted around her waist suddenly felt as sheer as silk instead of the sturdy terry cloth she knew it to be.

Jack reached out and put his hands around her waist.

"You're stalking me like some wild animal on the prowl. Stop."

"I'm not…" He paused and then grinned. "Okay, maybe I am."

"Why?"

The question stopped him short and his playful smile slipped a notch. "Something happened tonight."

"Something that never should have happened," she said. "We're friends and that…"

"Kiss," he supplied when she paused. "That kiss, Carrie."

For years she'd maintained the mouth-to-mouth was a kiss, but Carrie wasn't about to call what they'd done tonight a kiss. The mere thought made her nervous. "That momentary lapse of sense should never have happened. We're friends. That's all. It was a mistake.''

"Tonight was unexpected, but I don't think it was a mistake.'' Jack reached out and put his hands around her waist. "You're a beautiful woman, and what happened was special.''

"You're stalking me again.''

"No. I've caught you. And I want to try another lapse of sense, if you don't mind.''

"And if I do mind?''

His hands were no longer on her waist, but had traced the belt to the knot. He tugged at it.

Carrie knew she should run, she should scream and shout. It wasn't right, she knew that. Carrie didn't want Jack on the rebound. She just wanted him to see her as more than a little sister, and slowly, maybe he'd see her as a woman, someone he could learn to care for.

"We shouldn't,'' she said, with absolutely no conviction in her voice.

The knot gave way and Jack's hands moved beneath the robe. "Shouldn't what?'' he said, his lips moving to her shoulder, nibbling delicious little circles there.

"You'll hate me in the morning,'' she said with despair. The thought of him hating her broke her heart.

"Oh, honey, I don't think that's possible.'' His lips crept a little lower, his hands were stroking her, soft and slow as if she were some kind of cat.

Carrie resisted the urge to purr and arch against

him. One of them had to keep their sanity. "It will change everything."

That stopped him.

Jack's hand went under her chin and tilted it upward until she was forced to look at him. "It doesn't have to," he said with certainty.

What had changed between them? Jack couldn't figure it out. Ever since he'd waxed Carrie's legs, there had been something between them he'd never suspected before. And when he'd brought his tipsy best friend from the airplane to the hotel? The feelings he'd entertained hadn't been friendly, they'd been hot. He'd been relieved when she'd kicked him out and undressed herself. He'd thought he could walk away from those feelings.

But now, standing here with her, only a robe separating him from the woman he wanted to claim in the most primitive way a man could, Jack knew he couldn't escape these feelings. They were growing stronger minute by minute.

He wanted her. Wanted her in a way he'd never wanted anyone else, not even Sandy. What had changed?

"But it will make things different," she said. "If you, if we... Jack, if we do this, things can never go back to what they were."

"Maybe they'll move forward instead?" Moving closer, Jack feathered kisses down her neck. Holding Carrie, kissing Carrie felt right. It felt as if after years of searching he'd finally come home—home to Carrie.

"I don't know if this would be moving forward. I don't know if it's what I want," Carrie said, though she knew it for the lie it was. She just didn't know if it was what he wanted. He needed more time to recover.

He didn't believe a word of what she'd just said. And the look he gave her told her so, more clearly than any words he could have ever chosen.

"You're sure that no's your answer?" His hands dropped from her body and Carrie almost wept from the pain the loss of contact caused.

"It's the only answer I can give," Carrie said, reknotting her belt.

"Well, if that's it, then that's it. Good night, Carrie." Without another word, Jack turned and walked into the room, threw the comforter and a pillow onto the floor and crawled into his make-shift bed.

Carrie stood on the patio, watching the ocean for a long time. Tonight was a memory akin to the chem lab kiss-that-wasn't. It was a memory that she'd hang on to for the rest of her life. And hard though it was, she was sure she'd made the right decision. She couldn't allow herself to use Jack that way.

She wouldn't do it. He didn't realize how precarious his emotions were. He was on the rebound. It had been months since the breakup, but rather than healing, he just seemed to plod forward. It broke Carrie's heart, knowing he wanted something he could never have. That he wouldn't talk about Sandy only reinforced her belief in his grief.

Tomorrow she'd try to get him to forgive her and put their friendship back on track.

Her fingers brushed her lips. No, after having been really kissed by Jack, there was no way she'd ever mistake his mouth-to-mouth as anything but.

It was almost six before she tiptoed into the room and crawled in bed, with her bathrobe still knotted in place. Her dreams that night weren't filled with sweet fantasies about her life if only Jack had loved her.

These dreams were X-rated.

JACK JOGGED UP to Carrie's perfect hiding place. Still, she'd known he'd find her. Jack had always found her when she was hurt and confused. Most of the time he was able to ease the tempest, this time he was the cause of it.

She hugged her legs to her chest and watched the dark clouds rolling in off the ocean. The weather suited her mood. Dark and troubled.

She watched him jogging toward her and her heart gave a little flip-flop. She checked the emotion, having become accustomed to the longing after all these years. However, having experienced a taste of what loving Jack could be like, the feeling only intensified.

"Good morning," he said easily as he reached her rock. "Got room for someone else on there?"

There was enough room, barely, but it would

require them to sit awfully close. Too close. Carrie shook her head. "Why don't you take that one next to me."

What looked like disappointment flitted across Jack's face, but he sat on the stone she'd indicated. "You're up early" was all he said.

She shrugged, unwilling to admit she couldn't sleep with him so close. Those dreams hadn't helped. No gentle vignets of companionship with Jack, but wild dreams of what making love to him would be like.

"So, are we just going to pretend that last night didn't happen?"

"If you wouldn't mind," she answered, ever the hopeful optimist.

"And if I do mind?" he asked gently.

"I'd still rather not talk about it. I do owe you an apology, and I offer it now, but couldn't we just chalk it up to an aberration?" Carrie was desperate. It was too soon for him. He was still mourning the loss of Sandy.

Jack was looking at her, there was a quiet desperation in her that he'd never seen before. She had as much as admitted to him that she'd had a crush on him once upon a time, but he'd been too young, too inexperienced to recognize it.

And then there was Sandy.

Sandy Baker, flight attendant, every guy's fantasy. And she'd chosen him. Four years they had been together. Somewhere along the line he fell into the habit of thinking he loved Sandy. But, nine months ago when she'd moved out of their apartment, they'd both admitted what they had wasn't love. It was merely comfortable. And yet, they'd never gone further than living together. With Sandy's job as a flight attendant she was gone for long stretches of time.

It took Sandy's injury to force them to examine their relationship, or lack of one.

They had nothing in common.

Their parting had been easier than either had thought possible. That was what had been eating Jack for the past few months. Maybe he'd never have the ultimate dream. Maybe he wasn't capable of truly loving a woman.

And now?

If last night was any indication, there was something between him and Carrie, and it was scaring her to death. The last thing Jack wanted to do was scare her, to hurt her.

He found himself saying, "If that's really what you want."

Carrie just nodded, but still didn't look at him. Jack reached for her and she pulled away. Convincing Carrington Rose Delany that they could be more than friends was going to take some work. Convincing her that the something they could be was even better than what they had been was going to take even more.

"Mrs. Richardson called after you left," Jack said, keeping his distance.

"Oh?"

"I hope you don't mind that I told her we'd have dinner with her and Herb tonight."

"Dinner?" she asked absently. She watched the water as if she expected some cousin of the Loch Ness monster to appear at any minute.

"Yes, Carrie. Dinner. You know, that meal that comes after lunch." She nodded and he beat down his frustration and added. "We're meeting them at seven. I hope that's okay." Again, just a nod.

"Are you just going to keep nodding your head at everything I say?" he asked.

She shrugged this time.

"You know, we're going to have to talk about this sometime, don't you?"

"Talk about what?" she asked, feigning ignorance.

Jack sighed. Dealing with Carrie was something he thought he'd perfected over the years, but he was beginning to see that he'd just scratched the surface. "Have it your way. We won't talk, won't even mention it."

"And won't repeat it," she said firmly.

"If you say so, we won't. Just stop this silent treatment and talk to me again."

She finally turned and really looked at him, not through him or past him. "Okay, what should we talk about?"

"How about what we're going to do today?" he asked. He'd broken through her icy reserve and that was enough for now. Later he'd worry about what to do next.

The last of her reserve melted. "They have that water park, I thought it might be fun."

"A water park?"

"Yeah, you know with slides and wave pools. It'll be fun." She smiled at him encouragingly and Jack knew he'd do anything she wanted, from water slides to bathing with piranha, if she'd just kept smiling at him.

"Okay. If we go in and change we can pick up something for lunch and then go."

She was off the rock, seemingly relieved that they were done talking about last night.

Jack just smiled as he watched her scamper toward the hotel. He was a lawyer, something Carrie frequently forgot. He'd promised they wouldn't talk about it again, but when she asked him to promise not to repeat last night, he'd simply promised not to repeat it if she said so.

Jack didn't plan on her saying so.

He planned to have her begging so.

CARRIE SLIPPED the sundress on and scuffed her feet into her sandals. Her sunburn had faded to a dull pinkish brown. She wasn't even sure that she'd peel. Oh, how she hoped she didn't peel. There was nothing attractive about a woman who was shedding her skin.

She took it back. She hoped she peeled. She almost wished she hadn't slathered sunblock all over her abused skin before they had headed for the water park that afternoon. She hoped she peeled so bad that children screamed when they saw her. She'd look so bad that Jack wouldn't even begin to think about kissing her.

But peeling skin wouldn't stop her from thinking about kissing him. Carrie doubted anything would.

She didn't want to kiss him again. At least not until he was over Sandy. Four years he'd been with her, and under a year without her. He was still hurting; Carrie could see it in the way he threw himself into his cases, by the tiredness in his expression and the lack of women in his life.

Maybe, after he'd had more time and truly healed, maybe there wouldn't be more women. Maybe he'd finally notice that Carrie wasn't his little sister—that she'd never been his *sister*. Maybe...

She put away the maybes and checked herself in the mirror. Despite wishing herself peelie, she was pleased she didn't resemble the woman who'd spent the afternoon at the water park. She'd come back to the room with her hair resembling Medusa, her face devoid of makeup and she'd wanted to scream.

It had been worth her looking like a witch, though. Jack had enjoyed himself. He'd laughed and smiled and run around like a little boy. For a while at least he was the old carefree Jack she used to know, not the stodgy, workaholic lawyer who had been hanging around the past few years.

She jumped when she heard the pounding on the

door. "Come on, Carrie. This is just dinner with an old teacher, not a night at some award show."

"I'll be right out." Men.

"You said that twenty minutes ago."

"And now I'm twenty minutes closer to being done." She could hear him muttering outside the door and smiled as she ran eyeliner under her lashes. They were back to normal. She and Jack had put the kiss behind them, at least for now, and they were back to being friends. Good friends.

Best friends.

Things were normal and this afternoon just proved it. She looked at her reflection and patted a stray strand of hair into place. Things were back to normal all right and tonight would just be a dinner with an old schoolteacher.

THINGS WERE NOT BACK to normal, she swore an hour later.

"And then we went to the Cayman Islands..." Mrs. Richardson continued. Carrie didn't mind letting the woman monopolize the conversation. As a matter of fact, she doubted she could have conversed if her life depended on it. She was too busy fending off her ex-best friend.

Jack's arm kept creeping over her shoulders and she kept shrugging it off. Then his hand would fall, oh so innocently, on her knee and she'd try to nonchalantly smack it off. He'd reach past her for the salt and accidentally graze her breasts with his forearm, though she knew their size made them difficult to accidentally graze. Their size made them almost impossible to purposely graze.

"Damn it, cut it out," she growled in his ear when Mrs. Robertson paused and said something to the silent Herb.

"Temper, temper. You don't swear, remember?" Jack smiled.

"I do when you…"

"When I what, darling?" he asked, the picture of innocence.

"Don't call me darling," she said a little too loudly.

"Oh, I just love it when Herb calls me darling," Mrs. Richardson cooed.

Carrie was sure she did. The woman was probably thrilled when Herb said anything, much less whispered an endearment. "I just don't care for public displays of affection," Carrie said as primly as she could manage.

That famous Mrs. Richardson finger bobbed in reprimand. "Now, Carrie, that's not how I remember it. As I recall you and Jack have had some very public displays of affection."

"See, *darling*," Jack said, a heavy emphasis on the darling. "You're just going to have to get used to my public displays."

As discreetly as she could, Carrie elbowed him. He let out a very satisfying grunt. "Oh, I'm so sorry, *dear*. You're just sitting a little closer than I'm used to." She batted her eyelashes at Herb and said, "You never told us just what you do."

"Oh, Herb," Mrs. Richardson answered for him. "He's a telephone solicitor. Talk, talk, talk. That's my Herb. Lucky for him I just love listening to his dulcet tones."

Jack started choking on the water he'd just sipped. Carrie momentarily forgot her annoyance, and hid her smile by turning and smacking his back with all her might.

"Thanks," Jack gasped.

"You should be more careful," Mrs. Richardson. "I knew a woman once..."

Ten minutes later, when the entire table knew Sophie Garret's life history—a life that was tragically cut short when she laughed while drinking a soda and choked herself to death—their dinners arrived.

"Sir, you ordered the shrimp?" the waitress asked and she set the plate in front of Jack when he nodded and then passed out the rest.

Jack took the first bite and discreetly set a shrimp on Carrie's plate of fettuccine alfredo. "Did I ever tell you how fettuccine and shrimp brought Carrie and me together?" he asked the instantly alert Mrs. Richardson.

She shook her head. "Carrie did mention it last night, but she didn't go into any detail."

Carrie elbowed him again, but Jack liked Mrs. Richardson's response better and he started, "Well, she had been dating this guy, Jed."

"Ted," Carrie corrected, taking great delight in biting the shrimp in two.

"Jed, Ted…anyway, they were out to dinner and he ordered the fettuccine."

"Fettuccine?" Mrs. Richardson asked.

"Fettuccine. You see, Carrie here loves fettuccine, but she also loves shrimp." So saying he passed her another one. Carrie resisted the urge to toss it back into his face.

"And Ned…"

"Ted," Carrie corrected again.

"Ted, he ordered fettuccine, just like she did. Well, there was no variety and she realized that she needed something more in a man. Carrie needs a man who knows how to order correctly—a man who can kiss. And, of course the first man she thought of was me. After all we'd ordered enough dinners together and she had kissed me in chem class."

"It wasn't a kiss, it was mouth-to-mouth," Carrie muttered.

"Well, she'd had experience, and knew that I was the one for her."

"Oh, Herb, isn't that the sweetest story you've ever heard? I'll never order shrimp or fettuccine again and not feel a flutter in my heart." To Carrie she said, "To think, all that time you'd been dating the wrong men. It was Jack here who turned your litmus paper blue."

Even Herb groaned over that one as a poor excuse for a joke. Mrs. Richardson laughed a kind of laugh that didn't sound at all like the teacher Carrie remembered. "Oh, you all liked that? Well, how about—and all those years it was Jack who could make your Bunsen burn.''

The tension that had Carrie's back rigid disappeared and she found herself laughing with the rest of their group through the main course and dessert. When their good-nights were said, Mrs. Richardson hugged them each in turn. ''Now, when those wedding bells chime, Herb and I will expect our invitation. Remember, I'm a chemistry teacher and I know a chemical reaction when I see it. The two of you are almost combustible.''

Herb just winked at both of them, wrapped his arm around his wife and the couple walked down the hall.

''Well,'' Jack said.

''Yes, well,'' Carrie echoed as they started toward their own room. ''Do you remember her being quite so...'' She searched for a word. ''Ah, funny?''

''As I recall, the most exciting part of the whole class was when you and I had our kiss.''

''It was mouth-to-mouth,'' Carrie said.

Jack just continued talking right over her. ''The rest of it was a bit dry.'' His arm slipped over her shoulders.

Carrie tried to shrug out of it, but he held tight. ''Jack, I think it's best if we keep our distance.''

''I'm sure you do.'' His voice sounded anything but distant.

''I mean, we're friends. We've been friends for years, and I'd hate to jeopardize that.'' She tried to quicken her pace. If she could beat him to the room she could be safely locked in the bathroom, pruning her skin in the bathtub, before he caught up.

Jack matched his pace to hers. "I'd never want to lose your friendship."

"Then we're agreed." She sighed her relief. He was going to be reasonable after all.

"Agreed," he said, hugging her closer to him.

Her smile slipped. He wasn't acting like her old friend. "Jack," she warned. "You just agreed we'd be friends."

"Oh, I'm feeling very friendly." His hand rained featherlight caresses on her upper arm and she felt her resolve slip. He must have opened their door because she was suddenly safely inside the room.

He leaned over and nibbled her neck as desire nibbled at the center of her being.

"We can't do this," she managed to say.

"Oh, but we can."

"What if—"

He interrupted. "What if we find that Mrs. Richardson is right? That we do have a chemical reaction. What if we find that we were meant to be more than friends? I let you have last night and today to think about it. I was hoping you'd notice that there's something special here."

"What if we find that we weren't meant to be more than friends? You're on the rebound. After all those years with Sandy, you don't know what you want." She pushed against him, needing some distance.

Jack allowed her to push him back, but not far enough. His voice was soft. "Rebound? It's been months, almost a year. I'm over Sandy. Truth be told, I was over her long before we split up."

Carrie shook her head. "You hold everything inside. You always have. There hasn't been anyone since she left. If you were over her, there would have been."

"Rebound. You think that's all you'd be? Just a rebound relationship?"

"I think there's a chance—a very good one— that we'd end up hating each other. And then I'd lose the best friend I've ever had."

"I always thought you were the bravest woman I knew. The reason you're always in those scrapes you get yourself into is that you're not afraid to try something new. Of course, it doesn't always work out, and you run the risk of having a problem, but you try. Are you telling me that you're just going to let this thing that's growing between us die without giving it a chance?"

His hands were still on her shoulders and the sensation was just too much. Carrie wanted to melt into him, and forget about being reasonable, forget about all her doubts, all the reasons why they should wait.

Did he really see her as brave, as someone who takes chances? Carrie had always secretly been afraid that Jack had seen her as a flake. The thought that he saw her as something more than she'd ever seen herself was new, and almost as terrifying as risking her friendship with Jack. He couldn't be over Sandy already. She'd meant the world to him.

They were all valid concerns, but they all boiled down to one overwhelming obstacle. "I'm afraid," she admitted.

No longer content with distance, he pulled her into his arms. "Honey, so am I. Despite all the men you've dated and——"

"Sandy," she said, voicing the one wedge that stood between them.

"She isn't here in any way. None of your ex's are, either. It's just you and me."

Carrie stared at him, wanting to believe him, but not quite able to make herself do it.

"You're the longest lasting relationship I've ever had."

"Because we're friends, not lovers," Carrie maintained stubbornly.

"Maybe, or maybe we have something that's meant to withstand time. Maybe what we have isn't just friendship. Maybe it's——"

"Stop," she practically screamed. She didn't want to hear him say words that would move this physical attraction to a new level. If he said them they'd always hang there between them. She pushed against him again, but this time he didn't give an inch. "You're getting ahead of yourself." She gave one more shove and he let go.

"Am I?" he asked.

She turned and looked anywhere but at him. Her heart was racing. Maybe she was having a heart attack. That would serve him right, backing her into a corner like this. Saying she was brave, saying that there was something between them.

She stood a minute and willed her racing heart to beat faster. Jack would have to rush her to the hospital and, in the confusion would forget all about this nonsense between them. When her heart didn't oblige her, she retreated to her last resort. Anger.

"Who do you think you are?" she shouted, turning back to him. "I waited years for you to notice me, but you never did. I kissed boys, practicing to make myself what you wanted. But, you fell for pom-pom perfect Patti, who was followed by others, and that's all there was. Any chance I ever had of making you see me as a woman disappeared in their shadows. Now, after all these years, after we've built a terrific friendship and know where we stand with each other, now you think you can just change the rules?"

"Yes," he whispered. Like a yo-yo, she was back in his arms. This time he held on like he'd never let go and his lips moved forward to seal her fate.

Carrie had kissed boys in high school when she was practicing for Jack and she'd kissed men since, but nothing had ever prepared her for what was happening between them.

"Jack," she gasped, though she had no idea what she wanted to say.

"Yes or no, Carrie? I want you, want you more than I've ever wanted any woman, but I want you willing. Yes or no?"

6

HE WANTED HER.

Not loved her. Moments ago she'd been terrified of hearing him say he loved her, but now the tiny section of Carrie's heart that had always held out some hope wilted. She should say no. He still loved Sandy. He was just turning to her on the rebound.

She shouldn't take the chance of losing a friend over a physical itch. Her head knew that, but her body wasn't paying any attention, and neither was that broken piece of her heart. If she couldn't have his love, maybe she could settle for his body?

He liked her, maybe even loved her like a friend. And he wanted *her.* Maybe it could be enough? Maybe she should take a chance.

"Yes or no, Carrie." He held her but his hands and his lips didn't even try to coerce her.

Yes or no? Carrie didn't know which way to answer until she heard herself say, "Yes." She loved him. She said the words to herself, unwilling to burden Jack with them.

He wanted her. It might be enough. She repeated the phrases over and over in her mind.

Jack groaned and scooped her up in his arms. "I can walk," she said, forcing a laugh.

Jack looked into her eyes with such a hunger that Carrie shuddered. "I don't want to take a chance of your getting away. I need you tonight, Carrie."

Tonight. Ever the lawyer, Jack had qualified his actions, making his intent clear. She could still say no, Carrie thought as Jack laid her almost reverently in the center of the bed.

He pulled his polo shirt over his head. When had Jack turned into such a gorgeous creature, eye candy, a mouthwatering feast? Had he always looked this good?

"Like what you see?" he asked with a deep chuckle that sent Carrie's already overworked heart into overdrive.

She tried to speak, but couldn't seem to get any words out, so she settled for a simple nod. Oh, yes, she liked what she saw.

It wasn't just the package, though Jack's package was quite nicely wrapped. No, it was Jack himself. Her best friend. She faced the truth once and for all. She couldn't say no.

Jack had been her best friend for years, and now he was going to be her lover. She remembered his qualification—for *tonight*. He was going to be her lover for tonight.

It was enough.

It had to be.

Carrie sat up and took off her sandals, but her

eyes never left Jack as he continued stripping. As she reached to take off her dress, his hands stopped her. "Let me," he said.

She groaned and flopped back against a pillow. "I want you now."

He chuckled, not the normal Jack chuckle, but that husky sound that sent shivers of desire racing up her spine. "Honey, I've waited for what seems like a lifetime for this. I want to take it slow."

"Jack, maybe we could go slow the second time?" She needed him now, this second; she needed him so much she ached with it.

"Oh, we can go slow the second time, too." He slid onto the bed next to her and his finger traced the line of her jaw. "Have I ever told you how beautiful you are?"

Carrie laughed nervously, studiously looking anywhere but at Jack. "I don't believe you have, though you might have mentioned I was too thin, or that I should just shave my head because my hair would never behave, or…"

"I see I've been sadly neglectful. You're beautiful, Carrington Rose Delany." He eased one strap of her dress from her shoulder, tracing the skin it had hidden with a trail of light kisses.

"And not only are you beautiful, you're delicious." He moved to the other shoulder and repeated the process.

"Jack!" Carrie gasped.

"Sh," he whispered.

He sampled her, tasting, touching. He left her

dress on, kissing her through the thin fabric. The sensations were so much more erotic than if he'd simply stripped her bare.

The heat was growing and Carrie couldn't remember why she'd ever considered saying no. Now all she wanted to say was *yes, oh yes.*

"Please?" she asked, reaching for him.

He just shook his head and went on with his assault.

Carrie couldn't stand it. She couldn't take much more. He was teasing her, driving her to the edge. She was at the point of begging when she realized he had finally slipped her dress off. Feeling his bare skin against hers was the most sensual thing she'd ever experienced.

"My turn," she whispered as she gently pushed him onto his back. She traced the lines of his body with her lips, memorizing them. Needing to squeeze a lifetime of longing into this one moment in time.

Jack was beautiful. And, at least for tonight, he was hers.

"Mine," she murmured.

He hissed as she caressed him, needing to brand him with her desire. She felt his throbbing need. She'd done this to him—the thought was empowering, liberating. She could go on memorizing his body forever.

But Jack had other plans. In one fluid movement he rolled, ending her exploration by pinning her beneath him. He didn't say a word as he cupped her breasts and hungrily besieged her taut nipples. Sensations swirled as he resumed his intoxicating assault. But Carrie was no longer a passive partner. She joined in, deliberately continuing her own siege. Hunger met hunger, but beneath their need there was a tenderness that Carrie had never known.

There were no words, but with their bodies they spoke to each other more clearly than they ever had. Carrie was on the edge of something wonderful, the pressure building until she wanted to scream her need, to beg for completion.

Suddenly he poised over her, touching but not fully joined.

"I need you," Jack moaned, not moving, waiting at the brink.

Jack needed her. It *was* enough.

"Now," she commanded. Now. The urgency was too great to be put off.

Their bodies merged in one explosive thrust. And with that joining, Jack and Carrie ceased to exist. In their place was one body, one hunger, one need. Carrie matched the beat of Jack's desire—rising to meet him again and again. Her longing as great as his—greater even.

Rise and fall, beat and counter-beat. The world faded and all that was left was this new being where once there were two. Jack screamed her name as he reached the peak of his desire.

Her name.

She thought she shouted his name as her

thoughts spun in the whirlwind of her release, but she couldn't be sure. All she knew was that she'd never reached the place she'd been tonight and she'd never know this sense of completion again without him. Even through her fog of passion Carrie sensed the import of what they'd become and that they could grow to be even more.

Jack collapsed on top of her, pressing her against the mattress. His body still molded to hers, as if he was as reluctant to lose the moment as she was.

If she had the power, Carrie would have frozen this moment in time. Lying beneath Jack, physically sated, but more than that, feeling protected and safe, feeling as if she was a part of something greater than she'd ever imagined, Carrie didn't want to move.

What she wanted was to whisper that she loved him; the words burned in her mouth and she longed to let them slide off her tongue. But she couldn't, wouldn't, make Jack feel guilty, or even worse, obligated. So, she simply said, "Thank you."

"Happy to oblige, ma'am." Jack kissed her, and rolled onto his back, then pulled her into his arms. "And if you'll be kind enough to give a gentleman a chance to recuperate, I'm thinking we could give it another...shot," he said in his cowboy accent.

"Oh, kind sir, I'd love to." Carrie inched closer to his warmth and drew a long breath. Instead of *I'd love to,* she'd almost admitted the truth. I love you. She whispered the words silently to herself.

Burrowed next to him, Carrie felt torn between

the greatest happiness she'd ever known and the knowledge that it wouldn't, couldn't last. A sigh escaped.

Jack's hand brushed her wild hair away from her face. "What was that for?" he asked.

"Nothing. Just go to sleep," she whispered and tightened her arms around him. She'd hold on and keep him safe. She'd hold on...for as long as she could.

It was a dream, that's all this was. Just a dream and in the morning she'd wake up and real life would slap her in the face. But for now, she was just going to dream a little longer. "Go to sleep," she whispered again.

IN THE MORNING SHE DIDN'T wake and find her dream over, she woke to find Jack wheeling breakfast toward her. "You have permission to get up and use the facilities," he said with a smile. "But that's it. We're going to see if two people really can spend a day in bed. I've never quite managed it, have you?"

Carrie rubbed her sleepy eyes. He was here and he was smiling—joking even. Who was this man? And where had he hidden Jack Templeton?

"Let me just..." She blushed and settled for, "I'll be right back." Carrie wrapped the sheet around herself and dashed to the bathroom and shut the door. She leaned against it for a moment, trying to collect her scattered thoughts. What had she done and what did Jack's reaction mean?

She stared at the woman in the mirror and didn't recognize her.

"Carrie, are you going to stay in there all day?" Jack called.

Oh, if only she could. Quickly she took care of her morning needs and hurried out the door. "Jack, we have to talk."

He just shook his head and pulled her back into bed. "Not this morning we don't. I said we were going to see if we could spend an entire day in bed. There was no mention of talk, at least not the serious sort. We'll save that sort of talk until tomorrow."

"If we can't talk, what do you plan on doing all day?" she asked and when he leered at her she had to resist smiling. "All day?" she asked. "You really think we can do it all day?"

"Oh, we may need a break from time to time, but, yes. If last night was any indication, I think we can do it all day and all night besides."

"Jack, really, we have to talk."

"Later," he whispered. "I'm so hungry."

Deciding she'd earned her reprieve, Carrie asked, "What did you order for breakfast?"

"You." He began unwrapping the sheet like a little boy unwrapping a Christmas present.

"Jack, we can't...I mean, we haven't eaten breakfast even. It will get cold."

"I just ordered bagels and fruit. Waiting won't kill it, but waiting might kill me. I need you."

There were only three words in the English language that could have lessened Carrie's resistance any quicker. "Yes," she whispered.

"That's all I want to hear today. *Yes, Jack. Oh, yes* will do in a pinch as well." He chuckled and ran his fingers down her back.

"All I'm supposed to say is yes?" she asked. "You think that might really happen?"

"A man can hope."

"Jack." She was going to say more, but the words evaporated as Jack's lips met hers. He moved from her lips to her neck and then to her shoulders.

"Do you want more?" he crooned.

"Yes," she murmured and then realized what she'd said and giggled. Her laughter and Jack's didn't dim the heat, it merely added another type of fuel to it. "Okay, that was one yes, but I can't keep it up all day."

He smiled wolfishly at her and then renewed his efforts. As he and his kisses moved lower and lower, Jack murmured, "Oh, I think you can."

"YOU DON'T NEED TO LOOK so smug," Carrie said between a huge bite of her hamburger.

"*Smug* isn't the word I'd use," Jack said, grinning as he watched her inhale the sandwich. A birdlike appetite had never been one of Carrie's vices. Jack was finding himself extremely thankful of the fact that her appetites so aptly matched his own. He'd made some headway at tearing down the walls of her doubt. Soon she'd admit that they were meant for each other.

"What word would you use?" She slurped her strawberry shake.

"Well, let's see. I'm sitting here with my naked lady eating lunch at a romantic resort. When we're done, I plan to see if I can make her scream again…"

"You can't…I mean, it's physically impossible for a man your age to keep up this pace."

"My age?"

Nodding, she shoved a fry into her mouth. It shouldn't have looked sensuous—it was a French fry after all—but Jack knew that physically impossible wasn't a phrase his body would acknowledge. In fact it seemed bound and determined to prove that with Carrie there were no limits.

"My age?" he asked again.

"Well, Jack, let's face it, you're not getting any younger. I read somewhere that men reached their physical peak somewhere in their late teens or early twenties. So, you're well past that. And—given the fact that you lead a rather sedentary, lawyerish sort of life—I'm afraid you might permanently damage something if you try again."

"I would not." He was torn between indignation and delight. This was his Carrie. The person who had always kept him on his toes, challenged him and thwarted him in turn. He'd never met any woman like her.

He had to be the dumbest guy on earth not to have noticed what he had before this trip.

Well, he might be dumb, but he wasn't dumb enough to let her slip through his fingers now that he'd noticed her for the beautiful, intelligent woman that she was. "Are you finished with your lunch?" he asked, smiling.

It was the smile that made her nervous. When Jack smiled like that she was reminded that he was a lawyer, a modern-day hunter going after his quarry. This time it wasn't a witness on the stand he was after, or some obscure phrase in a contract—it was her.

"No, I don't believe I am."

"Ah, ah, ah. We agreed that *yes* was the word you were using today, not *no*."

"But I'm not through," she said, hoping to keep her hamburger, fries and shake between them.

"Let me rephrase the question. Carrie, do you truly believe I'm past my sexual prime?"

"You know, they say women hit their peak in their mid-thirties," she hedged, popping another fry into her mouth, even though she'd suddenly lost the taste for them. "I'm on the upswing, while you're definitely on the downward end of things."

"Well, the studies were right about women, but I think, if they'd tested men who were sharing a bed with the delectable Carrington Rose, they might have gotten different results, no matter what the age of their test subjects."

He lunged across the bed and pushed her food

to the floor even as he pinned her to the mattress. "Let's just see if you can remember what word you're supposed to be using as I try to prove to you that men of my considerable age have as much staying power as boys in their teens."

"Yes," she murmured a half hour later.

"Your Honor, I rest my case," Jack said, a hint of laughter mingling with desire.

HAPPY.

No, that seemed to mild a word.

Ecstatic. Joyful.

Carrie couldn't come up with a word that seemed adequate to describe the emotion that was filling her to the bursting point.

She checked in the mirror. Her hair was tamed, at least momentarily, and her heart was in her eyes. Anyone who saw her today wouldn't be able to help but know the truth of things. Carrington Rose Delany loved Jackson Eric Templeton.

Of course, she wasn't going to tell him. Not, just yet. She wasn't completely sure he had healed. Sandy had been a part of his life for years. Until she was convinced that he was over Sandy, she'd take her time. They had all the time in the world.

Even thoughts of Sandy couldn't dim her mood. Not after the way she and Jack had spent the past twenty-four hours.

She opened the bathroom door. "Jack?"

The room was empty. Maybe he'd gone down to the restaurant to get them a table. They'd decided today that they would leave the room, for a while at least.

Carrie smiled as she grabbed her key card.

Yes, for a while. They'd eat, maybe take a walk on the beach and then come back to their room, and she'd let Jack work his delicious magic on her again.

The thought was enough to send a wave of desire coursing through her bloodstream. She quickly pressed the elevator button. She was anxious to find Jack, to eat, to take that walk and then get back to the room.

Oh, how she wanted to go back to their room.

She practically bolted off the elevator, so great was her need to see Jack. Walking through the lobby she stopped short.

In that one moment, her dreams didn't just fade away, they died.

Jack was sitting on a couch next to Sandy. No, not just sitting—hugging. Clinging to each other. Wrapped in each other's arms, as if their separation had never happened.

Carrie stood, locked in place, watching her dreams shatter before her eyes. Jack and Sandy. Sandy and Jack.

They ended their embrace, but didn't move apart. His hand rested on her thigh, like it had countless other times. They were talking, Jack was smiling.

Carrie backed out of the room. She had to get away. Jack had Sandy back. His true love.

Carrie had just been a momentary aberration, just as she had feared.

Friendship had mingled with loneliness and for a just a flicker of time they'd had each other. Now Jack didn't need her anymore. He had Sandy.

It was a couples' resort, a small voice in the back of her mind whispered. Sandy had to have come with someone, with a man. But the image of Jack and Sandy hugging overrode that voice. Whoever Sandy had come with meant as little to her as Carrie had meant to Jack.

Sandy and Jack were together again and nothing, and no one else mattered to them.

The pressure in Carrie's chest threatened to cut off her oxygen. She couldn't breath. Couldn't think. She had to get away.

Away.

That's what she'd do.

She'd see when there was a flight leaving the island and she'd be on it.

She couldn't stay and witness Jack and Sandy's reunion. She couldn't witness the look in his eyes when he had to tell her their short fling was flung.

Over. Finite.

Just like the dreams that had been revived. They were over as well.

7.

"YOU'RE HOME EARLY," Eloise said the next day between a mouthful of pins.

"You know, that's why God created pincushions." Carrie tossed her bag on the bench in Encore's workroom and went to her desk. She was going to force herself into normality. Going back to work was a start. "One of these days you're going to swallow one of those things, trying to talk around them like that and you'll kill yourself."

"What happened?" Eloise asked again.

Carrie should have stayed at home. Eloise was like a pit bull—when she grabbed hold of something, she didn't let it go. "Nothing. I just decided the life of decadence wasn't for me."

Eloise didn't look up, she just continued pinning a pale pink dress on the dressmaker's form. "So, what did he do?"

"Nothing." Carrie went through the motions of looking through the letters that were waiting for her.

Eloise didn't look up again, she just continued pinning the dress. "You might as well just tell me and save yourself the inquisition."

Carrie tossed the letters down and walked toward Eloise. She sank onto the floor next to her boss. "I slept with him."

Eloise stabbed another pin into the material. "Ah."

"That's all you're going to say? Ah? You browbeat me into telling you—"

"I didn't browbeat you, I just threatened to." Eloise looked up and grinned through her mouthful of pins.

"And I tell you, confess that I've slept with my best friend, and all I get from you is 'Ah'?"

"What would you prefer?"

Carrie rested her head in her hands. She was so tired and every time she thought she knew what she was doing, doubt whispered in her ear. "You could have said something like, Carrie, you poor thing."

"Was he that bad?"

"He wasn't bad...it wasn't bad. As a matter of fact, I've never experienced anything quite like it."

"Did he snore?" Eloise asked.

Despite herself, Carrie felt a hint of a smile light her face. "Nothing I couldn't cope with."

"So, the problem was...?" Eloise left the question hanging.

"He's my best friend, and he's on the rebound, and..."

"And?"

It was time to say her deep, terrible secret out loud. "Sandy."

"So, she called."

"Not called. Came to the island. I found them in the lobby together. They were hugging." Carrie doubted she'd ever get that image out of her mind. Jack embracing Sandy.

"And what did Jack say?" Eloise's expression furrowed as she studied Carrie.

Carrie felt like a bug under a microscope as she admitted, "Nothing."

"He slept with you and didn't say anything when he went back to Sandy."

"He didn't have a chance to say anything. I saw them hugging and I left. I packed, wrote a note and just left. I couldn't face him. I just got in this morning and came straight here. I didn't want to go home. I wanted—"

"You wanted me to say, *poor baby* and comfort you."

Carrie nodded. "Something like that."

"Sorry. I'm fresh out of sympathy for fools."

"Eloise."

"Listen, I'm offering you a partnership in this business because I think you've got a lot on the ball. You're talented, creative and have been an asset to the business. With you at the helm here, I can move forward with starting a new store in Pittsburgh. But, now I'm rethinking—"

"Partnership?"

"Oh, didn't I mention it?" Eloise smiled, pins sticking oddly out of the corner of her mouth. "While I was working on that Carrington Rose line, I was also working on a partnership between us. The papers are on your desk. You'll be taking over the store here in Erie.''

''Oh.''

''Is that a yes?''

''Yes.''

Eloise took the pins from her mouth and stuck them in a pincushion. She extended her hand. ''Put it there, partner.''

''Partner. I've thought about starting a place of my own, but I liked it here, liked you…'' She let the sentence trail off. Partner. It was a dream come true.

''Encore will be the exclusive home of Carrington Rose Originals.''

A partnership. Her own label. It might not be New York, or Paris, but Erie was home and this was her dream. A dream come true.

Some dreams could come true.

She thought of Jack.

And some dreams never would.

IT WAS EIGHT BEFORE she ventured back to her loft. More out of habit than an interest to know who had called, Carrie poked the message button on her answering machine.

''Message one of sixteen,'' the disembodied voice said.

''Carrie. Where are you? And what the hell kind of emergency does a dress shop have?'' Jack's voice pleaded to Carrie.

"Message two of sixteen."

"Carrie. There's some front moving in and no planes are leaving until it passes. I'll be in the first available seat. Call me here. You must have the number."

"Message three of sixteen."

"Carrie. What the hell happened? Call me."

She shut the machine off. She didn't need to hear anymore.

She'd left a note. Of course it was brief, but he had a note and he had Sandy. What more did he want from her?

The phone rang three times and the machine picked it up.

"Carrie. Damn it. I know you're there. Pick up the phone. Is this about us? Did I rush you? Scare you off. Damn it, Carrie, it scared me, too. You've been my pal for as long as I can remember. If you want to slow things down, I'll try. I'm sorry. I—"

Sorry? He was sorry? Carrie couldn't stand listening to any more. Jack was going to play the wounded party? He had Sandy back. Why keep up the charade? "Jack. It's me. I'm here. I just got in from the shop."

"And the emergency?"

"Eloise made me a partner. Isn't that wonderful?" She tried to infuse her voice with a happiness that she didn't feel.

"It couldn't have waited until the end of our vacation?"

"Eloise knew the whole thing was a setup to get

you out of town. And she's hit on this fantastic site in Pittsburgh, but she had to move fast. So, I'm back, holding down the fort here. When she's done there's all kinds of paperwork to do. You deal with contracts, so you know how it is when people are setting up a partnership.''

''I'm glad for you, but that doesn't explain why you didn't tell me.''

''I couldn't find you and I had to hurry to catch my flight. I left you that note.''

''What about us, Carrie?''

''Us? Why, we're friends, Jack. Nothing could change that.'' Even as she said the words, she realized it was a lie. Their friendship had changed, and she wasn't sure if they'd ever get past those two glorious days they'd spent together.

''Friends? That's all?''

''I know things will be odd, after we…well, you know.''

''After we made love?'' There was frustration in his voice.

''Had sex,'' she corrected. ''It was the atmosphere, just a fluke. We'll just forget it. Put it behind us and get back to reality. The reality of the situation is we're friends. Nothing more, nothing less.''

''That's it? Whatever else we'd started to discover was just a fluke? You can discount it that easily?''

''Jack, you know that we're not meant for each other. You've…'' she started to say, *you've got*

Sandy, but he hadn't mentioned his ex's return. Maybe he felt guilty. Maybe he was just putting up a fight to help Carrie save some self-respect. He'd tell her about Sandy later. Well, Carrie wasn't going to ruin his illusion.

"You've got someone out there who can be what you need. It's not me. I mean, can you see me fitting in with your lawyer friends?"

"Yes."

"Listen, I've got to run. There's so much to do here. Call me when you get home and we'll get together as *friends.*"

"You're sure that's the way you want it?"

"It's the way it has to be. Goodbye, Jack."

MONDAY, Carrie mechanically began to review Encore's books from last week, getting herself up to speed. Her books. Her store. The thought should thrill her, but it didn't. Nothing did.

She forced herself to focus on the numbers. It was easier to concentrate on work than to worry about Jack and what she should do.

The phone rang. "Hello, Encore, where yesterday's clothes are rediscovered for today's woman. Carrington Delany."

"Carrie, you didn't answer the phone at home all weekend," Jack stated emphatically.

Carrie decided another reason why a woman shouldn't fall for a friend—they knew too much. "I've been busy."

"Busy?"

"I needed to get back to work. Things are going to be crazy here until we settle into the new routine," she finished lamely.

"Yeah, all those emergencies at the dress shop."

She wasn't going to fight with him. She avoided him after his return for just that reason. "What can I do for you, Jack? Shouldn't you be out defending the American way of life, or something?"

"I'm at work," he said.

Carrie tapped her pen against the ledger. "Well, you should be thinking about your next case, not your friends." Carrie sighed in defeat. He was back at work—right back on the merry-go-round.

"Well, I wanted to see if you wanted dinner tonight."

"I'm sorry, Jack, I can't. I'm...uh, busy." She needed some time apart from him, time to let their relationship get back to normal.

"Doing what?" he asked.

"What?"

"Yes, what?" Jack said again.

"I...uh, well..."

"It's an easy question, Carrie. What are you doing tonight that you can't go out to eat with me? Are you waxing your legs again?"

She snorted and felt a reluctant smile erupting. "I'll never be that desperate. There's not much I'd ever go that route for again."

"Okay, is it a date? Are you seeing someone else?"

Carrie only wished she was. For years she'd wanted Jack, but she'd ignored what she felt and dated other men. Now, after having experienced what truly being with Jack could mean, she wasn't sure she'd ever want another man again. "No date. Work."

"I wanted to ask you at dinner, but I'll ask you now. I have a favor and I'm hoping you'll help me out."

"What favor?"

"I need a date for Simpson's retirement party—"

"And you want me to suggest someone?" *What about Sandy?* she wanted to ask, but she didn't. She was maintaining the act that she didn't know they were back together. When Sandy flew, Carrie had played fill-in date numerous times.

"I want you...to come with me."

"I don't think that would be wise."

"Ah, come on, Carrie. You've gone to office stuff with me in the past when Sandy was out of town."

She didn't want to cut Jack out of her life entirely, she just needed distance. But it didn't look like she was going to get it. "Fine."

"Great. Tomorrow at seven."

"Fine."

"Oh, and wear that dress. You know, the one you wore to the club after I waxed your legs," he said.

"I thought you didn't like that one."

"No. The problem was I liked it way too much."

Carrie shook her head. "Then I probably shouldn't wear it." A sharp pain shot through her hand and Carrie realized she had the phone in a death-grip. She forced herself to relax.

"Well, I thought, since we've decided we're just friends again, you might want some introductions around the office. That dress certainly shows your...assets to their best advantage."

AS JACK SPOKE TO CARRIE on the phone, he was torn between wanting to kiss her senseless and the urge to throttle her for what she was putting him through. He had no plans of introducing her to anyone at the party, at least not any single, available men. But he wasn't about to tell her that. Something had spooked her, and it was up to him to fix it.

She sputtered. "You're going to show me off to your friends, parade me around like some offering?"

Jack grinned at the annoyance in her voice. She might be running, but she wasn't going to run fast enough to escape him. "Sure. I mean, I'm sure we can find you someone better than Fred."

"Ted."

"Whatever."

"Fine."

"Fine."

Jack tried to resist grinning as he hung up the

phone on Carrie, who was obviously furious. She wasn't going to know what hit her. Over the years he'd allowed himself to be manipulated time and time again by his *friend*. It wasn't until recently that he began to wonder why it was she always got her way. The answer was so painfully simple now that Jack smiled just thinking about it.

He loved her.

Carrie always won because he couldn't bear disappointing the woman he loved. That's why a lawyer, who didn't take anything when standing in front of a judge, could be pushed and pulled by a tiny dressmaker.

Well, love had toppled mightier men than Jack Templeton.

But for the sake of that love, Jack was about to use all his lawyerly wiles to rescue the damsel one last time—he was going to rescue her from herself.

FOR YEARS CARRIE HAD LET Jack play her white knight, but who was going to save the damsel in distress when it was the knight who was distressing her?

"Come on, Carrie," he called again as she walked into the room where the party was in full swing.

"I feel like I'm popping out," Carrie complained.

"You're not popping out." Jack gave Carrie's dress a little hike in an upward direction for good measure.

She slapped his hand. She was certainly capable of hiking her own breasts back into the dress if necessary. Being near him was doing things to her system—dangerous things.

Things like making her imagine what he'd do if she stripped off his suit and had her way with him right in the middle of her living room.

Friends, she reminded herself. They were back to being friends. Remembering they were just friends was going to be one of the hardest things she'd ever done.

"How long do we have to stay at this?" The sooner it was over, the better.

"Your enthusiasm is flattering. What's wrong, Carrie? You've never minded being with me in the past," Jack inquired.

She'd never been in his bed before. The memory of that night kept cropping up at the oddest times. Apparently Jack was able to put it behind him, but Carrie wasn't having such an easy time. Picturing him naked was only part of the problem. It was the little things. Like when he'd showed up at her door to pick her up, she'd had an overwhelming urge to straighten his tie.

She didn't. It was an intimate thing to do. Maybe not as intimate as making love to him on her living-room floor, but too intimate for the way things stood between them.

Oh, she might have done it before that darn trip, but now she couldn't. She didn't want Jack to read anything into it, because there couldn't be anything between them. They were friends. She'd been chanting the phrase since he'd picked her up—it was rapidly becoming her mantra, but it wasn't working. Only friends, she tried again.

Nope, it wasn't working at all. A friend would never look at another friend and imagine removing his clothes and kissing her way down his body.

No, a friend would never do that.

A woman in love might.

Only friends, only friends, only friends, she kept chanting, while she studiously kept her eyes off the man she'd like to strip naked.

"Stan," Jack called, waving his hand at an older gentleman. "You remember Carrie, don't you. Carrie, Stan Simpson, the guest of honor."

"Congratulations," she said. "What big plans do you have?"

"Oh, the wife and I are thinking about taking a romantic little second honeymoon, then I'm going to settle into some serious golf and teach an occasional class at the college."

"If you're thinking about sneaking off somewhere with Wilma, think about Amore Island," Jack said.

Thinking of the island brought images of Jack flashing through her mind and Carrie kept chanting her mantra, hoping to override them.

Only friends.

"Amore Island?" Stan asked.

"It's off the coast of the Carolinas. Carrie and I just got back last week from a vacation there.

Couples only and romantic. Stan, if the island does for you and Wilma what it did for Carrie and me...well, hang onto your socks.''

Carrie glared at Jack. He wasn't making this easy, not easy at all.

Only friends—and friends don't want to make love to friends. And they certainly didn't want to rip their clothing off and go wild with them. Only friends.

Stan laughed. ''I always thought the two of you belonged together. That nonsense about being friends.'' He laughed. ''Never believed in it. Everyone who knows the two of you, have seen you together, has known for a long time you belonged together.''

''We're not together,'' Carrie protested. What was Jack thinking? Why didn't he tell her he was back together with Sandy? He was deliberately giving the poor old dear the impression they were a couple.

They weren't a couple.

A couple of fools, maybe.

They were friends—only friends.

''No, we're not a couple. We're just friends, right, Care?'' Jack winked, a blatant kind of wink that said he didn't believe his last statement any more than Stan should.

''Oh, I know all about those kinds of friends. It just so happens Wilma and I have always had that kind of relationship.''

Both men laughed and Carrie said, ''If you both

will excuse me a moment?'' and slithered out from under Jack's arm.

Men. They were such fickle creatures. He made love to her, then he took up with his old girl-friend—and where the hell was Sandy?—and now he was acting as if he was engaged to her. Well, they most certainly weren't a couple. He had Sandy. And at the rate things were going, they weren't even going to be friends by tomorrow.

''Wine,'' Carrie said to the bartender.

''White, or red?''

She thought about it a moment. ''Never mind the wine, give me a Scotch.'' She'd always wanted to try the stuff, it sounded intriguing. Suddenly to-night sounded like a great time to give it a shot, literally. She took the glass and tilted, allowing the liquid to flow down her throat. Maybe she should have sipped, but she wasn't in a sipping mood.

She wasn't in a choking mood, either, but it didn't look like her throat or the Scotch cared be-cause she promptly and inelegantly began to cough uncontrollably.

''Ma'am?'' asked the bartender.

''I'm fine,'' she gasped. ''Just fine. Give me an-other.''

The stuff was vile, burned going all the way down, but with any luck it would calm her nerves.

She took the glass and suddenly was holding only air.

''I don't think so,'' Jack said and emptied the glass himself. He slammed the glass on the bar and smiled. The darn man didn't even have the decency to choke a little. He had always been a show-off.

"That was mine," Carrie protested.

Jack shook his head. "I've had experience with you drunk before, I don't relish reliving it, especially not here with all my co-workers."

"Who you are deliberately misleading," Carrie pointed out.

"How am I misleading them?" he asked, the picture of innocence.

"Just friends...wink, wink. Sound familiar."

"I had something in my eye?" he asked.

She balled her fist and thrust it toward his big, fat head, but stopped short, her fist hanging menacingly between them. "You're going to have something in your eye—something that looks suspiciously like my fist—if you don't give that sort of stuff a rest."

"Carrie." He laughed, obviously not intimidated in the least.

She was on a roll and wasn't going to stop for him. "Listen, I'm sorry about Amore Island."

"The hell you are," he bellowed.

"You said you were sorry," she reminded him. When he'd said that on the answering machine Carrie had wanted to die. Now she just wanted to kill him. He was such a man.

"Not for what we did, but for scaring you," he explained.

"Scaring me? I'm not afraid of anything."

"That's what I used to think, before this. You ran away, you must have been scared to do that."

"Jack, what do you want from me?" Carrie felt as if every time she got her feet firmly planted, Jack ripped the rug out from under her.

"I want you to be honest with yourself, with me," he said quietly.

"When have I lied?" she asked in frustration. He was the liar. He still hadn't said a word about Sandy being at the hotel.

Out of the corner of her eye she could see the bartender whispering to the people at the other end of the bar, nodding in their direction.

"You lied when you said you'd give us a chance. I want that chance, damn it."

"Jack, you're old enough to realize that most people don't get everything they want." She was an expert at that, years of experience had given her plenty of opportunity to learn.

Jack leaned close, his breath caressing her neck. "Ah, but sometimes people get lucky and get everything they want."

"Well, if you want my friendship, it's here," she said stubbornly.

"Lucky for you, your friendship is something I never want to be without." Jack ran his fingers against her spine and watched with delight as she shivered. She might be trying, for whatever illogical reason, to convince herself that friendship was all they had going for them, but Jack knew better.

Soon he planned to make sure Carrie knew it as well.

"So you'll stop this winking nonsense and just enjoy the evening with me?" she asked.

"I very much plan to enjoy the evening with you, if you'll let me," he said.

"Fine. There are the Cowells. Let's go say hi."

Jack watched Carrie breathe her sigh of relief and he let her have it. He was a patient man, a lawyer who was used to winning. And Carrington Rose Delany was a prize worth winning.

He watched her work the room, talking to his friends, people she knew from years of being a part of his life, and just as easily mixing with those she didn't know. Carrie's hair started slipping from the twisty sort of hairdo she'd worn for the evening. While she was immersed in a conversation with Terry Lester, she pulled at something, and the mass of silky blond strands came tumbling down.

For years Jack had thought it was cute the way her hair would maintain no style for more than an hour. Now, after having those silky strands cascading over him, spreading over the two of them as they made love, Jack longed to reach out and touch them, and have Carrie in his arms.

He wanted her with a passion the likes of which he'd never experienced before. It wasn't just sex. Hell, with Carrie it wasn't sex at all. It had something to do with desire borne deep from the core of his being instead of a reaction he was much more familiar with. What he felt for Carrie was unlike what he'd felt for any other woman.

She laughed at something Lester was saying and the sound burned into Jack's heart.

She thought they were back to being just friends.

Well, they were friends and he didn't intend for that to change. But if Carrie thought that was all there was between them, then she was mistaken and it looked as if it were up to Jack to teach her the error of her ways.

And he would, just as soon as he got away from this party.

CARRIE EYED JACK NERVOUSLY.

"Isn't that right, Jack?" Carrie asked, pulling him into the conversation. He'd been giving her those looks again.

The kind of looks that made her legs turn to jelly and melted that little block of ice that had recently taken residence in her chest. But she was going to ignore it.

Jack was her friend. Nothing more, nothing less. Only friends. Things were back to where they'd always been. They were right back where she wanted them.

She'd just ignore Jack's nonsense and eventually he'd stop. He had Sandy. She wasn't sure why he was going through this charade, but if she played it cool, he'd stop soon enough.

"What?" he asked.

"I said, the water park on Amore Island was

wonderful, but nothing compared to the one we have here at Waldemeer.''

''Oh. I guess.''

She glared at him and continued, ''You know, we're so lucky here in Erie. We have all the amenities of a big city, and yet we've maintained that small town mentality. There's a great big lake in our backyard, beaches to swim in, snow for skiing... I can't imagine living anywhere else. The island was a fun place to visit, but really there was nothing there that we don't have in Erie. It's like a vacation every day.''

Carrie glanced again at Jack. He was acting strange, drifting in and out of the conversation, a totally un-Jack-like thing. ''Maybe we should get something to eat?'' she asked him, hoping food would help him regain his focus.

''Maybe you're right. I'm hungry.''

He looked at her then, his eyes reflected hunger, but not for food. He looked like he wanted to reach down and feast on her, something Carrie wouldn't allow. Couldn't allow.

''Someone said the chicken salad was great. I think that's what I'm going to try.''

Jack leaned over and whispered huskily in her ear, ''You're welcome to try anything you like.''

Forcing herself to keep smiling, Carrie beamed at him. ''Chicken salad it is then.''

They were moving toward the buffet table when someone called Carrie's name.

''Carrie?''

She turned. "Oh, Mrs....?" She was embarrassed she couldn't remember the lady's name, though her face seemed familiar.

"Mrs. Marsh," the woman supplied, then added, "we met at Encore."

Mrs. Marsh. Carrie could have kicked herself. The elderly lady was one of their regulars. It just went to show how flustered Jack was making her feel. "Mrs. Marsh. Of course."

The woman tugged at an older gentleman's sleeve and said, "This is my husband, Clarence."

Clarence Marsh—Judge Clarence Marsh? Carrie sighed. "Your Honor," she said.

The older man, who looked more like Santa Claus than a judge, let out a merry chuckle that matched his look perfectly. "Oh, my dear, don't you Your Honor me here. Here I'm just Clarence. Unless you're Harriet then I'm *My Dear,* if she's in a good mood, and *Oh, You,* if she's not."

"Oh, you. I'm always in a good mood," Mrs. Marsh humphed. Realizing what she said, she blushed. "Well, I am."

"Yes, dear," Clarence said meekly.

Mrs. Marsh gave him the evil eye and then turned those eyes on Jack. "And you must be Carrie's friend that Eloise was talking about?"

Jack shot her a look. "Yes, ma'am, I am."

What had Eloise said to Mrs. Marsh? "Just a friend," Carrie emphasized.

"Yes, dear, I remember Eloise talking about how much of a friend he was when I asked where you were last week. Maybe I can offer you a bit of advice today, from someone who has had to deal with a lawyer for forty some odd years.''

"Ma'am?" Carrie asked, praying the woman wouldn't say anything to give Jack any ideas. He kept looking at her as if he had plenty of ideas of his own and didn't need a lick of help.

"Keep them guessing. Lawyers are an orderly lot. They like to have all the facts so they can manipulate them. If you keep them guessing—hold onto some things, keep them for yourself, at least for a little while—you have an edge.''

Carrie was an expert at keeping things to herself. The thought of holding onto those thoughts, those feelings made her overwhelmingly sad. "I'll keep that in mind. If you'll excuse us, we were just heading for the buffet," Carrie said, though she had little appetite for food.

"Oh, you two run along. And remember, if you need someone to perform your ceremony, Clarence would be happy to do it.''

"Oh, that I would, Jack my boy. When did you say it was?'' he asked all three of them.

All three answered at once.

"We didn't," Jack said.

"There isn't one," Carrie said.

"Soon," Mrs. Marsh said with a knowing wink at Carrie. She took her husband's arm and led him away as Carrie beat her retreat to the buffet table, praying Jack wasn't following.

"Just what was Eloise saying in front of Mrs.

Marsh?'' Jack was smiling in a way that said he thought the entire situation was funny.

Funny wasn't the word Carrie would use to describe it. ''I have no idea, but you can be sure I'll find out. She was probably just saying what a good time we had on the island.''

Carrie was going to kill her boss—no, her partner. Whatever Eloise had said, it left Mrs. Marsh with the impression that she and Jack were more than friends.

They weren't.

''We did have a good time,'' Jack agreed. He leaned over and whispered in her ear, ''My favorite day was the one we spent in bed. The only flaw I found was that I didn't have nearly enough time to try everything I wanted to.''

8

"I'VE TOTALLY FORGOTTEN." Carrie gulped, trying to indeed forget.

The look in Jack's eyes said he remembered more than that, and as he dragged Carrie into the coatroom, she realized her mistake. "I mean, it was nice, but that's not what our relationship is about."

"Isn't it?" Jack asked, shutting the door.

"No," she said firmly. She knew it was more to convince herself than Jack.

"Why don't you remind me just what our relationship is about," he said, backing her against the now closed door.

"We're friends," she tried.

He nibbled on her earlobe. "Friends," he echoed in between bites.

"Good friends," she added.

His lips moved from their in-depth study of her earlobes and Carrie breathed a sigh of relief only to suck it back in as Jack's lips began tasting her neck and shoulders. "You were saying?" he asked.

"Ah..." Carrie couldn't think.

"Friends," he prompted. "Good friends even."

"Oh, yes. Good friends. That's what we are."

"I agree."

"I'm glad you're being reasonable." His lips continued taunting her and now his hands joined in the party, slowly skimming the sheer fabric of her dress. "Uh, Jack, I don't think this is what most good friends do."

"No?"

"No."

"I think if more friends did this, then their friendships would be better off," he assured her, his hands continuing their sensuous touch.

"I think this gets in the way of a friendship," Carrie said, trying to keep her voice even and stem the tide of feelings that were flooding through her body, begging her to reach out and touch him.

"I think it enhances it."

"Seems we're at a stalemate," Carrie declared.

"Seems so," he said, agreeably. His hand sliding along her leg, inching its way up past her skirt.

"Maybe we should cool this off then?" If they didn't, Carrie was very much concerned that she might spontaneously combust.

"That's one idea," Jack whispered in her ear as his hand inched up another millimeter. "Another approach might be to heat things up."

"Ah, Jack, I don't think that would be wise. We're at a retirement party."

"I can think of nothing I'd enjoy more than to retire somewhere quieter with you."

''That's not what I meant,'' Carrie said desperately.

''What did you mean, sweetheart?''

''Ah.'' Carrie tried to think, tried to remember just what her point was, but she didn't have a clue.

''I missed you,'' Jack murmured. His hand ran along the waistband of her panties.

''I'm right here.''

''Carrie, I—''

What he was going to say was lost when someone knocked at the door.

''Who is it?'' Jack barked.

Carrie slapped at his hands and tried to disengage them so she could straighten her dress. ''Ah, Jack, we're in a coatroom. I think maybe whoever is at the door might be more interested in a coat than in us.''

''Oh.'' Despite the fact that they were in the closet, Jack didn't look very pleased at being disturbed. He pulled his arm, and then stopped abruptly.

There was another, louder knock on the door and Carrie pushed at Jack's hand again. ''Get it out,'' she demanded.

''I'm stuck.''

''Stuck?''

''I think my cuff link is caught on your underwear,'' he explained.

Lace panties. Carrie groaned. Lace panties were going to be her downfall.

''Here,'' she said, pulling at the panties, which

seemed to be glued to Jack's shirt. The lacy span-dex undies just stretched out and gave no indica-tion of loosening their hold.

"Take the damn things off," Jack hissed.

Another knock.

What else was there to do? Carrie inched the offending panties down her legs, while Jack, and his arm, followed. As she stepped out of them, he chuckled. When she saw what was at his eye level, what he was staring at, she smacked him. "That will be enough of that."

"Oh, I don't think so," he said, a promise of things to come in his voice.

He stood and tucked his hand, the one with the panties attached, into his pocket as Carrie straight-ened her dress. The door handle twisted. "Let's go."

Slowly she opened the door. "Oh, I'm so sorry. We were just—"

"Making out," Jack supplied.

Carrie blushed and hit him. "We were looking for my coat, but then I remembered that I didn't wear one."

The man grinned and gave Jack an exaggerated wink. "Honey, if I weren't with a date, I might consider asking you to help look for my coat as well."

Carrie didn't say anything, but stalked down the hall, and didn't look back to see if Jack followed. Actually she hoped he was anywhere but near her. What she did hope was that Jack Templeton, attorney-at-law, decided to take a long walk off a very short pier.

"Carrie, wait up," he called.

"No."

"Why are you mad?" he said, matching his strides easily to hers.

Carrie glared at him. Was he insane? He was back with his old girlfriend, but he was making out with her in a coat closet. "Mad? I'm not mad."

"You could have fooled me."

"That was simply one of the most embarrassing situations I have ever found myself in, so maybe I'm a bit put out." She could feel herself blushing still. The way she was feeling now, she might never erase the red stains from her cheeks.

"I hate to disagree," he said, "but I can't believe that's more embarrassing than the time you set the kitchen on fire in home ec?"

The problem with having the same knight-errant since grade school is that he tended to know every little mishap. Even worse, he tended to remember each and every one in vivid detail. "Well, I'm not doing too bad if you have to go all the way back to high school to find a more embarrassing moment."

"Or the time the straps of your bikini broke when you dived off the high board. That was just last year," he said with a grin.

"Not as embarrassing at all. I don't have enough to warrant any ogling."

"Oh, there was plenty of ogling. What you've

got is perfectly proportioned. And how can exposing yourself be less embarrassing than necking with your boyfriend?''

"Well, you are a boy, and you used to be a friend, but right now you're not much of one."

"Don't say that," he snapped.

Tears began forming in her eyes. "Why shouldn't I say it? All night you've been going out of your way to show people we're more than just friends, but you know we can't be more. There's Sandy."

"Sandy and I are over. We've talked this to death. Is that why you've got me in this hell? You're jealous of Sandy? You think I'm still pining for her? It's over. How many times do I have to say it?"

Carrie didn't believe a word of it. She didn't know why he was lying, maybe he wasn't lying to her, as much as lying to himself.

"You apologized for making love to me."

"I only said what I thought you wanted to hear," he yelled. "The only thing that happened on that damn island that I'm sorry for is letting you out of my bed."

"Sure, that's what they all say. You just couldn't wait to get rid of me." She sniffed, trying to hold back the flow of tears that could easily flood the room.

"Hell, Carrie, I've done everything I can think of to let you know how much I enjoyed myself, how much I'd like to see that side of our relationship continue.'' He ran his fingers through his hair, a totally uncharacteristic display of annoyance, one that was marred by the fact that Carrie's white lace panties were still attached to his arm.

Even worse than that Carrie suddenly became aware of the fact everyone in the room was unnaturally silent.

Worse still, when she looked up to see why her eyes met dozens of other sets of eyes. ''Jack,'' she whispered.

''Don't argue, Carrie. Sandy and I are history. We've been history. You and I, on the other hand, we're just beginning. We were good in bed and I think our friendship has gone beyond going backward.'' His hand, done trailing through his hair, was folded along with its pantyless mate in front of his chest.

''Jack,'' Carrie whispered again. She now knew for certain the blush that was covering her entire body was probably permanently tattooed in place.

''Ah, Jack, your arm,'' someone from the crowd called.

Jack looked down and quickly tucked his hand back into his pocket.

Carrie thought she'd been in trouble before, but this...this went beyond trouble. She spied Judge and Mrs. Marsh coming from the coatroom. ''Pardon me,'' she said, rushing from Jack to the couple. ''You look like you're leaving. I know it's rude to ask, but would you mind dropping me at my place?''

"We'd be happy to, my dear," Judge Marsh said.

Jack grabbed her arm. "Carrie, you're going home with me and we're having this out once and for all."

She yanked it free. "I am not, I'm going home with the Marshes."

"There's still that little matter that I find myself rather stuck to, to discuss," he warned.

"Keep them." She followed the Marshes, desperately needing to get away from him.

"Carrie, I want to know what's going on in that convoluted mind of yours," Jack called to her.

"Did you hear what he said?" she said to Mrs. Marsh. "He thinks I'm stupid. He's always thought I was stupid, but I need to tell you that I've always been smarter than him. I've let him play white knight for me for years, thinking Mr. I-Need-to-Save-the-World needed to feel needed. When all the time he needed a boot in the butt."

"Men need a combination of both, dear," Mrs. Marsh said knowingly.

"Well, he'll have to find a maiden in distress somewhere else. The role was getting sort of old," she said, talking to Mrs. Marsh and studiously ignoring Jack, who was still trailing after them.

"I imagine it would after a time," Mrs. Marsh said sympathetically.

"Carrie, I'm serious," Jack said.

"Call the girl in the morning," the judge said.

"Don't bother," Carrie said, crawling into the

back seat of the car. "Call Sandy. If she chased you to the island, I'm sure she wants to hear from you." She slammed the door and pushed the lock button.

"Are you going to be okay, honey?" Mrs. Marsh asked as the car pulled away.

Carrie watched Jack, standing on the sidewalk, fade into the distance. "Fine. Just fine," she said. After giving Judge Marsh her address, she sank into the leather seat and gave way to her remorse. She'd done it this time.

She'd lost the best friend she'd ever had.

She sniffed, wishing for one of Jack's never ending supply of handkerchiefs. No, she took that back. She was over Jack Templeton, the underwear-stealing, two-timing, black knight. He'd fallen off the pedestal she'd put him on so many years ago.

He was a mere mortal. Worse than that, he was a *man*.

Well, she was a woman, an independent, intelligent woman who was definitely over her little case of lust. She was relegating hormones to the past, she was going to ignore unwanted spurts of physical attraction, she was over Jack Templeton.

It had taken her a decade, but she was over him.

She was a woman finally ready to stand on her own two feet.

"Are you sure you're okay, dear?" Mrs. Marsh asked.

"Yes, I'm just fine."

And with all her heart, Carrie hoped she hadn't lied.

THE NEXT MORNING CAME, the sun was streaming through Encore's window, its merry rays mocking Carrie. She took another slug of her coffee and tried to pretend she was enjoying the brilliant Erie sunshine.

She took the thought back. She wasn't pretending to enjoy it, she *was* enjoying it. She was going to enjoy the rest of the day, the rest of her life. She didn't need Jack, the panty-thieving, coatroom-kissing, bane of her existence.

She didn't need him.

The bell above the front door rang, as merrily as the sun shone through the window. Disgusted with the lovely weather and the sweet chiming of bells, and most of all, disgusted with herself, Carrie took another quick gulp of coffee to fortify herself. She walked into the main room and pasted her customer smile on her face.

"Hello?" she said to an unknown back.

The gray-haired patron turned and a smile creased her face. "Carrie, I'm here for Jaycee's dress."

Carrie's business smile was replaced by a genuine one. "We just finished it this morning, Mrs. Smith," Carrie said.

"I wish Jaycee was here," the older lady worried.

Carrie patted the woman's back, trying to reassure her. "We had her measurements and, as long as they were accurate, there shouldn't be a problem."

"But we're pressed for time. If I get it to the awards and there's something wrong with the fit, I'll never be able to get it fixed in time," the older lady worried.

"I'm sorry. I can get one of the forms out if you'd like to see how it hangs on that, if it would reassure you," Carrie offered. She dug through a rack and pulled out the dress Mrs. Smith had come to pick up.

It was a deep turquoise silk, elegantly simple and one of the best things Carrie had ever designed and made. She was so thrilled to sew in the little label that proclaimed the dress was an original. Eloise had given her two hundred labels. *A Carrington Rose Original,* with a tiny picture of a rose.

"I don't know," Mrs. Smith fretted, stroking the turquoise silk.

"Mrs. Smith, I made this to the exact measurements Jaycee sent us. It should be perfect."

The bell on the door rang again and both women turned.

Her professional smile stood her in good stead as she pasted it on her face, as if the person entering was just another customer. "Can I help you?" she asked, as blandly businesslike as she could muster.

"You can explain this," Jack said, tossing a package on the counter next to Jaycee Smith's silk.

"And when you're done I'll explain why Sandy was on the island."

Carrie drew herself up and met his glare with one of her own. "It should be pretty self-explanatory. You've been asking for it back for a long time. I finally got around to having the darned thing cleaned and sent it to you."

"You couldn't bring it yourself?"

"I didn't think that would be wise. Now, as you can see, I'm with a customer," Carrie said, praying he'd take the hint. She turned her back on him and concentrated on Mrs. Smith.

"I can wait," Jack said at the same moment Mrs. Smith said, "That's fine, dear."

Her smile was feeling brittle, but she kept it in place. "No, it's not fine, Mrs. Smith. Here at Encore, we value our customers and personal matters are just that, personal. If you want to talk to me, Jack, you can call me this evening." She didn't want to hear his explanations, and she didn't want to offer any of her own.

"Oh, as long as Mrs. Smith doesn't mind, I'd rather talk now." Jack moved back into Carrie's line of sight.

Mrs. Smith got a good look at Jack and she beamed. "I don't mind at all. Ah, how tall are you, Mr...."

"Templeton, but please, call me Jack." He smiled, his courtly manners in place. "And I'm five foot eleven."

Mrs. Smith's smile grew broader. "I wonder if

you'd mind doing a little favor for me while you continue your conversation with Ms. Delany.''

Carrie, sensing where the woman was going, jumped in. ''Mrs. Smith, I'm sure Jack doesn't have the time. He's a lawyer, probably in the middle of some very lawyerly business.''

Jack glared at her and smiled at the older woman. ''I'd be happy to help a lady in dire circumstances. I've had years of practice.'' He gave Carrie a significant look.

He was actually throwing her little catastrophes in her face? All those years she let him play the gallant, allowed him to be the white knight who rode to her rescue, and he was going to throw it out there as if it was some sort of trial he'd endured? She'd let him hang.

''Well, if you're sure,'' she said, smiling at him sweetly.

Mrs. Smith beamed. ''Oh, I'm so relieved. I don't have any friends who wear the same size as my Jaycee.''

''Pardon?'' Jack asked.

The smile on Carrie's face wasn't her professional one at all. It was total, utter jubilation. ''Just follow us, Jack. Mrs. Smith won't take up all that much of your time.''

He followed, looking at both women with suspicion in his eyes. ''Maybe I should have asked just what the favor was.''

''Maybe you should have, but you didn't.'' She might have pulled Jack into a troublesome situation or two, but he'd done this one all by himself. Yup, Carrie was prepared to let him hang. As a matter of fact, it looked like she had front row tickets for the hanging.

"Ah, Mrs. Smith, just what did you want me to help you with?" he asked nervously.

"You're just about the same height as my Jaycee, heavier, to be sure, but close enough. She's in the WNBA," Mrs. Smith said, wearing her pride in her daughter like a garment. "She's getting an award from Tennessee—she graduated from there, you know—this weekend and we ordered this dress weeks ago, but before I take it, I want to see how it's going to look on."

"And she's coming to the shop now to try it on?" Jack asked. "Her car and yours are both on the fritz and you'd like me to go pick her up?"

Carrie could hear the hope in his voice and watched it wither away to resignation when Mrs. Smith said, "No, silly. She plays for the New York Liberty and couldn't afford the time it would take to stop over in Erie just to pick up a dress. I'm meeting her in Tennessee, so I'm picking it up for her."

"Then who..." Jack started to ask. Carrie could see the moment of realization hit him. "Oh, ma'am, I don't think—"

Carrie just laughed and led Jack into a back dressing room. "Carrie?" he said.

Like she might help him. She was feeling uncharacteristically vindictive. "Come on, big guy.

It's just a little old dress. Why, in Scotland, men wear skirts all the time.''

"Kilts," he corrected. "And we're not in Scotland. I don't think Mrs. Smith has a kilt in her hand." He eyed the turquoise cloth as if it were a guillotine just waiting to drop on his head.

Carrie patted his shoulders. "Ah, you're manly enough to handle this, and if you want to talk to me on company time, you're going to have to do something for the company."

At the door to the dressing room Carrie handed Jack the dress. "We'll overlook your hairy legs, after all, you didn't know you'd be dressing today. Although, for future reference, hairy legs are frowned upon when wearing silk."

"You shouldn't tease the poor boy," Mrs. Smith admonished. "Really, Jack. I do appreciate this."

Jack snatched the dress and went behind the curtain.

"You can leave your socks on," Carrie called. "The floor can get cold."

"Dear, you're not nice," Mrs. Smith whispered, though her merry eyes sparkled with humor.

"So, do you want to talk now?" Carrie called to Jack.

"Wait until I'm out," he said. Minutes went by before Jack called, "How do you fasten the back of this?"

"If you're decent, I'd be happy to give you a hand," Carrie called through the curtain.

"Come on in," Jack hollered.

Both women could hear a muttered string of curses in a male voice.

Carrie smiled at the older woman. "Just have a seat, Mrs. Smith. We'll be out in a minute." She walked through the curtain and would have turned around and walked right back out if Jack hadn't caught her wrist. "You're not decent," she said. The dress wasn't even on his body yet. He was standing there in just his boxers and a smile.

9

"I NEVER SAID I WAS. I said come in," Jack argued, always the lawyer. "And I want to know why you sent that package."

"You asked for your jersey back right before the trip." Carrie squirmed, trying to break free from his grip. She'd never noticed how strong he was.

"I've asked for it back for years, but it didn't do me a bit of good. You always had some excuse. We both know I only ask out of habit, to tease you. So, why now? Why did you return that damned worn-out jersey now?"

"I thought I should," Carrie said quietly.

"Why?" he pressed.

"Because of Sandy. I should have returned it years ago. I..." She'd heard confession was good for the soul, but Carrie's soul didn't feel the need to make full disclosure. It was too late. Sandy was back. Maybe if she was out of the picture, Jack and Sandy would make a go of it.

"Sandy's out of my life, has been out of my life. What you must have seen—"

Carrie didn't want to know. "Come on, Jack,

Mrs. Smith is waiting.'' She helped him slip the dress in place and then fastened the back for him. ''It looks good,'' she said, trying to tease him like she used to, but it sounded hollow even to her ears.

''We're not through talking,'' Jack argued, following her from the dressing booth.

''Oh, don't you look lovely,'' Mrs. Smith cooed as she rose from her seat and walked toward Jack. ''Oh, but Carrie, look the hem isn't quite straight here.''

''I can fix that in a jiffy, Mrs. Smith.'' Carrie went behind the counter. She took the pin cushion and, eyeballing the dress, grabbed the appropriate spool of thread.

''Right here,'' Mrs. Smith said, pointing to the offending dip in the hem.

Thankful for the distraction, she said, ''Jack, would you mind climbing on the stool here, so I can hem this. It's always best to hem on a real person. The forms just aren't the same.''

Jack climbed on the stool and Carrie walked to the left side of the dress. ''There, let me pull this out and reposition it.''

''Carrie, what did you mean about Sandy?''

''Pardon?'' she asked, her mouth full of pins. Why wouldn't he just let it go? Why was he here, why was he pushing like this? She'd thought he'd come to her yesterday, but he hadn't. She'd gone for her Sunday run by herself, actually running the whole way. She hadn't even bought a single piece of junk food. Her heart wasn't in it.

"You heard me," Jack said, turning slightly as Carrie gave him a little push. "You said Sandy was back. I want to explain."

"Who's Sandy?" Mrs. Smith asked.

"Sandy is the woman he loves." Carrie sighed and ripped out a little more of the seam. "I took him away to get over her. He's been pining away for months, throwing himself into his work. And, while we were there, Jack and I, well we... Oh, it's not important. She came back, you see. Jack's always loved her. He'll see that after he's over being mad. He just feels guilty about me."

"He doesn't look guilty," Mrs. Smith said knowingly.

"But he is. He wants Sandy, but doesn't want to hurt me. He'll remember what's important soon, though, and we'll go back to being friends." Carrie felt her voice hitch. Well, she wasn't going to cry. She'd been crying for days and it hadn't done her a bit of good. She was done with that—done pining for Jack Templeton.

"Which was?" Mrs. Smith asked.

"Was what?" Carrie whispered. She'd been lost in her train of thought and had misplaced the uncomfortable conversation for a minute.

"What was important?" Mrs. Smith asked.

"Yes, what?" Jack added.

She sucked in a deep breath as the needle bit into the silk. The time had come to tell Jack the whole truth. "Sandy and Jack. They're what were important. I thought I was taking him away to get over her, but I really was being selfish.''

"How?" both Jack and Mrs. Smith asked.

If she confessed what she'd done, maybe Jack wouldn't feel so guilty. Maybe he'd take Sandy back and get on with the life he was meant to have. "I took him away because I wanted him, I wanted to have my evil way with him," she said in one burst, needing to get it off her chest.

Jack choked as Mrs. Smith asked, "Your what?"

"My evil way. I took Jack to Amore Island because I've wanted him since high school and I don't mean I wanted him as a friend, though I've always treasured his friendship. I wanted him in a totally sexual way. I thought I was over it. After all, I've dated a lot of men since then and some were better looking than Jack—"

Mrs. Smith looked him up and down. "Oh, I find that hard to believe."

"No, really. Why Tucker was a model. He was cute." Carrie remembered the man whose biceps had bulged and whose good looks put most other male models to shame.

"So, what happened to Tucker?" Mrs. Smith asked, as Jack just glowered.

"He was cute and built and smart...but he didn't have a sense of humor at all. I mean, after I borrowed his little car and put a tiny little ding in the door, through no fault of my own," Carrie hastened to add in her own defense. "Well, he just wouldn't listen to reason. Jack always has. Well, until now anyway.'' Jack would have understood that it wasn't her fault that the tree's branch had whacked the door when she opened it. Who would plant a tree that close to a driveway, anyway?

''And there were others. Some were very nice men, but none of them were Jack. Why Ted, the latest guy I was dating, was wonderful.'' Nauseatingly perfect.

''But?'' Mrs. Smith asked.

''But he ordered fettuccine and didn't kiss as good as Jack. At least that's what I thought, but Jack convinced me he'd never kissed me. What I thought was a kiss was mouth-to-mouth, which when you think about it means all those guys I dated were really bad kissers because none of them kissed as good as Jack gave mouth-to-mouth.'' Carrie sighed.

''And what does this all have to do with Sandy, with my jersey?'' Jack asked.

Carrie looked up startled. She'd almost forgotten he was modeling Jaycee Smith's dress. ''Jack.'' It was time to confess her sins and be done with it. ''I've kept that jersey all these years, slept in it almost every night, because…''

''Because?'' Jack prompted.

''Because I've lo…it doesn't matter. I saw you and Sandy, and I know how miserable you've been without her. You felt guilty about me, but you don't have to. Take her back. I'm sure that's what she wanted. It's just best if you and I, if we, well, if we didn't see each other for a while. You're mad because she walked out on you, and you feel obligated to keep seeing me because we, well, you know.''

Love. Jack was almost sure that's what she was going to say. She loved him, and had loved him for years. She loved him. She'd always loved him. He was almost giddy with relief. "Carrie, Sandy and I, we—''

"Please, Jack. Just go" was Carrie's only reply, made as she bolted from the room.

"Better go after her, boy. She has no idea how much you love her. She thinks you love this Sandy.''

"She's confused. But she won't be for long,'' he promised, jumping from the stool and running through the door after Carrie. His steps were shorter than they normally would be, held in check by tight fabric. Carrie was in her office, staring out the window at the parking lot.

"You've got to go,'' she said softly, without turning around to face him.

"I have to talk to you first,'' Jack said softly in return.

"Jack, there's nothing to talk about. You've got Sandy. Our friendship will be in the way. I should never have let things go so far. After we…''

"After we made love?'' Jack helped. He was standing behind her and longed to pull her into his arms, but he held himself back, sensing she needed to finish.

"After we made love, I decided I must have brought you there when I knew you were overworked and vulnerable, for that reason. When Sandy left, I was sorry for you, but this little spark of hope lit in my heart and I used your vulnerability. I seduced you." Her shoulders slumped dejectedly.

"Carrie, sweetheart, you didn't manipulate me into your bed." Her silence told him she didn't believe a word of it. "Would you believe that these past few weeks, ever since that day I waxed your legs, have opened my eyes to a few things."

A sniff was her only response. Jack reached for his handkerchief, but realized that he was still wearing turquoise silk. That he was going to confess his love for Carrington Rose Delany wearing a dress, a half-hemmed dress at that, seemed strangely appropriate.

"Carrie, I've always thought I was smart but it took me all these years to realize..." He hesitated. The words were so big, so new that he savored them on the end of his tongue for a moment.

"It took me all these years to realize what I had sitting right under my nose."

"A huge pain in the butt?" Carrie asked, still sniffing. "The hemorrhoid on the backside of your life? The barnacle on the hull of your existence?"

His arms finally crept around her, pulling her back against his chest. Holding her felt so natural. This was where she belonged. She'd known it all along, but it had taken him years to figure it out.

She might think he was the smart one, but he knew the truth—Carrie was one of the bravest, smartest, most loving people he'd ever known. "Not a pain in the butt. The love of my life. When I think of all the years, all the time we wasted."

She shook her head, her hair tickled his nose. "No, you don't. You just feel sorry for me. You love Sandy."

"Honey, Sandy was there, you're right. You were sleeping and she called the room. You see, she wanted me to know she was engaged."

"Engaged?"

"To someone else," he carefully emphasized. "Carrie, when she had her injury, we were forced to spend time together. Really spend time. And we both realized that whatever we once felt was gone. We were friends, but we weren't in love and hadn't been in years. We were used to the idea of loving each other."

"You don't love Sandy?"

"No. I should have talked to you about it, then we wouldn't have gone through this mess. But how do you admit, even to your best friend, that you've wasted years of your life? I wasn't working so hard because I missed her. These past few months I've been looking at my life, trying to figure out what was missing. I didn't realize what was missing because I had you in my life, I just didn't know I needed something more."

"Jack, I don't want you to say this because you feel sorry for me."

"And you. You've made this whole thing harder than it needed to be. If you'd asked me for a kiss back in high school instead of kissing half the male population, I might have figured things out back then."

"You're going to blame me? You went away to college. There were always women in your life."

"You were still the girl next door, I looked on you as a sister. We were friends.

"Now, don't get me wrong, Carrie. Friendship with you is amazing and is a treasure I've valued, but I want you to honestly tell me that this feels like a friend feeling sorry for you." He pulled her into his silk-covered arms and kissed her with a week's worth of frustrated love. More than that, a lifetime's worth of frustration that he'd only just recognized.

She felt so right in his arms. And he knew that if he'd kissed her, really kissed her, years ago they might not have wasted all those years.

"Wow," Carrie said. Articulating anything more wasn't within her capabilities at the moment. She'd missed the feeling of being held by Jack. She missed their easy banter. She'd just missed him.

"I want you, Carrie. It has nothing to do with sympathy. It has everything to do with the way you make me feel."

There was a discreet knock at the door.

"Mrs. Smith," they both said at the same time.

"I just wanted to make sure everything was okay," she called to them.

Carrie and Jack just looked at each other and started laughing. "I think everything is finally fine, Mrs. Smith," Carrie called.

"We'll be out in just a minute," Jack added.

"Jack, we should go now. As soon as Mrs. Smith leaves, we'll continue this."

"I just want to make sure you know what you'll be finishing," he said, pulling her back into his arms, but she pushed away.

"I didn't get any tears, or makeup or anything on the dress, did I?" she asked, checking for potential damage.

"I don't think so, but it wouldn't have mattered if you had." Jack smiled indulgently as she examined the dress.

"Maybe not to you, but I bet it would have mattered to Mrs. Smith and to Jaycee." She got back down on her knees. "Now, stand still a minute and let me get this hem in for poor Mrs. Smith."

"Just hurry up. I think you're taking the rest of the day off."

"Jack, I can't. I'm responsible for Encore now and…"

"Carrie, you know Eloise would tell you to lock the door."

She looked stubborn. Her work was important to her as his was to him. He might as well learn that right up-front. "But I won't."

Instead of looking annoyed, Jack just smiled and

stroked her chin. "Has anyone ever told you that you are a stubborn woman?"

Carrie grinned. "Someone might have mentioned it."

Carrie snapped the thread and surveyed the hem. "I think that does it."

"You mean I can get out of this dress now?"

She leered at him wickedly. "Yes. Though I have to confess you look very sexy in a dress, Mr. Templeton." Running her eyes up and down his silk-clad form, she added, "I think turquoise is definitely your color."

"Just think what this could do to my career? I can see the headline now—Local Lawyer's Legs More Compelling Than His Litigation."

Carrie was still laughing as she opened the office door. "What do you think, Mrs. Smith?"

"I think that dress has already seen some action, and I hope my Jaycee sees just as much in it. I have my eyes on this very nice boy..." She looked at the two of them and chuckled. "But, I'm guessing you two have other things to discuss."

Carrie gave Jack a push toward the dressing room. "Actually Jack understands any discussions will have to wait till after business hours. I might have dragged him into more than one adventure over the years, but never in the middle of court."

From behind the curtain Jack called, "So, why don't we finish this discussion later at the club?"

"That's fine. I've been missing Felix's cooking." Thinking about the wonders Felix would prepare for her, Carrie's stomach growled, despite the uneasiness she felt by settling things with Jack.

He didn't love Sandy? She was engaged to someone else?

Carrie wasn't sure what to make of it. It was easier to concentrate on food.

"Whose cooking have you been eating?" Jack called.

"Mine."

They both groaned in unison.

"That bad?" Mrs. Smith asked.

"Worse," Jack said, coming out of the changing room, no longer wearing the dress. He handed the silk to Mrs. Smith.

"I'll see you tonight then," Carrie said, anxious for him to leave. She needed to figure things out. Where did they go from here?

"Tonight." In his eyes was a wealth of promises. He held her gaze for a moment, as if he was trying to figure out things, too, then he turned and walked out of the shop.

"That's some guy," Mrs. Smith murmured.

"You can say that again." Carrie gave herself a little mental shake. "I'm so sorry you had to witness our..." She hesitated, unsure what to call what had happened.

"Actually, watching a man go to those lengths to declare himself." Mrs Smith gave a little sniff. "Well, it was one of the most romantic things I've seen in a long time."

Carrie looked back at the door. "Yeah, I thought so, too." She pulled herself up and smiled at her customer. "But, romantic or not, it wasn't the way I like to run a business."

"Honey, if you could give a performance like that every day, people would flock to the store." She shook her head. "Now, if I could only find my Jaycee a man like your Jack. I've been trying, but she's not real cooperative. I've got a man in mind, and since your Jack seems to be taken, I'll have to just go ahead with my original plan." She looked at Carrie. "He is taken, isn't he?"

"Maybe," Carrie said, her heart suddenly lighter than it had been in a week. She smiled. "Maybe. We really do try to cater to our customers here, but I'm afraid Jack's one order I won't be filling."

Mrs. Smith gave a dramatic sigh, but her eyes twinkled as she smiled. She looked Carrie up and down. "Just what were you planning to wear tonight?"

"Oh, I hadn't thought about it. It's just the club, with Jack. Before all these problems, we used to go a couple times a week."

"But tonight is special."

Carrie thought about the look Jack had given her when he left. Shivers of anticipation crept up her spine. "Yes, I think tonight might be very special."

"And a special night requires a special dress, particularly for a girl who works in a dress shop."

"Well, there is that."

"And there's also this..." Mrs. Smith walked up to a rack and pulled off a simple blue sheath.

Only it wasn't so simple or quite blue. It was a blue that bordered on black, the color of the sky half an hour after the sun has set. It suggested dark nights and whispered secrets, sin and deliverance. It practically shouted, "Sex" from the hanger.

"I couldn't," Carrie whispered.

"You could," Mrs. Smith assured her.

"It's too much," Carrie protested, though she fingered the dress that had caught her eye and her imagination since the first moment it had entered the shop.

"It's hardly enough."

"I'd look silly."

"You'd look irresistible. I don't think Jack will be able to eat a thing."

"Felix would be insulted. He's the cook and he takes such things very seriously." Realizing what she said, she corrected herself. "Chef. See, if he heard me make that mistake he'd burn my food for a month, and he likes me."

"If Felix sees you, he'll understand why Jack can't eat. Carrie, honey, if the chef sees you he'll probably burn your food only because he'll be as flustered as every other man in the place."

"Mrs. Smith," Carrie protested, weakening.

"You know you want to," the older woman said, playing the devil's advocate.

"But I shouldn't."

"I've dealt with Eloise often enough to know she'd tell you to go for it. Since she's not here, I suppose I'll have to stand in for her. Try the dress on, Carrie."

"Mrs. Smith, I'm supposed to be the employee, you're the customer."

"And the customer is always right. Try on the dress, Carrie."

"Mrs. Smith, have you ever thought about working retail?"

The older woman laughed. "Actually, since Jaycee is out of town and her father retired, I've been thinking that I should find something part-time, just to get me out of the house."

"Since Eloise is starting the store in Pittsburgh, I've been thinking about looking for someone who was interested in flexible part-time hours."

Mrs. Smith held out the dress. "Well, let's look at this as my first sale. Try the dress on, Carrie."

"Did you boss Jaycee around like this?" Carrie grumbled, taking the dress and heading to the dressing room.

Mrs. Smith laughed good-naturedly. "Next time she's in town, we'll all do lunch and the two of you can compare horror stories. Now, climb out of those slacks, and slip that dress on."

"I think you'll do fine in this business," Carrie muttered.

"I was a teacher for thirty years, I can certainly handle an uncertain customer or two."

Carrie slipped the dress over her head and before she looked in the mirror, she knew she was sold.

When she opened the curtain, Mrs. Smith whistled. "He'll never know what hit him."

10

MARTIN DIDN'T LOOK UP as he asked, "Hello, do you have a reservation?"

"Martin, it's me." This time he did look up. Carrie smiled at his bemused expression. "I'm meeting Jack."

"Carrie?" he whispered, his eyes finally moving from her cleavage to her face.

With the help of a good push-up bra and the dress itself, she actually appeared to have a silhouette. She tugged at the dress. "Do you think Jack will like it?"

The maître d' cleared his throat. "Ah, I think he's going to like it a lot better when he gets you home." He started walking into the dining room and Carrie followed.

"Tonight is sort of important," she admitted in hushed tones.

Martin nodded. "Finally the two of you are going to get together."

She stopped. "What do you mean, finally?"

Martin turned around and smiled. "Carrie, the entire staff has been ready to shake sense into the two of you for years, waiting for you both to realize what was under your noses."

"What was that?"

"Love." He cleared his throat again. "Jack's already here. He's waiting."

She glanced at their usual table. "I don't see him."

Martin shook his head and beckoned her forward. "He decided to try something different this time."

Jack had called her a half hour ago and said something had come up, could she meet him? Carrie's stomach rocked back and forth, rolling to the cadence of her heart, as she followed Martin. She was beyond nervous.

She kept telling herself that this was just Jack. They'd eaten at the club a hundred times—it was old hat. But it wasn't. She'd been on many dates over the years, but Carrie couldn't remember ever being so nervous. "Where are we going?" she asked Martin, who was leading her through the main dining room.

"I said he had something special in mind."

"Yes, but where are we going?"

Martin walked through the open patio doors and pointed to a table by the cliff that overlooked the lake. "There." He kissed her cheek. "Now, go."

Carrie started down the path by herself, trying to take in the scene. The table was lit by dozens of flickering candles, their flames dancing merrily in the warm still air. "Jack," she said, as she approached the table. He was standing on the edge of the cliff staring at the water.

She waited in nervous anticipation for him to turn and when he did her nervousness fled.

"Carrington," he said, using her full name like a caress. "I've been waiting for you."

She'd been waiting all her life for this moment, she realized. "I'm here. I've been here for a very long time."

"And I was too blind to see you." He held out a chair for her and took his own after she was seated. "I'm seeing you now."

He poured a glass of champagne and handed it to her, then poured one for himself. "To us."

Hesitantly she allowed her glass to clink with his and just watched as he took a sip. "You're not drinking," he said.

"I'm anxious, and we both know where drink and nerves get me."

"Come on, Carrie."

Carrie had never been able to deny Jack anything. She took a sip. "You went to a lot of trouble," she murmured. The word *ambience* hardly touched what Jack had managed to accomplish.

Moonlit skies bathed their banquet and the cadence of the waves beating against the shoreline beneath the cliff provided the music. And lovely as it all was, Carrie couldn't fully appreciate any of it because her entire being was focused on the man.

That he was here, that he'd gone to this kind of trouble for her sent feelings rolling through the center of her being, which she still wasn't used to.

Feelings of love that she'd tried to deny for so long. "So much trouble."

Jack smiled. "Not all that much. Martin helped."

"That was nice of him." She sat there, unable to think of anything else to say.

Jack lifted a domed lid. "Oyster?" he asked.

Carrie's stomach rolled. "I don't think so."

He looked disappointed. "Just try one. Here," he said, picking out a big one from the top of the pile. "This one looks good."

"Jack, I know you went to a lot of trouble, but I've never had oysters and can't imagine ever having them. They're gray. I mean, I'll eat my greens, oranges and yellows, but I don't do gray. Plus they're slimy."

"You just open it and swallow," he said and proceeded to do just that.

"Then why bother?"

Jack looked annoyed. "I just want you to try one."

She shook her head. "I'm sorry. I'll stick to the champagne."

"You're not making this easy," he muttered.

Suddenly she laughed, more from nerves than humor. "When have I ever made your life easy?"

His frown disappeared and his grudging laughter joined hers. "Point taken."

"Were we just having oysters and champagne?" Carrie's nerves were settling a bit and she thought she could eat something. Actually, if she was drinking champagne, she better eat something, just nothing gray.

He shook his head. "Martin is bringing our dinner out in a few minutes."

"Good."

They both sat in uncomfortable silence. Carrie looked at the water. The lights from various boats lit the lake, flicking much like the candles that lit the table. "This was a beautiful idea."

"Not as beautiful as you," Jack said.

"Oh." She couldn't think of a thing to say. Jack had never said things like that to her. She'd dreamed one day he would, but she'd never really believed he would.

"Carrie?" Jack said, causing her to jump as he broke their silence.

There was something in his voice that made Carrie apprehensive. "Yes?" she managed to say.

"Listen, I might as well get this over with." He sounded like a man on his way to an execution.

Suddenly Carrie knew what tonight was about; he was going to let her down easy. Her heart began to shatter in her chest, but she ignored it. She'd get through this somehow. "Don't worry about it, Jack. I understand. You've thought it over. I knew you would eventually and that when you did put that lawyerly mind to it, you'd understand that it can't work." Her heart was breaking, but she wouldn't let him see it.

"Damn it, Carrie. Do you plan to make the rest of our lives this difficult?" Jack rose from his seat and moved around the table. He sank to his knees beside her and plucked an oyster off the pile. "Here, open it."

"I said I don't want an oyster," she said.

Jack shook his head. "You are" was all he said.

"Are what?" What was with him? He was losing his mind, maybe she'd taken him away on vacation too late and now he was certifiably nuts.

"*Are* going to make things difficult for the rest of our lives. Probably going to drive me crazy, too, for good measure." He pried the oyster open and looked annoyed. He tossed it onto the ground and pulled another off the pile.

"Jack?" Carrie was nervous. "What did you do that for?"

He talked as he pried open another oyster. "When we first moved in next to you and you started getting me embroiled in your escapades I thought, *good grief, what a pain.*"

"I know. I don't mean to get myself and you into..."

Gently he placed a hand over her mouth, silencing her. It smelled overwhelmingly fishy and Carrie drew back and remained silent, not wanting his hand on her again until after he'd washed it.

He tossed the oyster on the ground and reached for another one. "But, over the years, you've changed."

She gave a bitter laugh. "Yeah, I went from kicking you while hanging from basketball hoops to making you rip hair off my legs."

Again he gave the oyster a toss and reached for another, grinning at her. "Yeah, that was a real hardship, right up there with rubbing lotion on your back during our vacation. You irritated me at first, when we were kids. But you know after a while, you weren't irritating anymore. You were just something that was a part of my life, part of me.''

"Well, thanks for that I guess.''

"Sh,'' he said. "I worked all day on this.''

He straightened himself and grabbed the next oyster.

What the hell was he doing? she thought to herself as he shucked oysters and tossed them onto the ground.

He continued his odd behavior as he talked. "Anyway, you weren't annoying anymore, you were a part of me. Kind of like a grain of sand that gets caught in the oyster's mouth. After a while, he doesn't notice it's irritating because it's changed into something beautiful.''

"Are you saying I'm as irritating as that grain of sand?'' Carrie asked, her voice little more than a breathless whisper.

"No, I'm saying you are one of the most beautiful women I've ever known. You're that pearl that the oyster finally notices one day, a pearl that has literally been sitting under his nose.''

Carrie's lips found his, fish smell be damned. "Mmm. Much better than any of those practice boys.'' She leaned back and stared at him. "A pearl, am I?'' she asked.

He reached for the last oyster on what had once been a nice little pile. "You ruined my proposal, you know,'' he said. He cracked open the oyster and said, "Aha." He held it out to her. A pearl ring sat inside the shell.

"Will you marry me?" he asked.

Carrie didn't touch the ring. She just stared at it. "I drive you crazy," she whispered.

"But I'm used to it after so many years."

Her finger ached to take the ring, but she held herself back. "I manipulated you into bed," she confessed.

"You can say it as much as you want, but it doesn't change the fact that I wanted to be in your bed more than I've ever wanted anything."

"Are you sure?"

"Carrie—this sounds so disgustingly mushy, but you're my pearl. Irritating, but beautiful."

"That's what you worked on the whole day?" She laughed with the giddiness of it all. "That's so flattering."

"Not as flattering as you telling me about how you practiced kissing all those boys. You do know that your practicing days are over, don't you?"

He took the ring and held it to her finger. "Say yes, Carrie."

"Yes." A piece of her heart that had been bleeding for years suddenly was made whole again and seemed ready to burst from her chest. "Oh, yes."

Jack slipped the ring in place and kissed her. It was tender at first, but within seconds it moved beyond tender and became eager and demanding.

"I don't think you'll be needing any more practice," he practically growled.

"You, either," she warned, breathlessly.

"You're sure about this?" she asked, needing to be certain he was certain. She didn't need to search her heart—it had belonged to Jack Templeton for as long as she could remember.

"Carrie, remember that night I ripped the wax from your legs?" he asked.

"Vaguely," she said, laughter suddenly bubbling from her lips. He loved her. Jack Templeton wanted to marry her.

"Well, it's as if I ripped something off my eyes that night as well. I looked at you, really looked at you and I didn't see good old Carrie, my friend."

"What did you see?" she asked.

"I saw you as a woman...a woman I wanted. A woman I loved. I've just been trying to figure out how to tell you without damaging our friendship."

"You mean, I waxed my legs for *this?*" She giggled. "You mean, if I had waxed my legs years ago we wouldn't have wasted all that time, all those years? Geesh, Jack. If I knew dehairing my legs was all it would have taken, I would have done it back in high school." She giggled again at the thought.

Jack gave a tug and she joined him on the grass. Both of them laughing like loons.

"Ah-hum," came a voice.

Carrie, who was sitting in Jack's lap, looked up and there was Martin, trays in hand, staring at them, with amusement in his eyes.

"Food?" Carrie asked.

"Food, you'd call Felix's creations food? You

do know if he found out, you'd be eating elsewhere for a month at least.'' There was a twinkle in Martin's eyes.

''Ambrosia,'' she corrected herself as she tried to stand without exposing anything. She planned to do some exposing later for Jack. A smile lit her face as she thought about it.

''So, I take it you two have fixed everything?'' Martin asked as he set another bottle of wine on the table.

Carrie thrust her hand toward him. She flicked her fingers back and forth.

''What's this?'' Martin took her hand and peered at the ring glowing near the candlelight. ''Does this mean what I think it means?''

''What do you think it means?'' Carrie asked, laughing.

''That you two fools finally figured it out?''

Jack now stood behind Carrie, with his hands wrapped around her waist. ''I know it's last minute, but do you have enough clout to get us the club for a reception in, oh, say about a month?''

''A month?'' Carrie cried. ''Jack, no one can pull together a wedding in a month. And with your job there are so many bigwigs we're going to have to invite, it will have to be something really special.''

''Oh, it has to be special, all right, but not for any bigwigs. There's been a slight change in my career, by the way. Bigwigs aren't much of a problem, you see.''

''Change?''

"We'll talk later." Jack looked at the maître d'. "So, what do you think?"

"Let me go check the reservations and see what I can come up with. I'll be right back," Martin said.

"No hurry," Jack said. "Tomorrow's soon enough."

"No, problem. I'll be back in a minute."

Carrie stopped their friend. "Martin, I think what Jack's saying, in his polite way, is get out so we can talk."

Jack laughed. "Polite, hell. Get out of here...I plan to woo my lady."

"Hey, doesn't the lady have anything to say about the wooing, or wedding?" Carrie asked.

Jack shook his head. "The only thing you get to say tonight is yes."

She looked at the maître d'. "Sorry, Martin. I plan to be a dutiful, obedient wife, and must agree with everything my future husband says."

"That will be the day," Jack humphed.

"Yes, that will be the day," she said, laughing.

"See what I'm going to have to put up with?" Jack said.

Chuckling, Martin left them.

"Alone at last," Jack said.

"Was there some reason you wanted to be alone?" Carrie asked, desire mixing with her laughter. It was a heady combination.

"I've got plans," Jack admitted.

"I like the sound of that," she purred.

"Dinner, Carrie. I plan on eating dinner with my fiancée. We need to talk."

"I *don't* like the sound of that," she muttered. Whenever Jack got that tone in his voice, things weren't looking too good.

He pulled out her chair and she sat down. She lifted the lid that covered her plate and almost burst out laughing. "Let me guess, there's shrimp under yours," she said, staring at her fettuccine.

"Well, just think, if poor old Ned had known how to order appropriately I might not be here now."

"Ted," she corrected. "And all you ever had to do was ask."

"Well, I'm asking now. How do you feel about a man who's no longer a potential partner in a firm?"

Her fork stopped midway between the plate and her mouth. "What happened?"

"Well, remember when you asked me if I was happy doing my job?"

She nodded.

"And when I asked who is, you said you were?"

What had she done? All that Jack had ever dreamed of was the law. "Jack, you didn't have to quit your job for me. I've been around you long enough to realize what kind of hours you have to work. It's not a shock or anything."

He reached across the table and took her hand. "And remember when I said I wasn't pining for Sandy all those months? I was trying to figure out what I wanted. You asked one question, and it all fell into place. I quit for me. You were right, I was so tense because I no longer loved what I was doing.''

"You're sure?" she asked.

Jack smiled, a smile that said everything was all right and so Carrie relaxed. His hand tightened on hers. "I'm sure."

"So, what are you doing now?"

"I'm setting up a small practice on my own. I can take cases that interest me, that make me feel that rush that's been missing in my work for a long time."

"Jack, that's great." That old spark was back in his eyes and Carrie sensed that he had really thought this out, that this was what he wanted, not something she had manipulated him into.

"And guess where my office is going to be?" he continued.

She shrugged her shoulders and took a bite of her fettuccine. Ambrosia was a perfect word for it.

"Next to Encore. See, I know the new boss and thought she might enjoy lunch breaks with her husband."

"Oh, she has a husband? Lucky woman."

"Lucky man." He speared a shrimp and reached across the table, handing it to her.

She took it and ate it with vigor. "Jack, are you sure about all this?"

"Carrie, I've never been so sure of anything in my life. How do you feel about marrying a man whose income just went down a couple zeros."

She grinned. "As long as he's happy, I feel just fine."

"Sitting here with you tonight, he's got everything in the world he's ever wanted."

She reached across the table and laid her hand over his. Her heart was close to overflowing. "If I wasn't worried about hurting Felix's feelings, I'd ditch this meal and take you home right now."

Jack stopped chewing and managed to ask, "And what would you do with me?"

She took a single noodle and gently pulled it into her mouth. "Oh, I think I'd think of something."

"Carrie?" he asked.

"Yes?" she answered, taking another slow, seductive bite.

"How fast can you eat?"

TWENTY MINUTES LATER they were back at her place. "Have I mentioned that you had better never wear that dress out of the house?" He wrapped his arms around her and tugged the zipper downward.

"You don't like the dress?" she asked, her voice sounding strange to her ears.

His hands were on her shoulders, gently tugging them down her arms. "Oh, I like the dress," he said. His lips replaced the straps on her shoulder.

"So, I can't wear it why?"

His lips didn't move as he pushed the dress downward, leaving nothing in its place. "You didn't have anything on under it?" he croaked.

Carrie's trembling fingers worked at the buttons

of his shirt. "I had high hopes for this evening," she muttered.

"New rule—you don't leave the house in only one layer of anything. Think multiple layers, Carrie."

"I'm not thinking layers."

"What are you thinking?"

"I'm thinking you have too many clothes on. See the advantage of one layer," she said. Laughing huskily as he swore, his fingers no steadier than her own.

Finally, both free of clothing, they stood gazing at each other. "I love you," Jack said, pulling her onto the bed.

"I love hearing you say that," she whispered.

"I'll just have to keep telling you then," he said, his lips finding hers as his hands started to travel her body, lighting her skin as surely as a match had lit the candles at dinner. Only she was burning hotter than any candle had ever burned.

"Jack," she murmured, her hands starting a journey of their own. She'd been friends with this man for so many years, but she wanted to memorize his body, know it in a way she'd never known before.

They made love long and lazily. Mouths replaced hands, traveling over the width and breadth of each other, tasting, learning the textures and pitches of the other. Finally the teasing was over. "Jack," she screamed.

"Say the words, Carrie," he commanded as he drove home.

"I love you, I love you," she chanted, lost in a sea of passion. "Jack," she screamed as she rode the crest of the wave.

"I love you," Jack echoed as he finally lay against her, still—complete. His hand roamed up and down her body. "Now, aren't you glad you waxed your legs?"

"You mean, I waxed my legs for *this?*" she asked. He grimaced and she grinned all the wider and moved closer to him. Suddenly a thought occurred to her. "Does this mean I get your football jersey back?"

"Honey, this means you get whatever you want."

At that moment, Carrington Rose Delany knew she already had everything she'd ever wanted. "I love you," she whispered, just to hear herself say it out loud.

"Love you, too," Jack murmured, half-asleep.

She snuggled closer. Yes, she waxed her legs for this.

Author in the Spotlight

In February 2001

HARLEQUIN
Duets™

brings you

The Swinging R Ranch
&
Whose Line Is It Anyway?

Both by

Debbi Rawlins

Both available in one book for one low price!
Available at your favorite retail outlets.

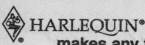

HARLEQUIN®
makes any time special—online...

eHARLEQUIN.com

your romantic books

❦ Shop online! Visit Shop eHarlequin and discover a wide selection of new releases and classic favorites at great discounted prices.

❦ Read our daily and weekly Internet exclusive serials, and participate in our interactive novel in the reading room.

❦ Ever dreamed of being a writer? Enter your chapter for a chance to become a featured author in our Writing Round Robin novel.

• • • • • •

your romantic life

❦ Check out our feature articles on dating, flirting and other important romance topics and get your daily love dose with tips on how to keep the romance alive every day.

• • • • • •

your community

❦ Have a Heart-to-Heart with other members about the latest books and meet your favorite authors.

❦ Discuss your romantic dilemma in the Tales from the Heart message board.

your romantic escapes

❦ Learn what the stars have in store for you with our daily Passionscopes and weekly Erotiscopes.

❦ Get the latest scoop on your favorite royals in Royal Romance.